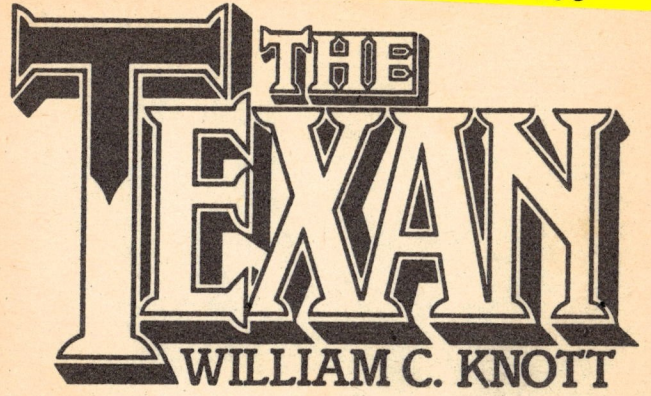
THE TEXAN
WILLIAM C. KNOTT

POPULAR LIBRARY

An Imprint of Warner Books, Inc.

A Warner Communications Company

POPULAR LIBRARY EDITION

Copyright © 1987 by William C. Knott
All rights reserved.

Popular Library® is a registered trademark of Warner Books, Inc.

Cover art by Harry Schaare

Popular Library books are published by
Warner Books, Inc.
666 Fifth Avenue
New York, N.Y. 10103

 A Warner Communications Company

Printed in the United States of America

First Printing: January, 1987

10 9 8 7 6 5 4 3 2 1

For Kathy Malley

Prologue

During that long morning ride to the Nordstrom ranch Bart Hardison had tried to keep his mind off saying good-bye to Kristen. He had loved her from the first moment he caught sight of her peeking out from behind her mother's skirts so many years before. Since then he had come to regard the Nordstrom ranch as his second home. And Kristen as *his* girl, just as Kristen always knew that he would be the man she would someday marry.

They had secretly decided on marriage this spring, but the Civil War was about to change all that.

Now, as Bart rode into the yard alongside her father, he saw Kristen slip out onto the porch and realized she must have been watching for him. Seeing her like this—her long hair caught like spun gold in the early-morning light—Bart felt a terrible, numbing dismay. Not only was he leaving her behind for months or even a year, but there was always the chance he might never return.

Men died in wars.

Two saddled horses were standing at the hitch rack, bedrolls and gear tied snugly on the cantles. They belonged to Kristen's father and brother, Bart realized. As he rode past them one of the horses nickered and swished its tail impatiently. Bart heard the squeak of leather as his father reined his horse in to let Bart ride up to the porch and say his good-bye to Kristen in some privacy.

Dismounting, Bart stepped up onto the porch and took Kristen's hand. They retreated to an area where they could speak out of earshot of Bart's father. Kristen looked wanly up into his face. Her eyes were red-rimmed and swollen. She looked like she had been up half the night crying. He shucked his hat back off his forehead, searching for words to make this leave-taking bearable.

"Then you *are* going with your father," Kristen said.

"Kristen, how can I stay behind?"

"You talked of doing it. You said you agreed with me. You said this was not a war for Texas to get mixed up in." There was an edge to her voice Bart had never heard before.

"I know it, Kristen," Bart admitted miserably. "But we're already in it. It's too late to pull out now."

"It's never too late. Not if you meant what you said—that you loved me."

"That ain't fair, Kristen."

"Is it fair to me—you goin' off like this?"

"Now, Kristen, there's no sense in you carryin' on this way. Ain't no fight in a Yankee. You'll see. We'll be back before next spring."

"Do you really believe that, Bart?"

Bart knew at once that he sounded worse than silly—stupid, even. But Kristen had backed him into a corner, and he had no recourse but to bull his way out of it. "Of course, I believe that," he insisted miserably.

"Then maybe the good Lord's doin' me a favor—preventin' me from marryin' a damn fool!"

Before Bart could say anything more, Kristen's mother strode out onto the porch. Bart read pure despair and fury on her bold, handsome face. She directed her fierce gaze to Matthew Hardison, still astride his horse a few feet from the porch.

"Matt!" she told him. "This is your doing!"

Matt Hardison leaned forward calmly and patted his horse's neck. "It ain't me, Kate," he replied. "It's them blamed Yankees. They won't let the South go free."

3

"What business is that of ours? This is Texas!"

Matt shifted uneasily in his saddle. It wasn't in Matt Hardison to argue with a woman about politics or war. He had always considered these matters best left to men. "Kate, I ain't goin' to argue with you. It's up to you and Seth to work it out. Is he coming?"

"Yes, he's coming. Damn him to hell! And he's taking Nils with him!"

Seth Nordstrom walked angrily out of the house, his powder horn slung over his shoulder, a rifle in his hand. Nils followed behind him, a lanky version of his father with a mop of light, unruly hair poking out from under his black, floppy-brimmed hat.

"Go on back inside, Kate!" Seth scolded her.

She turned to face her husband, arms akimbo. "Is that your good-bye to me, husband? A surly command for me to get back inside?"

"You heard me, Kate."

"What am I, then—some whipped cur who's messed on the rug!"

Seth's face showed the awful tension he felt. "Dammit, Kate! We been over this all night! I'm goin', and there's nothing you can do to keep me here."

"All right, then! Go! Leave us to the Kiowa and the Comanche. But don't take Nils!"

"It's what Nils wants. I can't tell him to stay, not if he wants to go."

"That's a lie! You *can* tell Nils to stay! Tell him!"

"I can't do it, Kate!"

"Then I'm warning you, Seth. Don't return without him!"

Seth turned without another word to his wife, descended the porch steps, and mounted his waiting horse. Nils hesitated for only an instant before mounting up also. During all this unpleasantness the young man had kept his eyes averted, his face crimson with embarrassment.

Matt Hardison looked over at Bart, still standing on the porch with Kristen. "Let's go, son," he said.

Bart stepped back from Kristen. He felt cheated. Instead of telling Kristen what he felt—and how much he hoped she would wait for him—all they had done was argue.

"I... guess this is good-bye, Kristen."

"Stay!" she whispered urgently. "Don't go! Stay here with us! Don't leave us to the savages!"

"I *can't* stay, Kristen."

Her blue eyes turned ice cold. "*Go*, then."

Bart felt as if she had slapped him. He gazed at her for a long, desperate moment, hoping to see her soften. Instead her face hardened into a cold, bitter resolve.

Bart strode off the porch and reaching up blindly, swung into his saddle, keeping his eyes straight ahead—even though, more than anything else in the world, he ached for one last look at Kristen. But his pride would not allow it.

Matt Hardison gathered up his reins and cleared his throat. "Kate," he said harshly, "you got no call to carry on like this. The Comanch' are done. The Kiowa too. The pox and the cholera have taken the wind out of them for good. When's the last time you seen a mounted Comanch'? Most of 'em are up there in the Topeka Agency, gettin' fat and stayin' drunk."

"It ain't *them* Comanch' I'm a'feared of and you know it, Matthew Hardison," Kate snapped back. "It's them other devils still out there waiting on the Staked Plains!"

"You won't be alone, Kate. There's the Baileys not too many miles from here, and there'll be a home guard. Captain Warren of the Rangers has already organized a militia to patrol this valley. And there'll be patrols from Fort Kyle."

"The soldiers have pulled out of Fort Kyle. All the forts are abandoned! When the Comanch' see this, they'll come back!"

"Dammit, Kate," Matt insisted, "it's too late in the mornin' for this!" He glanced at Bart. "Ready?"

Bart nodded. Matt Hardison pulled his mount around. Keeping pace with his father, Bart wheeled around and rode away from the house. Seth pulled up alongside Matt while Nils kept up with Bart. They had just passed through the gate when

Kate's voice, as clear as a trumpet, came after them.

"Go!" she cried. "Abandon us! The smoke from our ruined homes will darken the sun! The air will be filled with the screams of women and children... dying!"

A cold hand closed around Bart's heart as he thought of his own mother and his sister, Jill, even though they had moved off the ranch into Burnt Creek for the duration. Bart turned his head to catch one last glimpse of Kristen. He saw her standing next to her mother, Kate's powerful figure outlined starkly against the skyline, her dark hair blowing wildly in the hot wind.

He turned back around in his saddle. As a boy, Bart's mother had read to him about the Greeks and the fall of Troy—and how the woman Cassandra had foretold the fate of the Trojans. But no one had listened to Cassandra. And no one was listening to Kate Nordstrom.

PART ONE
Bart

Chapter One

In June of 1865 Bart Hardison and Tim O'Hare crossed the Sabine and headed for the Brazos frontier. The two men had left with the bloom of youth still on their cheeks. They now returned as bearded, battle-hardened veterans clothed in ragged Confederate gray.

In a shallow grave beside Fourteen Mile Creek, Bart had left his father. That obscure but bloody engagement had decimated the 7th Texas. Part of a futile rear-guard action to stop Grant's forces outside Vicksburg, the fighting had not even slowed Grant down. After taking Vicksburg, Grant offered the Confederate prisoners parole, assuming they would take advantage of his offer to return home. And many Texans did. But Bart had signed up for the duration—as had his father. It was not until the last battle of the war at the Palmito Ranch in the Rio Grande that Bart and Tim started for home.

Six feet when he left, Bart had grown two more inches and was now a lean, granite-jawed blade of a man who rode with the ease and proficiency of a Comanche. He had let his sandy hair grow until it reached clear to his shoulders; his nose was sharp, his brow craggy. His piercing, sky-blue eyes peered warily—as if he were still charging a ridge defended by Yankee sharpshooters.

Tim O'Hare was smaller and blockier than Bart, his hair reddish-brown, his cheekbones scalded from the sun and wind. Unlike Bart, his features were gentle. Many women in the Confederate towns through which they marched found them pleasing.

The two men rode silently. Companions since childhood, they did not need the comfort of incessant chatter. After the mutter of guns and the screams of dying men, they welcomed the awesome stillness that brooded over the high plains. They knew there was enough—more than enough—to see and hear in this world without adding talk that only mutilated any real feeling or sentiment.

Besides, both men's thoughts drifted ahead—to home and loved ones. Bart was thinking of Kristen, as he had throughout the war. Was she much taller? he wondered. Did she still wear her hair long? And would she forgive him for leaving her? Though there had been no formal announcement, the two of them had almost decided for sure on a wedding that fall. It had been their secret.

But now another fall was approaching. And as soon as Bart saw to his mother and sister, who were staying with Tim O'Hare's parents in Burnt Creek, he was going to ride out to the Circle N ranch and win Kristen's heart all over again.

On the fourth morning after crossing the Trinity, Bart caught sight of a thin, black trace of smoke lifting from the horizon to their right.

"How far would you say?" Bart asked, his mouth a grim line.

"Eight, maybe ten miles."

"Comanche."

"Or Kiowa."

They could see close to a dozen miles in every direction. Yet they knew how deceptive the faint roll of the prairie could be to the naked eye. A host of mounted warriors could be moving toward them only a thousand yards ahead yet be completely hidden in one of the grassland's deceptive swales.

"We better have a look," Bart said.

They had been riding northwest. Turning their mounts, they headed due north. The black plume of smoke hung on the horizon ahead of them like a solid exclamation point. They both knew they were probably too late to be of much help. Yet neither said a word as they rode on, hoping against hope.

Cresting a ridge, Bart caught sight of a Comanche war party and pulled his mount around so sharply, the animal almost fell over. Slamming into Tim as he swept back off the ridge, he nearly knocked Tim's horse out from under him.

"What the hell!" Tim cried as he galloped down the slope after Bart.

"Comanche!" Bart yelled.

They had just passed through a patch of willows alongside a stream. Dismounting behind a high cutback, they unlimbered their weapons and peered over its lip.

A line of Comanche appeared on the ridge they had just left. It was not a murder raid. There were too many for that. Bart counted twenty-four Comanche warriors in all. Each warrior was loaded with booty, and most of them were so drunk they were having difficulty staying on their ponies.

In a barbarous procession, some resplendent in bison-horn headdresses and buffalo capes, their iron lances glittering in the sun, they moved steadily along the ridge. Their finery had a wild eccentricity about it—a white man's vest here, a frock coat there. Pants they had confiscated no longer had seats in them. One barbarian had wrapped a bolt of red cloth around his naked chest; another had tied pink and red ribbons to his horse's tail. A few wore stovepipe hats, and one of them had an eagle feather stuck in his headband.

The usual tack of the Comanche was to slip down the rivers by night, hide by day, strike at sunset, then race back to the northern prairies before dawn. Yet here they were, drunk as lords, exposing themselves in the full light of day on the crest of a high ridge deep in Texas. The explanation for this was disheartening. These savages knew there was no longer any need for caution. They had little to fear from the Rangers or any of the men from Texas, who had vanished overnight from the Texas plains, leaving behind all that was precious and defenseless to the Comanche and the Kiowa war parties.

The Comanche kept to the crest of the ridge until they vanished to the northwest. After a judicious wait Bart and Tim mounted up again and continued north toward the burning ranch. There was no doubt in either man's mind what they would find when they got there.

* * *

The smoke had vanished into a cloudless blue sky. They kept riding due north, anyway. A good piece of the afternoon was gone when they topped a swale and hauled in their nearly spent mounts. Below them, sitting in the gentle embrace of the meandering stream, they saw what remained of the ranch the Comanche had hit. The main house still stood. It was the barn and the other outbuildings that had sent the heavy plumes of smoke pumping into the sky. Tiny, flickering tongues of fire still smoldered in the blackened ruins.

They spurred their mounts down the long sweep of grassland. Dismounting about twenty-five yards from the ranch house, Bart took from his saddle boot the Henry carbine he had liberated from a Union soldier and started for the house. On Bart's hip rode his huge Walker. Tim kept pace with him, his Navy Colt out and cocked. They did not expect any Comanche to be lying in wait inside the cabin. But sometimes a cut-up, crazed Texan could be as deadly as any Indian.

Bart saw blackened shingles and noted the spent torches and arrows that had been used in an attempt to set fire to the roof. It was the sod underneath the shingles that had held back the flames. The door was splintered and broken in—more than likely by a Comanche war pony backed up to it. What remained of the door hung askew on a single leather hinge.

They stepped inside, expecting to find bodies. There were none. The window shutters were smashed in. A kitchen table had been sliced in half by a single blow from a war club. In the center of the kitchen two steamer trunks were hacked open. Blankets, clothing, apparel of all kinds lay scattered over the floor. Above the stove, the hooks that had held the woman's brass pots and kettles were stripped of their burdens.

The two men looked silently, but alertly, around them. Bart could smell the terror, the hot stench of savage bodies as they whooped and *ki-yi-ed* through the small rooms. Bart led Tim from the kitchen and down a narrow hallway. At the end of it they found a smashed door and stepped into a small bedroom.

A boy not more than ten or twelve sat in the far corner of the room. His knees were drawn up to his chin, his sightless eyes opened wide. Most of his scalp was gone. Blood had dried on his forehead and cheeks where it had flowed freely from the open wound. Bart walked over and stared down at the dead boy, his mouth dry with fury. From the neck down the boy's shirt was caked with dried blood. A single stroke of a Comanche's knife had severed the boy's jugular.

Leaning his Henry against the wall, Bart lifted the blood-soaked body onto the bed. Using the bedspread for a shroud, he glanced up at Tim.

"See if you can find anyone else."

Tim ducked out of the bedroom. Bart tore the bed sheets into strips and tied them around the makeshift shroud, then carried the boy's body outside. He located a charred, long-handled spade behind the ruined barn. He selected a slight rise overlooking the ranch site and was digging a grave when Tim called to him from the yard.

"I found a trail," Tim cried. "Someone escaped, it looks like."

Bart tossed aside the shovel and hurried down the slope.

The trail led away from a root cellar behind the house. They had little difficulty following the bloodstained path through the grass leading to the bank of the stream. There they found a dead woman. She had been in her late thirties. Judging from the cut of her chin, she was the mother of the boy they had found. Her dark chestnut hair had been shaken loose and was so thick that at first Bart did not realize she had been scalped. Her long dress and undergarments had been sliced, ripped up the middle, and flung aside. Lying spread-eagle on her back, naked, she stared up at them mutely.

"Over here," Tim said. He was down behind the cutbank.

Bart joined him.

Without a word Tim pointed to the woman's small, naked footprints and the buckshot casings scattered on the ground among them. They told most of the story.

The woman had not let the Comanche take her without a fight. There were six casings in all, which meant that though she had been seriously wounded, she had managed to reload and fire her shotgun at least three times before the Comanche triumphed. Moving back up onto the bank, they saw the trampled grass and bloodstains as far back as ten or fifteen yards. She had wounded or killed at least one or two of the attacking Comanche.

They buried her alongside her son. Bart fashioned crude crosses for their graves while Tim picked wildflowers and set them down beside each one. Later, as Bart rode out with Tim, heading northwest once again, he remembered Kate Nordstrom's awful prophecy: "The smoke from our ruined homes will darken the sun," she had cried. "The air will be filled with the screams of women and children...dying."

Four days later, the sun hot on their backs, Bart and Tim rode into Burnt Creek. As they clopped down Main Street, gaunt townspeople turned out to watch them ride in. Lige Williams waved from his livery, a toothless grin lighting his ancient face. They cut down a familiar alley and emerged onto a dusty, tree-shaded street, then pulled up in front of a small, two-story frame house. It had a shingle roof and a porch that ran around three sides of it. Dan O'Hare, part owner of Anchor, had built this house six years earlier and then moved into town upon his wife Molly's urging, leaving Bart's father to run the spread.

The two men dismounted in front of the porch. After pausing for a moment to drink in the quiet of the street, Tim pushed eagerly through the picket fence, Bart on his heels. In two devouring strides he mounted the porch steps, winked broadly at Bart, and knocked loudly on the front door.

Dan O'Hare answered the knock. The shock of recognition momentarily stunned him. Then, uttering a joyous cry, he embraced his son.

"Molly!" he cried. "Come here!"

Sighting Bart, O'Hare reached past his son and clasped Bart's hand in both of his, then pulled them both into the house. They were just in time to run into Molly O'Hare in the small hallway. One look at her son and she cried out as if she had been struck, then rushed forward to embrace Tim, tears of joy tracing down her cheeks. Behind her, equally excited, appeared Tim's sister, Ellen.

The next few, excited moments were filled with

tears; foolish, happy laughter; and questions—a storm of questions. At times the clamor was such that no one seemed to know or care precisely what the other was saying. Not that anyone minded.

Looking around him, Bart saw that the O'Hare's kitchen looked just the same as it had the last time he had sipped Molly O'Hare's coffee. The wood floors were waxed to a high sheen. The walls were covered with plaster and were so clean, the light they reflected caused him to squint slightly. The huge black wood-burning range still dominated the room. Over it hung a row of gleaming copper pots and pans. Everything about the kitchen reminded Bart of how unkempt he must look and how rank he must smell.

Ellen, pulling back from Tim, glanced across the room at Bart and blushed crimson. When he had last seen her, she was little more than sixteen, a string bean of a girl, all knees and elbows. Now she was a tall, willowy young woman of eighteen with abundant dark curls that hung past her shoulders. Her lovely, brown, Irish eyes were filled, he noticed, with sudden concern for him.

As she came toward him he said, "Looks like I need to clean up some. And maybe cut off some of this hair. The washtubs still out back?"

"They're still there," she replied, her voice low,

a deep undercurrent of tenderness running through it. "I'll put the water on right now. You'll have hot water in no time."

"I'd sure appreciate that," he told her.

But she did not run off to draw the water. Instead she took a cautious step closer. "Do you remember me for sure now, Bart Hardison?" she asked.

"Guess you were a mite smaller when I left. But I remember you, all right."

"And I remember you—and your father, too—riding out with all those men. I can still see you disappearing into the damp morning. I prayed for you and Tim—and for your father, too—every night, Bart."

"Thanks, Ellen."

"We were all very sorry to hear of your father's death."

Bart thanked her and then saw something in Ellen's eyes that warned him. He had more wounds coming. In that instant he knew what it was. He had been expecting his mother and sister to burst in at any moment—drawn by the happy tumult. But they had not appeared.

"Ellen," Bart asked, "where's Ma? I thought she and Jill were staying here in town with you."

It was as if Bart had shouted his question at the top of his lungs. The room went deathly quiet. Molly looked over at him, her hand up to her mouth, an aching concern etched on her round, kindly face. Dan's face had turned ashen as well.

"Your mother, is it?" Molly said, hurrying over to him. "Why, Bart, she's still here. And she has her own room now. Let me take you to her."

Bart looked down into Molly's face. "What's wrong, Molly? Is Ma sick. And where's Jill?"

Molly started to speak, then abruptly ducked her head away, a tear gleaming on her cheek. Dan moved over to stand solidly behind Molly, his hands resting on her shoulders. He cleared his throat.

"Jill's not here, Bart," Dan said.

"Where is she?"

"Your mother and Jill were at the ranch alone. They just went out to clean the place. It was a Kiowa raiding party.... None of us knew they were in the area until it was too late. Before we could get out there, they'd hit Anchor and ridden off. Your mother was safe... but not Jill. She was taken. We went after her. Half the town did. We found her soon enough. As usual, Bart, them savage devils made no effort to hide her body. They wanted us to find her. We buried her right there on the prairie, Bart, and left a cross. It seemed to be the best thing to do."

Into Bart's mind flashed the mutilated figure of the woman he and Tim had buried on the way here. The horror of it swept over him again: the way her pitiful, defenseless nakedness cried out to him. Bart felt as if someone had just kicked him in the stomach.

"Your ma," Dan went on painfully, "just never got over Jill's death. When she got your letter about your pa, she just seemed to lose all hope."

"I want to see her," Bart said.

"She's right down the hall," Dan told him. "The room past the linen closet."

"I'll show you," said Ellen.

"That's all right," Bart told her. "I'd rather go alone if you don't mind."

"Of course, Bart," she said.

Bart knocked once. There was no response. From the other side of the door came a curious, metronomic tapping.

He knocked again. When there was still no answer, he pushed the door open all the way and saw his mother sitting in a rocker beside an unmade featherbed. She was wearing a black dress and a purple knit shawl. The steady tapping sound came from her rocking chair. A kerosene lamp on the dresser threw a dim, yellowish light over her shrunken figure.

"Ma...?" Bart called softly.

She was staring straight ahead into the room's farthest corner. She did not respond to his voice and kept on rocking. Bart closed the door, walked over, and knelt beside her. She turned her face to look at him, her large, sad, luminous eyes regarding him blankly.

"Ma," he said, "I'm here. I'm back."

He put his arms around her shoulders, dismayed at how thin and frail they felt. Her rocking slowed to a halt. She continued to look at him without uttering a word. Hanging about her was a musty smell that disturbed him deeply; and peering into her sunken eyes, he realized how close to death she was, huddled here in this sunless room. He shook her gently, urgently.

"Ma!" he said. "It's me! Bart! I came back from the war!"

A spark of recognition lit her eyes. Abruptly she reached out and touched his beard, then his brow, wonderingly.

"Bart?" she asked, her voice barely audible. "Is it you?"

"Yes, Ma!"

With a tiny cry she threw her arms around his enormous shoulders, hugging him tightly. Returning her embrace, Bart felt his mother's sparrowlike frame shaking as she cried softly. Pulling back from him, she let her eyes feed on him, her face alight with sudden, extravagant hope. Then she looked past Bart at the door.

"Your father—is he with you?"

Bart's heart sank. "Ma...I wrote you. He's...dead."

The glow in his mother's face went out as

quickly as a snuffed candle. "Yes, yes. I know. Foolish of me, wasn't it? Silly. Molly told me. She brought your letter. But I didn't have to believe it if I didn't want to."

"No, you didn't, Ma."

"But he really is dead. Of course he is. And now you're back. My big, strong son is back." She looked at him warily then, a strange, unsettling light glowing in her eyes. "And now you can go after Jill. Bring her back, son! Bring her back from them murderin' heathen!"

He saw then how little sense she was able to make out of the events of the past four years. It was too painful. She preferred her own private world, one in which nothing terrible had happened. A world where there was still hope, no matter how irrational that hope might be.

Pulling back, Bart felt a great weariness. "Sure, Ma," he said. "I'll bring Jill back. Don't you worry."

She leaned close, her eyes glittering. "It don't matter none what they done to her," she told him. "Even if she married a chief or got her face all tattooed. You hear? Buy her back! Pay the devils whatever they want."

Bart stood up.

"Will you...be joining us for supper tonight, Ma? Tim came back with me. He'd like to see you."

She pulled the purple shawl around her narrow

shoulders and leaned back in her rocker. Looking away from him, she resumed her rocking, the metronomic beat filling the room.

"No," she told him. "I'll wait here till you bring Jill back. You hurry up now and go after her."

"Sure, Ma," Bart said, backing out of the room.

"And shut that door tight," she said with surprising petulance. "I near got a chill when you came in."

Less than an hour later, clean-shaven, dressed in fresh clothes, and still sweating from the steaming tub, Bart planted his chair down in front of Molly O'Hare's table. Molly and Ellen had worked like a whirlwind. While he and Tim scrubbed themselves they could hear the sound of clattering dishes and happy chatter coming from the kitchen.

The result was a meal fit for returning royalty. Looking over the portions set down before him on the freshly ironed linen, Bart, for the first time, was ready to believe that the war was truly over and that he was home.

For the main course they had fresh roast pork cooked in honey; a pot roast that had been slashed open with small bits of garlic, pepper, bacon, and parsley; and a perfectly roasted leg of lamb. In deep side dishes there were mounds of mashed potatoes and plenty of thick, rich gravy. In addition there was mint sauce, a big dish of new peas, a platter of sweet potatoes, candied carrots, and thick slices of freshly baked bread with grape jelly and gooseberry jam.

Standing alongside his plate, Bart found an unopened jar of peppermint jelly. Molly had remembered that it was Bart's favorite whenever he and his father visited the O'Hares'. Thick wedges of apple pie topped off the meal, its crust so tender it melted in his mouth, and then Mexican pie made of dried buffalo berries. Served hot with plenty of sauce, Bart pronounced it "powerful good" and reached for a second portion.

Ellen beamed. This had been her special contribution.

Following four years of miserable food and even worse accommodations, Bart was tempted to regard this as the best meal of his life. But he could not forget his mother, alone in her tiny room, rocking endlessly as she picked at the single plate of food he had seen Ellen bring to her.

While the women were busy clearing off the table the men enjoyed coffee, and with a happy flourish Dan produced a bottle of Irish whiskey he had been saving for such an auspicious occasion. In his late fifties, he was a small barrel of a man, as tough as hickory.

Lacing his coffee with a generous dollop of

whiskey, Dan looked somberly across the table at Bart. "I want you to know, Bart, how bad I felt when I heard about Matt's death. We went back a long ways. I'll miss him, that's for damn sure."

"Thanks, Dan," Bart replied. "I'll miss him too."

Matt Hardison had died with his head cradled in his son's lap. Before he died, they'd had the chance to say what few fathers and sons ever get the chance to tell each other. Bart was grateful for it. Nevertheless, the raw sense of loss remained, and he knew it would never get any better than it was at that moment.

"What're you planning to do about Anchor?" Dan asked, sipping his coffee.

"Soon's I can, I'll be takin' Ma out there with me," Bart replied. "We'll build Anchor up again. Don't you worry none about that, Dan. Your investment is still good."

"That ain't worrying me none," Dan replied. "There's still plenty of mavericks runnin' wild, just waiting for the branding iron. Fact is, right now there's too many. There's no market for the critters. Not in New Orleans, anyway—and no one's anxious to get up a drive to California."

"Then we'll just have to find a new market," Bart said.

"Bart's already offered me the job of foreman," Tim broke in, smiling, his eyes gleaming at the prospect.

"You two'll be needing someone to cook for you," Ellen called over from the sink, a wet dish in her hand. "Someone to put some solid flesh back on your bones."

"And who might that someone be?" Tim asked, winking at Bart.

Ellen's eyes danced. "Who do you think?"

"I can't make promises now, Ellen," Bart told her. "But we'll sure give it some thought."

"You better."

"Let her do it, Bart," Molly said. "One woman in a kitchen is enough. And this one is already getting a mite crowded."

Laughing, Bart turned his attention back to Dan. "I haven't been out to see the place. How is it?"

"Some squatters were using it a year ago. I booted them out. The roof on the ranch house needs some fixin'."

"What about the horse barn?"

"Burned to the ground."

Bart thought of Kristen then—and Kate Nordstrom's prophetic words. "What about the Circle N?"

Dan grinned quickly at him. "You're thinkin' of Kristen, ain't you?"

"Guess maybe I am."

"She's fine. Prettier'n a picture and gettin' more so every day. When she and her ma comes

THE TEXAN

in to shop, seems like the whole town just stops to drink her in."

Bart swallowed. In his mind's eye he could see Kristen dismounting from the wagon, her golden hair tied in a neat bun at the back of her neck. Maybe she'd be wearing that wide-brimmed sun hat and the long white dress with the pink, frilly gather around her neck and sleeves.

"What about Kate," Bart managed, trying not to show what he felt. "And Seth? He back yet?"

Dan nodded, his jolly face suddenly grim. "Seth came back after Vicksburg. But he came home without Nils. Nils is dead, Bart. And from what I heard, Seth wasn't worth a pitcher of warm spit when he arrived at the Circle N. And now he's dead."

"Seth?"

Grimly Dan nodded.

"Comanche?"

"Yep. It happened a year ago. Last fall."

The irony did not escape Bart. Seth had survived the murderous fighting around Vicksburg—only to find the death he had eluded in Mississippi waiting for him in the Brazos Valley. And Nils too. Kate Nordstrom had warned Seth not to return without Nils.

He had, and now he was dead.

"How'd it happen?" Bart asked.

"Soon's you and your pa rode off, Bart," Dan

told him, "the Comanche and Kiowa started raiding us. It was the forties and fifties all over again. And what's more, it looks like it's going to get a whole lot worse before it gets any better—what with them damn carpetbaggers we got in Austin runnin' things."

"The Rangers still outlawed?"

"Yup."

"Tell him about last year," said Ellen, placing a fresh pot of coffee down on the table before them.

Dan fortified his coffee and proceeded to do just that. The fall before, he related, some thirty thousand Comanche and Kiowa, under Little Buffalo, a Kiowa war chief, crossed the Brazos about ten miles above Fort Belknap, near Elk Creek. They rode along both banks of the river bottom in the clear light of day, as cool as you please, hunting and killing the settlers they found, like coyotes flushing rabbits.

"What finally stopped them?" Bart asked. "The Rangers?"

"Nope. Thornton Hamby. He was forted up at the Bragg place. With the women loading for him, he kept up a steady fire that drove the devils back twice. Then he knocked the leader of the war party—Little Buffalo—off his horse and clear into hell's back alley. This nearly ruined the Comanche's concentration, and by the time Captain Warren rode up the next morning, the red devils had pulled back up the valley and were heading for home—beatin' their breasts and lamentin' the death of their late, great war chief."

"What was the toll?" Tim asked.

Dan compressed his lips grimly. "Doc Wilson got an arrow in the heart. And died as soon as he unplugged himself. Then there was Seth Nordstrom. He got caught out in the open before he could make it into his ranch house. All told, there were eleven killed and nine ranch houses burned to the ground. One woman and seven children were carried off."

"That sure as hell don't sound so good," Bart said. Then he glanced at Tim. "You want to tell him, Tim?"

Tim cleared his throat. "Pa, Bart and I came on a Comanch' war party about four days back. They'd just finished wiping out a settler's wife and his son. We never did find what they did with the settler."

"They probably took him along for amusement. Whereabouts was this?"

"About sixty miles southeast of here."

"Which way were the bastards headed?"

"In this direction."

Dan leaned back in his chair and regarded Tim and Bart thoughtfully. "How many in all, would you say?"

"Two dozen, anyway," Bart said, aware of the

two woman standing frozen at the sink, listening intently. "And most of them were as drunk as hoot owls."

"That's right, Pa," Tim seconded. "They sure weren't making any effort to keep themselves hid."

Dan blew out his cheeks. "That's the way it's been, all right. Each summer they been gettin' bolder. Guess they figure they got us licked, what with the soldiers pulled out and no more Rangers to keep after them." He frowned anxiously. "We better send a rider to Fort Murrah and alert Captain Warren and his Rangers."

"Didn't you just say they were outlawed?"

Dan snorted. "Why, hell, we'd all be rottin' in our graves if we paid any attention to that bunch of carpetbaggers in Austin. About a couple of weeks ago Warren and a few of his old Ranger boys just oiled up their Colts and reconstituted themselves. Right now they've set themselves up in Fort Murrah. 'Course, we don't call 'em Rangers, you understand, and no one's showin' any rank. But it don't matter what we call 'em or how they look as long as they do the job."

"Looks like I'll be ridin' to Fort Murrah, then," Bart said. "I'll leave first thing in the morning."

"I'll go with you," said Tim.

"I'd rather you stayed here, Tim," Bart told him. "Visit with your folks and maybe go down to Sam Bronson's store and see how much credit he'll allow for fixing up Anchor. Soon as possible I want to move out there."

Tim nodded eagerly. "Sure, Bart. You're the boss."

Bart got to his feet. "Before I hit the sack, I think I'll go in to see Ma."

His mother barely had touched the food Ellen had brought her. Bart experienced more difficulty arousing her than he had the first time. When at last he got her to stop her incessant rocking, he tried to get some food into her. But it was cold and unappetizing by this time, and she was stubbornly unresponsive, taking the smallest possible bites. Bart was about to give up when a light rap came at the door.

Bart put down the plate and opened the door. It was Dan. His face was flushed with excitement. Stepping out of the room, Bart pulled the door shut behind him. "What is it, Dan?"

"You won't have to ride to Fort Murrah."

"Why not?"

"That band of Comanche you saw has already hit."

"Where?"

"Kate Nordstrom's ranch."

Bart groaned inwardly. Cold sweat stood out on his forehead as he thought of Kristen.

"Who brought word?"

"Pete Bragg sent one of his hands. Bragg's all

right, but he saw the smoke coming from the Circle N. He lost plenty of stock, so it looks like a horse raid. Captain Warren and the Rangers are waitin' in the kitchen right now."

The kitchen was crammed with men smelling of horseflesh and leather. Dan hurried over to Captain Warren. Bart glanced around the crowded room and caught sight of a lean, older man standing in the far corner of the kitchen, sipping a steaming cup of coffee. His face was seamed and as worn as old leather, but his brown eyes were alert. What had caught Bart's attention was the fellow's Confederate cavalry officer's hat. The rest of his attire was leather and buckskin, a big Navy Colt stuck in his belt.

The older man saw Bart looking at him and smiled, as if he recognized him from somewhere. Bart returned the greeting with a nod. Putting down his cup, the stranger walked across the kitchen and stuck out his hand. Clasping it, Bart found the older man's grip surprisingly powerful. If Bart's father had been alive, he would have been this old—and just as powerful and alert.

"My name's Scott Tyrell," the fellow said, "and you'd be Bart Hardison, Matt's boy."

"That's me, all right."

"Recognized you right off, soon's you walked into this kitchen. You got plenty of your daddy in you. Sticks right out."

"You knew my father?"

"Back in the forties, down in Big Bend country. We did some hunting and fighting together. Took some Apache scalp amongst us—Comanch' too, whenever they got careless. I was sorry to hear about your pa. He was a fine man and a good friend."

There was an easy openness about Scott Tyrell that Bart liked. He wondered why his father had never mentioned Scott to him. But then, Bart's father had mentioned very little about his life before he settled down on the Brazos.

"You better get rid of that Confederate hat," Bart warned him with a grin. "You'll get in trouble with the carpetbaggers."

"That's just what I'm hopin'," Scott replied cheerfully, scratching the wiry red stubble that covered his chin. "But this hoss's seen trouble before." He took out a tobacco plug, sliced off a piece, and stuck it up into his cheek. "I knew your ma, too, Bart. Someone just mentioned she's feelin' poorly. I was thinkin' maybe I could duck in and say hello to her. Might cheer her up some."

"Sorry, Scott," Bart told him, "but I'd prefer you to wait on that. This here's a bad time for her. She's been through too much, I guess."

Scott nodded quickly, accepting Bart's refusal without resentment or comment.

At that moment Captain Warren's gravelly

voice boomed out above the loud talking that filled the room. He thanked Molly and Ellen for their hospitality, then told the men to finish their coffee and get outside. Bart left Scott Tyrell to pay his respects to Ellen and Molly. As the women bid him good-bye they did their best to hide their apprehension.

Then Bart followed Captain Warren and the crush of men flowing out into the night, bracing himself for the long ride to Kate Nordstrom's Circle N and trying not to think of what might have happened to either of the two women—especially Kristen.

Chapter Two

More than two years earlier, when Grant offered parole to the Confederate prisoners taken after Vicksburg, Seth Nordstrom was one of those Texans who took advantage of the offer. Kate Nordstrom was standing by the main corral with her foreman, Frank Kilrain, two weeks later when she caught sight of a horseman approaching the ranch. She and Frank watched the rider, straining to make out his identity.

Abruptly Kate's face hardened. "It's Seth."

Kilrain chucked his hat back off his forehead and squinted. "If you can see his face that far off, you got good eyes, Kate."

"It's the way he sits a horse. And he's alone."

"Yeah. So he is."

The ground seemed to shift under Kate's feet. She reached out and took hold of the corral post. Nightmare had become reality. Seth was returning alone, without Nils. And that could mean only one thing: Nils was dead. For a fleeting moment she wished she could lament in the fashion of Indian squaws who keened their sorrow aloud and slashed their breasts with knives.

But she was no savage. And she would not give Seth the satisfaction of seeing her weep again. In that cold dawn two years earlier, she had begged openly that he not take Nils. But her mighty lord and master remained unmoved by her pleas. Since that day she vowed she never again would humble herself before Seth—or *any* man.

Kate squared her shoulders.

"He looks pretty done in," Kilrain remarked.

"So he does."

"You want me to set off now?"

"It would be a good idea, Frank. We don't want them cattle to drift off too far."

Kilrain looked at Kate. She knew what was troubling him. He wanted to know if her husband's return meant the end of what they had found in each other—a brutal, uncaring passion that served a deep need for them both.

"I'll see you at supper?" he asked nervously.

"Of course."

"Inside the ranch house?"

She turned to look squarely at him, her dark

THE TEXAN

blue eyes coldly determined. "Yes. And tonight you'll be sitting at the *head* of the table."

He glanced quickly at the approaching rider. "But what about—?"

"You heard me, Frank."

With a relieved grin Kilrain pulled his horse around and mounted up. As he passed the gate he nodded curtly to Seth. Seth returned his greeting, a puzzled look on his face. He was curious about this stranger.

The interaction pleased Kate. She would let Seth wonder about this foreman she had hired. She would let him wonder about other things as well. Then, when he had wondered long enough, she would tell him.

As Seth came closer, his drawn face revealed the relief he felt at coming home. She could understand that. After returning from a terrible war that had taken two long years out of his life, his ranch house still stood. His wife and daughter were waiting for him.

He was home at last.

Had Kate felt any warmth for her husband, she would have been appalled at his gaunt, ravaged appearance. Seth had left a man in his prime and was returning a pale, withered husk. Yet, her husband's condition gave Kate a bitter satisfaction, a mean triumph she relished.

As Seth pulled his big gray gelding to a halt before her, she saw the hope in his eyes fade. He saw clearly the implacable coldness in Kate's eyes.

"Hello, Kate," he managed, his voice thin, hesitant.

"You've returned, Seth."

"Yes, Kate, I have."

"Without Nils."

"Yes."

"Where is he?"

"He won't be coming back. He's... dead, Kate."

"You know that for sure, do you?"

He nodded miserably. "We were separated. The Yankees were all around. He was hit twice. I saw him go down. He called out to me once. Then I took a ball in my thigh. I couldn't get up. I called out to him, but he didn't answer. I lay for most of a day in the mud until I was carried off to a field hospital. I tried to get someone to go back for him, but... they were so busy with the wounded and the dying..."

Kate snapped, "You buried Nils the moment you let him ride out of here with you and the Hardisons."

"It's done, Kate," Seth replied wearily, his shoulders slumping. "Done. And I've had a long ride. They're still killin' back there. But I came back."

"Without my son. Without Nils. It gives me no pleasure to see you, Seth. Is that plain enough?"

Seth dismounted and stepped toward Kate. "That's plain enough. You always were a direct woman, and I never wanted you any different. But you're my wife and I'm home."

He opened his arms to her.

She took a quick, angry step back. "Don't you touch me!"

"Kate, this ain't right! You're my wife. You ain't got no call to act like this."

She laughed contemptuously. "How should I act? Am I to open my arms to you once again so that we can make more sons for you to take off to war? No, husband. We will share no more embraces. Not you and I."

The hope in Seth's eyes faded. He looked for a long, miserable moment at Kate, then took up his horse's reins and moved past her, heading for the barn.

A sharp cry came from the ranch house.

Kate turned. Kristen was running across the yard to her father. Seth let go of the horse's reins and opened his arms to her. In a moment they were hugging each other, laughing and crying at the same time, tears of joy shining on their cheeks.

Kate watched them, unmoved, then walked past them into the ranch house and closed the door behind her.

In the months that followed, Seth Nordstrom seemed to accept the place Kilrain occupied in the running of the Circle N—and in Kate's life.

In fact, he was so resigned that Kristen sometimes wondered if perhaps her father was relieved to have Kilrain handling those husbandly responsibilities he no longer had the desire or will to assume.

But slowly, steadily, Seth regained his strength. His sunken cheeks filled out, and his eyes emerged from their dark hollows. Yet Nils's death had taken something vital out of his core. For hours on end he stared into the fire. And he often rode out without a word, to return late at night without explanation.

Once Kristen had ridden out after him. He had been gone all day and she was worried. When she finally caught sight of him, he was astride his horse on a knoll, staring into the distance. She turned back without hailing him, unwilling to break into his lonely vigil. Her father, she realized, was suffering from a profound spiritual weariness. Watching him, Kristen thought her heart would break. The gods had punished him mercilessly for having gone off to war with Nils, and now all Kristen wanted was to give her father some peace at last.

He had suffered enough.

During Seth's absence Kate and Kristen had survived three major Comanche attacks, plus "murder raids" by a few young bucks eager for action. The first attack was handled by Kate and

THE TEXAN

Kristen with the timely help of a surprisingly effective mounted force led by Captain Warren. But the Circle N had not escaped unscathed. Their toolshed, the blacksmith shop, and both barns had been burned to the ground. And they had lost many fine horses.

Surveying the damages grimly, Kate made her decision.

Leaving the Baileys to keep watch over the ranch house, Kate took Kristen with her to San Antonio. There they took a room in a hotel above the roughest saloon in town. From her window Kate watched the men in the street below. She studied them carefully, then made her choice. Kristen could not be sure what influenced her mother's decision, but the man she approached finally was Frank Kilrain. Offering Kilrain the job of foreman, she let him know that anything else he felt he was man enough to take, he could have. Kilrain—appraising Kate's handsome features and fine figure—understood what she meant. He accepted her offer, and along with three of his acquaintances he hired to serve under him as ranch hands, he rode north with Kate and Kristen to the Circle N.

Less than a month later Kilrain visited Kate's bedroom. He showed up around midnight and left before dawn to return to the bunkhouse. From that night on he slept with Kate whenever his or her needs required. His nocturnal visits followed the pattern they had set that first night, a condition Kate insisted upon.

Kilrain offered no objection to the arrangement and was careful to keep his relationship to Kristen polite but distant. Though Kate made no attempt to hide any of this from Kristen, she gave her daughter little opportunity to confront her on the matter and made it clear to Kilrain that unless he kept the arrangement discreet, it would end. The boundaries thus drawn were clear and unequivocal, and Frank Kilrain was smart enough not to cross them.

With the help of Kilrain and the three ranch hands, Kate rebuilt the barns, the blacksmith shop, and the toolshed. Then, under Kate's direction, more logs and adobe were added to the ranch house walls until they reached a thickness of three and, in some places, four feet. To protect the roof against the Kiowa's fire arrows they laid down a shake roof over two feet of sod. The doors were reinforced with massive oak logs designed to absorb bullets as well as arrows, and the windows were fitted with heavy battle shutters.

The Baileys, after an afternoon visit, christened it Nordstrom's Fort. Kate was pleased. A fort was what she needed in this outpost of savagery, and now she had it. She soon discovered that others along the Brazos were forting up their ranch houses, following her plans for the Circle N. She felt a certain pride in being the first.

THE TEXAN

Not long after—almost as if the Comanche had been waiting for the chance to test Nordstrom's Fort—a large war party of Comanche and Kiowa swept down upon the river valley. There was a bright Comanche moon that night, and the Indian force seemed determined to breach the walls of Kate's ranch house. From inside the fort, with two women loading and four men keeping up a steady, murderous fire, they held off each successive attack until morning. The savages picked up their dead and wounded, mounted up, and rode back the way they had come.

Another attack six months later was also repulsed. But this time one of the Circle N's ranch hands was killed by the Comanche. He had been overtaken and cut down before he could make it back to the ranch house.

On a golden autumn day almost a year after her father's return, Kristen was feeding the chickens when she saw smoke on the eastern horizon. It was a familiar sight, and she knew immediately what it meant. A ranch was going up in flames. Judging from the distance and direction, Kristen realized it was the Baileys' place. She dropped the pan of corn and ran back toward the ranch house to warn her mother. Before she reached the house, a hard-riding youngster rode into the compound.

The Comanche war party was a big one, the

boy told them excitedly. The Comanche and their Kiowa allies were spread out at least a mile wide and were taking their time as they moved down the valley, burning, looting, and raping with a ferocity surprising even for the Comanche.

As the boy rode off to warn others, Kate sent Kristen in to prepare for an attack. Then she hurried off to find Seth. Kilrain and her two remaining hands were in the bottomlands, rounding up stock. Seth would have to warn them.

Kate found Seth slumped forward on a table in the rear of the bunkhouse, a crock of moonshine sitting beside him.

"Seth!" she called, shaking him. "Get up!"

Seth stirred. He saw Kate and sat back in the chair, gazing at her through narrow, embittered eyes. "What do you want, woman?"

"Comanche! They're raidin' the valley!"

Seth reached for the crock. Kate snatched it from him and flung it against the wall. Furious, Seth grabbed the front of Kate's dress and drew her close.

"Damn you, Kate! I'm finished! I've had all I can take from you!"

Kate pulled herself out of his grasp and slapped him so hard, Seth was momentarily stunned. He leapt out of his chair and grabbed her around the neck. She struggled to free herself, but he tightened his grip, forcing her down to the floor. He was breathing heavily, his face distorted with rage.

THE TEXAN

Somehow Kate managed to grab hold of his wrists and loosen his fingers enough to get out a small, piercing cry.

It was enough. Startled out of his nightmare, Seth pulled back. He relaxed his fingers and released Kate. Kate gulped air into her lungs and struggled up onto her feet. Her breath was coming in painful gasps as she gazed at Seth with cold, withering scorn.

"You finished, are you?"

Seth looked down at his hands as if they had betrayed him, and then at her. "I...sorry, Kate," he told her. "I...must've lost my head."

"Yes," Kate said coldly. "So you did."

"My God, Kate," he told her. "We can't go on like this!"

"No, we can't."

"You've got to get rid of Frank."

"No."

"But I'm your husband! Not him. The whole valley's talkin'! It ain't Christian, you keepin' him on like this."

"I don't care what talk there is."

"You mean you love him?"

She laughed shortly. "I assure you, Seth, Frank means nothing to me."

Hope sprang into Seth's eyes. "Then you'll send him packin'?"

"I'll do nothin' of the sort. If anyone should be sent packin', it's you. You're not good for anything around here, Seth. You ain't been worth a pitcher of warm spit ever since you came back."

He rubbed his forehead and looked around him miserably. "Maybe if you hadn't froze me out, Kate." His face cracked, as if he were going to cry.

"For God's sake, Seth!" she told him scornfully. "Act like a man! I told you! The Comanche are raidin' the valley. Go after Frank and the men. Warn them!"

The word *Comanche* sobered him instantly. "Comanche?"

"Yes!"

"Where are they? Which direction are they coming from?"

"The Bailey place. They're sweeping down the valley, heading right for us. Frank and the men are out there. I want you to go after them. Warn them."

"All right," he told her. "I'll go after them. But before I go, I want you to know one thing, Kate. When I come back, things're goin' to be different around here. I've taken all I'm going to take."

"*Have* you, now."

"Yes, Kate. I have."

"We'll see about that," Kate replied.

She turned and strode from the bunkhouse.

Late that afternoon Kilrain, with Barker and Carl trailing behind him, rode in through the

THE TEXAN

gate on lathered horses. When they dismounted in front of the ranch house, Kristen ran out to ask about her father. Kilrain shrugged and told her he hadn't seen him. He and the two hands had heard about the Comanche raid from a family fleeing toward town. They had promptly driven the rounded-up stock into the cedar brakes on the near side of the Brazos, then headed back to the ranch. As they rode, they had glimpsed a few Comanche in the distance but had managed to outride them.

"Then Pa's still searching for you!" Kristen told them.

Kilrain nodded. "I reckon so, Miss Kristen."

"One of you has to go after him."

The three men looked at each other uneasily and turned to Kate. They were hoping she would contradict Kristen.

And she did not disappoint them. "They can't do that, Kristen," Kate said. "Them Comanche are getting close. Look at that smoke on the sky. That'll be the Clemm place."

"But, Mother! Pa's out there looking for Frank! He don't know the men're back! He'll stay out there and keep lookin'!"

"He's a man able to take care of hisself, Miss Kristen," allowed Frank. "He's been through a war and all."

"If you don't go after him, Frank, I will!"

"No, you won't," Kate told Kristen firmly.

Kristen spun around, then pushed furiously past her mother into the house. Following her, Kate heard the door to Kristen's room slam shut. She turned around and stuck her head back out the ranch house door.

"Ride out a little ways, Cullen," she told one of the hands. "Keep in sight of the ranch. Seth might see you and come in. If you catch sign of any Comanche, get back here. We'll get everything ready inside."

Reluctantly Cullen mounted up and rode out of the compound. Kate went back inside and knocked on the door to Kristen's room. After a moment a grim Kristen pulled open her door, her face streaked with tears.

"I just sent one of the men out to look for Seth," Kate told her. "Come and help me get things ready."

For the next hour or so the women and the men saw to it that each window had an ample supply of powder, cartridges, and percussion caps. For the inevitable fire arrows they lugged buckets of water into the ranch house, setting them down at strategic locations. Close on to sunset, they were going out for still more water when Cullen rode into the compound.

Flinging himself from his horse, he pulled up in front of Kate and Kristen. "Seth's riding here for sure," he said. "I just seen him. He won't be long now."

"You should've waited for him," Kristen snapped.

"I waited as long as I could, Miss Kristen. They're all around us now. There's smoke on every horizon."

"I haven't seen a single savage!" Kristen snapped, hurrying past the horse barn to peer into the fading light.

Pausing just outside the gate, she went up on tiptoes. Her heart leapt. Her father was moving steadily across the wide sweep of grassland. She ran a few yards into the tall grass and waved to him.

She thought he waved back, but she could not be sure.

Standing there, her heart pounding, she found it difficult to believe they were surrounded by Comanche warriors. Everything was so peaceful. The evening light was clear, enabling her to see so much farther now than in the full light of day. The prairie rolled away majestically, a great ocean of grass, apparently empty.

About a quarter of a mile off to her right a covey of quail exploded suddenly into the sky, and a meadow lark that had bedded down for the night shot into the air, circled unhappily, then zig-zagged away into the gathering dusk. Noting these signs, Kristen's heart almost stopped. Then she saw the bobbing heads and shoulders of mounted savages riding through the tall grass toward her.

Kristen looked anxiously back at her father.

"Kristen!" Kate called from the ranch house doorway. "Get back in here!"

Ignoring her mother's pleas, she waved frantically at her father. "Hurry, Pa!" she cried. "Hurry!"

He motioned with his arm, urging her to make for the safety of the ranch house. But she was determined to wait for him. By that time Frank and her mother had reached her. Frank had one of the Sharps. He fired at the closest of the mounted Comanche. The Indian peeled back off his pony, vanishing in the grass.

Kate grabbed Kristen's arm. "Kristen!" she pleaded. "Get back to the ranch house!"

"No! I'm waitin' for Pa!"

"Frank, take her!" Kate ordered.

Frank handed Kate his rifle and grabbed Kristen's arms, pinning them behind her so he could carry her back to the house. Furious, she kicked wildly at Frank's shins. Frank swore and let her go. Kristen ran a few yards closer to her father.

Again Seth motioned to her with his arm.

"Get back!" he cried, his voice faint but clear now. "Get back to the house!"

The sound of his voice calmed Kristen. Satisfied that her father would make it to safety, Kristen ran back to the ranch house with her

THE TEXAN

mother and Frank. As they neared the door an arrow seared past them, burying itself in the doorjamb. The three ducked swiftly inside, and Frank slammed the door shut. Cullen Barker and Carl were at the windows, rifles in their hands, the battle shutters in place.

Kristen ran over to the firing slit next to the door. Peering out, she saw her father galloping into the compound just ahead of the mounted Comanche. She left the firing slit and stepped to the door. Shoving aside the heavy wooden beam, she flung it open. But Frank Kilrain pushed her away and slammed the door shut, hastily sliding back the beam.

"Frank!" Kristen cried. "Pa's out there!"

"It's too late!" the foreman told her. "If we let him in, the Comanche will come right in with him!"

"Stand aside, Frank," said Cullen. "I can get Seth in. Just give me cover."

As Cullen spoke, he pushed the wooden beam aside and pulled open the door. But both Kilrain and Carl yanked Cullen back out of the doorway and slammed the door shut again.

"No!" screamed Kristen, throwing herself at the two men. "Open the door!"

Kate flung Kristen from the door so forcefully that Kristen fell to the floor. Dazed, she looked up to see her mother standing beside Frank Kilrain, her back to the door.

"Mother!" she cried. "Let Pa in!"

"You heard Frank!" Kate told Kristen, her face distraught. "It's too late! If we open that door now, we'll be letting the Comanche in too!"

Screaming, Kristen scrambled to her feet and rushed to the rifle slit. She was in time to see her father fling himself from his horse and bolt toward the ranch house, an arrow protruding from his arm. A moment later his booted feet pounded up onto the porch. He was out of Kristen's line of sight now, but she could hear him hurl himself against the door. Once, twice, he flung himself against it, pleading to be let in.

The Comanche swarmed up onto the porch after him. Kristen could hear the sounds of a struggle and saw her father driving the Comanche back off the porch with his thundering Colt. His Colt empty, Seth used it as a club and caught one Comanche on the side of his head, sending him reeling back off the porch. Then Seth disappeared from sight as the savages swarmed over him.

A moment later, as the Comanche dragged Seth back across the yard in the face of a murderous fire from the ranch house, one of the savages stopped to wave Seth's scalp at the defenders inside. A second later the Comanche pitched forward as a concentrated volley cut him down.

A fearsome night followed. Dense, choking clouds of gunpowder filled the ranch house as the men kept up a steady volley of fire. Through it all Kristen and her mother were kept busy loading and handling the nearly scalding rifles to the men at the firing slits.

The Comanche seemed deranged by their desire to reduce Nordstrom's Fort. Contrary to their usual tactics, they made repeated and costly direct assaults upon it, as if its impregnability had become a personal challenge. A little before dawn, using one of the barn's smoldering timbers for a battering ram, they ran up onto the porch and flung the ram at the massive door. Again and again they brought the battering ram against it. But it held, and those savages wielding the ram were cut to ribbons by the men's fire. With gradually diminishing enthusiasm the attack continued until near daybreak when—for some reason—the Comanche pulled back.

In the silence that followed, those inside the ranch house heard a series of high, broken screams. It was Kristen's father crying out in torment, pleading for death to come. As the first light of dawn broke over the prairie the screams continued until at last nothing was heard but the moaning, whimpering cry of a poor tortured creature who was no longer human.

Listening to her father, Kristen thought she would go mad. She flung herself repeatedly at the door, calling out her father's name. Kate and the others had to keep her from clawing open the door and rushing out to him.

It wasn't until full daylight that Seth's screams ceased.

A little later Kate saw the barbaric tide of Comanche and Kiowa, driving the stock they had captured before them, sweep past Nordstrom's Fort and move off down the valley.

Despite Kate's attempts to prevent it, Kristen was the one who found her father. Seth was lying in a charred depression behind the smoldering ruins of the toolshed. Kate heard Kristen's screams and dragged her back into the ranch house while the men saw to a hurried burial.

Closing Kristen's bedroom door behind her, Kate watched her daughter collapse onto her bed, dry sobs racking her. Kate sat down and placed a comforting hand on Kristen's shoulder.

Tears streaming down her face, she glared up at Kate.

"Frank killed Pa!"

Kate drew back. "That's nonsense and you know it!"

"Frank did it so he could have you!"

"You don't know what you're saying!"

"Yes, I do. And you helped him. You wanted him to kill Pa. You wanted him to!"

Kate pushed herself off the bed and stared down at Kristen. "My God, no, Kristen. I didn't!

THE TEXAN

We had no choice. If we let Seth through the door, that whole pack of savages would have come in! And you know it!"

"You did it for me, then."

"For all of us!"

"I don't believe you."

Kate looked for a long moment at her distraught daughter. Then she took a deep, miserable breath. There was no reasoning with Kristen, she realized.

"Then believe what you want," Kate snapped.

She turned and left the room.

A month or so after her husband's death Kate allowed Frank to resume his evening visits. With her new status as a widow and sole owner of a cattle ranch, she found it difficult to keep Frank in his place. But she managed by curtly refusing to discuss any future alliance with him.

Kate was determined that never again would she suffer under the petty, mindless tyranny of a man. If God himself appeared before her in chaps and Stetson to ask for her hand, she would have sent him packing.

Now, it was a year later, after still another Comanche raid—this time by a pack of drunken savages. A rifle resting across her pommel, Kate watched the arrival of Captain Warren and his men. As the horsemen rode closer, she recognized

Bart Hardison among them. So he was back from the war.

She took a deep breath. Seeing Bart made her think of Nils. Nils would have sat just as tall in the saddle. Perhaps he would have been slimmer— it had always been impossible to put meat on his bones. But his face would have looked as alive and strong as Bart's. And just as handsome.

The barns and outbuildings in the compound behind her were black, ashen ruins. Small tongues of fire still gleamed among the ashes, and a blue, smoky haze hung over the land. The raiding Comanche had swirled around the squat, solid adobe and log ranch house for most of the night. In their foolish, drunken attempt to smash through its massive door, quite a few had been cut down. But Nordstrom Fort had held.

Only this time they had ridden off with Kristen.

Chapter Three

As Bart rode up with the others, he saw Kate—ramrod straight astride a powerful black—waiting for them in front of the gate, a rifle across her pommel.

Though Bart was relieved to see the Circle N ranch house still standing, he wondered where Kristen was. He looked past Kate and thought he caught a glimpse of her inside at one of the windows. But when he looked closer, the image was gone, and he realized it must have been the grim, pale shadows of the morning that had tricked him. If Kristen was inside, he reasoned, she would have stepped out onto the porch to greet him—as she had that morning so many years before. But she did not appear, and his anxiety grew more intense.

Riding closer, Bart saw in Kate's face the same strength, the same indomitable force he had known before the war. But there was something else as well—a bleak, cheerless tenacity of purpose that left no room for weakness or temporizing. As Kate watched the Rangers ride closer, her gaze was cold and uncompromising. She uttered not a single word of greeting to the dust-covered, weary body of men who had ridden to her aid clear through the night, pushing themselves and their mounts to the limit. Noting this and seeing how still Kate sat her big black, Bart found himself thinking how little this Kate Nordstrom resembled the woman he had known before the war.

During those days Kate had presided over the Nordstrom household with a loving efficiency that was a comfort to all those within its warm embrace. Kate had a way of watching over her charges from a distance, then quietly providing what they needed without complaint or fuss. Her kitchen was filled constantly with the mouthwatering aromas of baking bread and simmering soups, of gingerbread men or brownies swelling in the oven, and always, it seemed, there was the deep, rich aroma of Arbuckle's coffee perking on the stove.

But that had been a long time ago.

Captain Warren and Dan O'Hare pulled to a halt in front of Kate, greeting her with a wary, subdued respect. The rest of the Rangers reined in close behind them. Kate returned Warren's greeting curtly, letting her glance sweep past him, resting for a moment on Bart before turning her dark blue, intent eyes back to Captain Warren.

"This all the men you brought, Captain?"

"That's right, Kate."

"We'll need more."

"Why, Kate? The Comanche are long gone from the looks of it. We can chase them, but they'll lose us soon enough. You know that."

"Captain, those savages have taken my daughter!"

"My God, Kate!" The captain's voice was hushed. "They've taken Kristen?"

"You heard me, Captain."

Bart did not want to believe his ears. As the impact of Kate's words struck him he felt an angry surge of helplessness. Around him the Rangers moved restlessly in their saddles, many many swearing softly, bitterly. Those who knew of Bart and Kristen pulled away to give Bart a chance to recover from the shock of what he had just heard.

"Kate, I'm sorry," Dan O'Hare said, his voice heavy with concern.

"Don't be sorry! Just get after them damn

savages! They ain't that far ahead of us. I want Kristen back! Frank Kilrain and the boys are on their trail now. They'll be leaving sign for us to follow."

"How many were in their war party?" Captain Warren asked.

"Two dozen at least. They was drunk as lords, most of them, too drunk to mount any real attack. We drove them off easy—but not before they caught Kristen hidin' in the brush along the river."

"They take anything else?"

"Most of my horse herd."

"Well, that might slow 'em down some."

"What are we palaverin' here for, Captain? I say we move out—now! They're only two—maybe three—hours ahead of us."

Captain Warren cleared his throat, his face suddenly red. He wasn't happy taking orders from a woman, even if that woman was Kate Nordstrom. He turned to his men.

"All right!" he told them. "You heard Kate! We're pulling out! No need for us to hold up for any coffee or breakfast."

There was no grumbling, even though the men were as weary as they were famished. With Kate riding at the head of the column alongside Captain Warren and Dan O'Hare, they set out.

Before long they spotted the first marker Kilrain

had left for them to find—a clump of grass tied around the middle with longer strands. As Bart rode on past it he saw that it resembled the little grass dolls Kiowa squaws made for their children.

By the third day the Rangers were beginning to grumble. They had come pretty far and were nearing the Staked Plains, that high, windswept steppeland stretching unbroken as far as the horizon—for years a Comanche stronghold. It was unsettling to ride this far into *Comancheria,* but Kate Nordstrom's tireless example kept the men from complaining openly.

On the fifth day, a few hours before sundown, the Rangers were making camp in a cottonwood clump—the first real break in the monotonous swells of grass they had put behind them—when one of the Rangers warned of approaching riders.

A moment later Kilrain and two other hands came riding toward them. Kate mounted up hastily and galloped out to greet them. A moment later the three men, exhausted and drawn from their long chase, were dismounting in the Rangers' midst. They were hardly on the ground before Captain Warren asked if they had found the raiding party.

Kilrain nodded quickly and pointed back to a low line of hills fronting a distant mountain range. "In them hills there's a canyon," he said. "They're camped down in it."

"How far is it?"

"It ain't far, no more'n a two-hour ride."

"Did you see Kristen?" Bart asked.

"I couldn't be sure," Kilrain replied.

"Well, what can you tell us?" Dan asked impatiently.

"They got a woman, all right," Kilrain replied hastily. "A white woman. We know that for sure."

Dan O'Hare turned to Captain Warren. "I say we move on them now. Maybe we can surprise them."

"We got two hours or so before dark," the captain replied. "We'll wait and catch our breath, see to our weapons, then attack. And for that our horses'll need some rest—and so will we."

The men saw good sense in that advice and moved away.

Finding a cottonwood for shade, Bart and Scott Tyrell sat down under it. Kate Nordstrom and Frank Kilrain were slumped on a low knoll, the other two ranch hands nearby. Studying Kate's choice for a foreman, Bart was not impressed.

Every man there knew why Kilrain had not been able to tell for sure if that was Kristen with the Comanche. He hadn't had the guts to get close enough to find out. The men were all eager to save Kristen from the Comanche. At the same time they were aware that if their attack wasn't a complete surprise, the Indians would have enough time to slit Kristen's throat.

To these men of the Brazos valley, Kristen's beauty and exemplary character were well-known. Never as austere and unapproachable as her mother, Kristen's capture was keenly felt. Unless they were successful this night, something very fine would be taken from them forever.

Every frontier family knew how the Comanche used the women they captured. If Kristen were to live with the savages for any length of time, then be ransomed or traded back, she would be regarded by every respectable family as just another savage. Though she might look the same and walk the same and still be a Nordstrom, no family would invite her to their home; no man would seek her hand in marriage. Defiled by the cruel violations of her savage captors, she would become a social leper.

Which meant Kristen had to be rescued from these devils this very night.

Scott held out his canteen to Bart. Bart took it. It was heavy but not with water. Bart hesitated.

"I don't need no bravo juice," Bart told him.

"I know you don't. Drink up."

Bart gulped down the raw whiskey and handed back the canteen. The fiery liquid burned a path down his gullet and sent its hot comfort clear into his bootstraps. Scott took a second lick, then glanced over at Kate and her foreman.

"Looks like them two are as close as peas in a pod," he said. "Can't say as I understand it. That man's a gun slick if I ever saw one—and Kate Nordstrom, from what I can see, is one strong woman and the owner of one of the biggest spreads in the valley."

"Bad things can happen to people," Bart said, "if you can believe it."

"Yeah," Scott grunted. "I can believe it. Especially in Texas."

An hour later, as the men rubbed their horses down with wads of dry grass, Captain Warren and Dan O'Hare approached Bart. He was busy checking his rifle's load.

"Bart," said Dan, "the captain here wants you to speak to Kate for him."

Bart looked at Captain Warren. "Why me, Captain? Kate makes a mean cup of coffee, but she ain't et nobody I can think of."

"We just figure she might be more civil with you," Warren replied uneasily. "You was pretty close to her and Kristen before the war."

"What do you want me to tell her?"

"It looks like Kate's getting ready to ride with us," he said. "She's been cleaning her rifle and Colt."

"That's her privilege, ain't it? Kristen's her daughter."

"She'll more'n likely get her head blown off," said the captain. His round, beefy face was growing red. "You got to ask her to stay back."

"Here, in these cottonwoods?"

"Yes."

"Alone?"

"No, of course not."

"So who's going to stay back with her?"

"I was hoping you would, Bart."

"Me?"

"Yes."

Bart had difficulty keeping his anger in check. "Forget it."

"You mean you won't talk to her?"

"I mean I'm not staying behind to watch over Kate Nordstrom. She don't need any help from me. She can look after herself. And if you want Kate Nordstrom to stay back here, you tell her. You're the one supposed to be in command."

"That's your last word?"

"Yes."

Captain Warren looked to Dan for help. Dan shrugged and turned away. The two men walked off.

Scott moved up alongside Bart, a sly grin on his face. "You didn't make Captain Warren very happy there."

"A man that foolish shouldn't ever be happy.

Besides, Kate will do what she wants, anyway. She has that right. Like I said, Kristen's her daughter."

With Kate and Kilrain riding alongside Captain Warren, they left the cottonwoods and crossed the moonlit stretch of prairie. They experienced no difficulty in finding the canyon where the Comanche were camped. Halting a few yards behind the rim, they dismounted and peered down into the encampment. Smoke coiled up from two of the three camp fires set close by the broad, shallow stream that wound through the canyon.

In all, Bart counted no more than ten blanketed figures lying around the fires. He didn't like that. It meant the war party had split up. But Kilrain had spotted a white women, and chances were Kristen was down there now, one of those huddled, blanketed figures. Farther down the canyon Bart glimpsed the Comanche horse herd. Mostly ponies. There was no sign of Kate's stock.

Scott noticed this as well. He grumbled to Bart, "I don't see any of Kate's horse herd."

"Maybe they're farther up the canyon."

Scott let fly a gob of chewing tobacco. "You know what's more helpless than a turtle on its back?"

"Nope."

"A Comanche afoot."

"So?"

"I say we circle around behind that pony herd and stampede it—right through the encampment. By the time them red devils realize what hit them, we'd be on them. And so would the Rangers. Our Comanche brothers would have nowhere to run. Without their ponies they'd be gone beaver, with no chance to hurt Kristen."

"Sounds good, Scott."

They pulled back from the canyon rim and described their plan to Captain Warren and Kate. They agreed to it instantly.

"We'll give you and your men an hour to reach the canyon floor," Scott told the captain. "When we start the stampede, move—and move fast."

"You figure you two are going to be enough?"

"Yes," said Bart.

"Good luck, then."

They led their horses along the rim until they found a narrow game trail and followed it to the floor of the canyon. They crossed the river, then swung to the canyon wall on the far side and, keeping close under the rim, kept on past the Comanche camp, then recrossed the river and circled back toward the Comanche pony herd.

When they judged themselves to be close enough, they tethered their horses and moved closer on foot, staying in the brush just under the cliff until they saw the herd ahead of them bunched loosely behind a rope corral.

Peering cautiously out from a clump of juniper, they looked for sign of any Comanche guarding the ponies.

"There's one," whispered Scott.

"Where?"

He pointed. "Over at them trees."

Wrapped in his blanket, the Indian was sprawled under a cottonwood, fast asleep. It was obvious this Comanche didn't expect anyone to trouble him or the ponies. Not this night, anyway. Bart understood. Comanches would chase something only until they got tired of chasing it. Then they would give up. That was their way. They had no conception of the white man's tenacity, his singleness of purpose when it came to going after what was his.

Bart lifted his head to peer over the backs of the ponies. The river was just beyond the herd and to their right. Straight ahead on the other side of the ponies, between the river and canyon wall, was the Comanche camp.

"I'll get that guard," Scott told Bart. "Wait for me by our horses."

"Like hell."

"What's wrong?"

"This here ain't your party."

"Sure it is, Bart. Besides, I need you at my rear. In case this here sleeper ain't the only Comanche guardin' these ponies."

"All right. Take care of that Comanche over there and I'll wait back where we left our horses."

As Scott circled around behind the sleeping Comanche, Bart moved cautiously back the hundred yards or more into the timber to their mounts.

He was reaching out to pat his horse when he heard a moccasined foot crushing the pine-needle floor behind him. Whirling, he brought up his Colt. The Comanche's war club came down just as quickly, knocking his weapon away. Bart was reaching back for his knife when the Comanche bowled into him and sent him flying.

His head struck the ground. Dazed, Bart felt the Indian grabbing his hair with one hand. He opened his eyes and saw the Indian raising his hatchet. Something hard smacked into the Comanche's chest—Scott's bowie knife. The Comanche sagged to his knees, trying to pull the knife out from between his ribs. Then he toppled forward onto its handle. Scott moved past Bart and kicked the dead Indian over onto his back. He withdrew his knife and wiped it on his thigh.

"Figured there'd be another one out here," Scott remarked. "I watched that son of a bitch stalking you." He grinned. "I guess maybe he thought *you* were the only one out here."

"We were both wrong," Bart admitted, rubbing

the back of his head. He blinked his eyes to clear his vision.

Scott reached down and helped him up. "You hurt?"

"Only my pride." Bart grinned and ran his hand through his hair. "I'm glad I still have this hair. Thanks, Scott."

Scott shrugged. "When you get the chance, return the favor."

"I'll do that. Did you get the other one all right?"

"Wouldn't be back here if I hadn't. You ready to move out?"

"Wait'll I get my Colt."

Scott mounted up as Bart found his Colt and dropped it back into his holster.

"Okay, partner," Bart said, swinging up onto his horse. "Let's give them Comanche ponies a ride."

A silver-dollar moon sat directly overhead. Its light sent a pale, bluish sheen over the canyon's grassy floor. With Scott on his right flank and the herd directly ahead, Bart urged his horse to a hard gallop. Scott did likewise. The pounding hooves alerted the ponies. For a moment they froze, their heads lifting, their ears flickering. Then Bart sent two quick shots into the night sky.

Like a single animal, the herd bolted down the

canyon, heading straight for the Comanche camp. As they approached the smoldering camp fires a sudden hail of gunfire came from the slope close above the encampment as Captain Warren and his force broke from the timber. Then the herd stampeded through the Indian encampment. Some Comanche were bowled over, others were trampled. A few Indians tried to stop or mount the spooked horses. They were dragged aways, then forced to drop off.

Meanwhile, the Rangers were rushing across the valley floor toward them while the remaining Comanche flung aside their blankets and leapt to their feet, reaching for any weapons at hand. As the stampeding ponies disappeared into the night Bart turned his mount toward three Comanche who were sending a rapid fire at the oncoming Rangers.

Flinging himself from his saddle, Bart took down the closest Comanche with a chopping blow to his Adam's apple, then sent two quick bullets into the belly of another. The third Comanche came at him from the side, flinging an arm around his neck. Bart saw the Comanche's knife ready to plunge into his chest. Something stopped the Indian. Dropping his knife, the Comanche sagged forward to the ground, a gaping bullet hole in his back.

Glancing up, Bart saw Dan O'Hare sweep past him, yelling like a Saturday night drunk, his big six-gun smoking as he picked off two more Comanche.

On all sides now, the Rangers came riding down upon the encampment. The high, unsettling battle cry of the Comanche could be heard above the gunfire, sending ice into the veins of the white men who heard it. No one liked hand-to-hand combat better than the Comanche—and not one of them gave quarter as the battle raged.

Bart saw Dan O'Hare—having galloped through the entire encampment—turning his mount to run down a Comanche, his gun still blazing. The Comanche collapsed, and as Dan swept past him, he sent one more round into the Indian for good measure. Then two Comanche rose from the thick grass beside Dan's pounding horse and loosed a quick flurry of arrows at him. One arrow caught Dan under his shoulder. Dan ripped out the arrow and flung it away. Then he turned his horse and ran down both Comanches.

Someone shouted a warning to Bart. He turned. A Comanche was rushing him. Bart fired, but his round went high and the Comanche caught Bart on the side of the head with his war club. The blow staggered him but he kept on his feet somehow and flung up his forearm as the war club came down a second time. The force of this second blow nearly shattered Bart's forearm and sent him tumbling to the grass.

THE TEXAN

On his back he cocked and fired up at the Comanche. Again his shot went wild. A Ranger rode toward him, pouring a stream of bullets into the Comanche's back. With a tremendous leap the Ranger's horse cleared Bart, and the Ranger galloped off. Bart jumped to his feet to see Kilrain being pulled out of his saddle by a Comanche.

Bart charged, bowling the savage off Kilrain. The Indian was staggered, but he did not go down. Swinging around, he jabbed Bart in the solar plexus with his war club. Bart reeled back and fired at the brave. The Indian sagged and came to a halt on his knees. He hung there for a moment in total surprise, a hole in his naked chest. Then he toppled forward, lifeless, to the ground.

As suddenly as it had begun, the fighting was over. An awesome silence fell over the moonlit battlefield. The only sound was that of horses blowing in the distance. And from the look of it there was not a single Comanche still alive.

But where was Kristen?

Bart glanced around quickly. His hope was that when the battle erupted, Kristen had had enough sense to keep down—or maybe break away from her captors. As Bart scanned the eerily quiet, moonlit field, he saw no blond figure rising from the ground.

"Over there!"

"We see her!" another cried happily.

Bart saw Kate, astride her black, charge across the clearing toward the two Rangers who were hurrying to the aid of a woman rising from a shallow depression in the ground. Elated, Bart raced toward Kristen—as did every other man there.

But when Bart reached the crowd of Rangers around the girl, Kate was already turning away, her face as somber and pale as death. Looking past her, Bart saw a frail woman accept a blanket from Dan O'Hare. Her light hair was awry, her eyes wild as she hastily pulled the blanket around her naked figure.

But this woman was sure as hell not Kristen.

Chapter Four

Kristen's captor was a renowned war chief of the Kotsoteka Comanche. Before coming upon and then joining forces with a smaller Nokoni war party, Iron Cheek had led his fourteen warriors deep into Texas, ranging among the isolated ranches at will, looting and killing with ridiculous ease.

For the past three years it was plain to him that some scourge—a new spotted sickness, perhaps—had taken the *tejano* warriors, leaving only old men and women alive to do battle or defend their lodges. It had been good to see this. No white eyes were more hated than the *tejanos*. To be able to loot and pillage their lodges, drive off their stock, rape their women, and take their children was sweet meat indeed. No longer did the Buffalo Eaters have to follow the trace deep into Mexico for plunder and fresh horses. The *tejanos* were closer and served equally as well. Soon the people would drive the hated *tejanos* from these plains, as they had the Apache before them.

But this would not be easy. One young Texan had recently proven that to Iron Cheek. Breaking out of timber near one ranch, Iron Cheek's warriors had flushed out a young *tejano*. One of the band's best warriors took off after him. As the boy ran, he shouted back a warning to the mounted warrior chasing him. The warrior laughed, drew up alongside him, and leapt from his pony onto his back.

But as the young *tejano* crumpled to the ground under the warrior's weight, he drew a knife from his boot and sank it deep into the warrior's chest, killing him. Racing up, Iron Cheek brought his hatchet whistling down. The blade split the boy's skull clear to his shoulders, sending a geyser of blood as high as his pony's belly.

It was soon after this that a Nokoni war party rode up. At once Iron Cheek saw the advantage of joining forces. But this move soon proved to be a mistake when the Nokoni warriors came upon an abandoned wagon and found it filled with crocks of whiskey. Despite Iron Cheek's protests, the stupid water was soon passed around. Even

Iron Cheek himself had been unable to resist. From that point on, their effectiveness as a raiding party diminished rapidly, convincing Iron Cheek that it was the young *tejano*'s headless spirit that had robbed him of his medicine.

After the unsuccessful assault on Nordstrom's Fort, aware that three *tejanos* were trailing them, Iron Cheek took most of the horses they had driven off and announced to the Nokoni war chief that he was returning to his village. He was taking the two women captives with him. He did not think much of the dark-haired one, but he was hungry for the woman with the golden hair. She was worth many scalps, and he had set her aside for his own pleasure. She had spirit, and he liked that.

When the Nokoni chief protested that Iron Cheek was taking too many of the horses, Iron Cheek explained to him patiently that his own warriors, no longer filled with stupid water, had done the bulk of the fighting. The Nokoni war chief, holding on to a whiskey crock, decided not to argue the point and led his warriors northwest, toward a small canyon where they planned to hold their victory dance.

Kristen sensed a lessening of tension and realized that her captors now considered themselves safely back in their home country. This filled her with despair. There was little chance that she would be found now, even if anyone tried to come after her. She would soon be swallowed up into one the Comanche tribes and forgotten.

To those she had left behind in the Brazos valley, she was as good as dead. Watching how another woman captive, Anna Mowbry, was being treated by the warriors, Kristen could only shudder and look away, praying that she would not have to endure such horror—yet knowing in her heart that if her turn came, there would be nothing she could do to prevent it.

The girl had already been a captive when Kristen was taken. Apparently Anna had been with the war party during most of its rampage through north Texas. Night after night she was raped by these warriors. The girl was no longer a human being, at least not in the eyes of her captors. She was but a poor, ravaged piece of meat they slid in and out of with the loutish brutishness of dogs raising their legs at a tree.

Kristen knew that Iron Cheek had chosen her for himself. It was her golden hair that attracted him, she realized. He was continually riding up alongside her to run his fingers through it, his coal-black eyes gleaming with pleasure.

Kristen knew the time would come when he would send for her. She tried not to think about it.

The warriors and the two women slept out under the stars with only a blanket between

THE TEXAN

them and the ground. As a result they usually tried to huddle as close to the camp fires as they could. On the fifth night after crossing the Canadian River, as Kristen was just beginning to fall asleep, she heard Anna scream.

It was so piercing, so filled with pain, that Kristen sat up instantly. What she saw horrified her. Two of the warriors had dropped live coals into Anna's nostrils. Anna's screaming was abruptly cut off as one of the warriors, grinning with pleasure, slammed his moccasined foot down over her mouth. In her agony Anna thrashed around like a speared fish, trying desperately to snatch the live coals from her nostrils. The stench of burning flesh filled the air.

Without thinking of herself, Kristen flew at the two warriors. Not expecting an assault, they were knocked to the ground by the fury of Kristen's charge. Ignoring them, Kristen tried to help Anna remove the charred, bloodied coals from her nostrils. The coals were no longer aflame, but the damage had been done. The skin covering Anna's nostrils had been burned away, leaving two charred holes in her face. The pain must have been unbearable.

The two warriors approved of Kristen's action. But they beat her nevertheless. They did so carefully, so as not to break any bone or scar her face. They did not want to alienate their war chief, who had no choice but to approve of this chastisement. No woman can be allowed to interfere in the pleasure of a warrior. A woman's job was to please a warrior, and a warrior's job was to please himself.

As Kristen finally lost consciousness the last thing she remembered hearing was Anna Mowbry's inconsolable sobbing. Yet when Kristen came to her senses the next morning, Anna was humming softly, almost gaily, to herself. The warriors were looking at her, puzzled. Kristen hurried over to see how she was. She looked terrible. The two scarred holes where her nostrils should have been had grown larger. A fly was crawling around inside one of them. Even so, Anna looked at Kristen and laughed with delight.

But she was not looking at Kristen. Not really. There was a bright glow of madness in her eyes. Suddenly Anna began a happy, animated conversation with someone standing to the right of Kristen. But there was no one there. A chill ran up Kristen's spine.

When the band set off that morning, Anna was still humming lightheartedly as the braves strapped her feet to the stirrups. By noon she had stopped humming, however, and when Kristen helped her down from the pony, her eyes were red-rimmed with a feverish madness, her face white, her expression stark.

When a warrior brushed past her to lead her pony away, she began to scream. It was a horrible, endless scream that seemed to have no beginning and no end. One of the braves who had dropped the coals into her nostrils the night before stepped up to her and slapped her repeatedly until she sagged, unconscious, to the ground.

That night she ran off. No one went after her, and near dawn they could hear her screams, distant and terrible. And after that, nothing.

Kristen was not surprised when Iron Cheek had her brought to him three nights later. The moon was high, the night cool. Despite this, the war chief had selected an open, grassy sward near a clump of beech trees.

He took her clumsily with his big hands, flung her down onto his blanket, then ripped off her tattered dress. Kristen wore no corset, but she had many petticoats, and these Iron Cheek disposed of with growing impatience.

When she was naked at last, Iron Cheek straddled her, his coal-black eyes shining in anticipation. The rest of the warriors, standing in a semicircle around them, watched with great interest. That she should have been stripped naked before this band of leering savages filled her with a terrible, searing shame.

Then she looked up at the savage looming over her.

From the first she had considered him to be the ugliest Indian she had ever seen. On the right side of his face he had a terrible knife wound, and in the hollow of the cheek the ridged tracks of two hideous scars crossed. The slashing blade evidently had severed vital facial nerves, so the chief's entire right cheek hung like a dead flap from his cheekbone clear to his jawline. Though the other side of his face had not been injured, the right side pulled this side down also. In truth, Iron Cheek's entire face was frozen into a malevolent downward cast.

And he was lice-ridden. A constant parade of gleaming lice marched across his forehead and back into his heavy shock of greased hair—and he stank like one who was too proud to wipe himself after squatting.

Kristen found herself inching back on the blanket.

What passed for a smile rearranged Iron Cheek's lifeless face. Reaching down, he tossed aside his breechclout. Kristen felt his already erect penis thrusting between her thighs. She glanced down at him in horror and saw his medicine bag dangling between his thighs like a third testicle.

Kristen had told herself she would not resist—that she had no choice but to endure this violation while trying to remain remote and untouched. She would pretend it was not happening to her but to someone else. With this strategem to give her what comfort it could, she closed her eyes and waited.

The moment she felt Iron Cheek's weight pressing upon her, she forgot everything she had told herself. He made her skin crawl as his big hands passed roughly, eagerly, over her body, then thrust her thighs apart.

Unable to restrain herself, furious at this awful invasion, she began to fight back with silent, unyielding purpose. Iron Cheek was stronger than she was, much stronger. He kept his temper, grunting in admiration at times. But when her raking fingers almost reached his eyes, he sat back calmly and struck her powerfully with his clenched fist. Her head snapped around, and for a moment she lost consciousness.

With a deep grunt he thrust into her. She was a virgin, and the pain was sudden and sharp. Iron Cheek was pleased to find her so tight and flung himself full upon her, rutting happily, one sweaty shoulder pushing heedlessly against the side of her face. Sobbing, she lay back, only dimly aware of the blood flowing from her split lip. She felt deeply outraged and a terrible sense of violation swept over her. A moment that should have been a source of wonder and joy, a gift from God, had been taken from her forever.

She lay there inert, sobbing wretchedly when the spent Iron Cheek pulled himself off her. He had taken her, but he was not pleased with his prize. He thought of giving her over to the other braves.

Only Kristen's golden hair saved her from that fate.

Chapter Five

Upon returning to his village, Iron Cheek relegated his first wife, Standing Willow, to the smaller tipi along with her mother and sister. Then he installed Kristen in his tipi. This was not because he preferred Kristen to Standing Willow. He did it only because he did not want it known that this woman with the golden hair had been such a disappointment to him. And he knew that if he sent her from his lodge, openly declaring his displeasure with her, she could be claimed by another brave immediately. He did not want this. He still wanted Kristen. His hope was that, in time, she would learn to please him.

But a month passed and there was no pleasure for him in anything Kristen did.

For one thing she made no effort to listen to or communicate with him. Worse, she made no effort to learn the Comanche tongue or converse with either Standing Willow or her old mother. This made for trouble. His household had two heads, but only one functioned. The Golden-Haired One did not cook. She could not light a fire nor keep one going. Her attempts at scraping hides or sewing beadwork were futile. She could only perform those duties of a slave: hauling water, gathering firewood, and sweeping the floor of the tipi.

Iron Cheek felt her hatred whenever **her cool** blue eyes rested on him. Not once did he hear her laugh. And, unlike his people—who saw in his scars evidence that he was a great warrior— he could tell that she found only ugliness in his face. She could barely stand to be near him, so that when he joined her in the night, it was like lying upon a slab of stone. She was a dead person, cold and unresponsive.

Sometimes, desperate to arouse her, he beat her. But even then she did not react. She lay there taking the blows without uttering a sound, her head drawn in for protection while he continued to strike her. Sensing a contest of wills, Iron Cheek at such times redoubled his efforts in a grim, determined attempt to draw some kind of response from her. Panting with exertion, he would flail at her until he succeeded in wrenching a single cry of pain from her.

But Iron Cheek soon realized that such miserable victories were pointless. He restored Standing Willow to her rightful place in his tipi and gave Kristen to Standing Willow and her family to be their slave. Perhaps his women might be able to teach her to be useful and obedient. But he was done with her. If the time ever came when, penitent and ashamed of her foolish behavior, she asked to be restored to his bed, he would laugh in her face.

Kristen was the only white woman Iron Cheek had ever possessed, and he had no desire to repeat his mistake.

Free at last of the chief's caresses, Kristen thanked God for her deliverance. Her life now was certainly more difficult, but it was infinitely easier to endure.

Standing Willow and her family had immediately despised Kristen as a threat to their own security. And since, despite Kristen's station as Iron Cheek's favored wife, they found themselves responsible for Iron Cheek's meals and all his other needs, they had treated her with a cruel and active contempt.

Now she became the only one fit to carry water from the stream, the only one left to carry the bundles of firewood to the lodges. She spent entire days hip-deep in the water, pounding clean Iron Cheek's buckskins. She spent hours in the hot sun bent over the staked-out hides, scraping them clean with bone knives, the blood from her worn fingers mixed in with the scrapings. She labored as she had never labored before, and if it seemed to any of Iron Cheek's women that she moved too slowly, they would take delight in laying willow switches across her back until more than once Kristen was unable to remove her buckskin dress at night without taking off scabbed-over patches of skin with it.

It was Walking Shadow Woman, Standing Willow's mother, who was the most persistent and ingenious in her cruelties and the most unforgiving.

One morning, a month after Kristen had been sent from Iron Cheek's lodge, she was carrying two buckets of water up a steep embankment when her smooth-soled moccasins slipped on the slick mud. She slammed forward, her face striking the side of the embankment, the buckets slipping from her grasp. Pushing herself off the ground, she turned to see them rolling back down the embankment. Scrambling hastily after the buckets, she managed to retrieve one of them, but the other one jumped lightly into the water, landed upright, and sailed swiftly downstream.

She tried to swim after it, but she was not a good enough swimmer. She almost drowned before her feet found the bottom and she was able to pull herself back onto shore. The women lining the bank laughed heartily at her dilemma, not one of them making the slighest effort to help her. Glaring up at them, Kristen realized that they would have let her drown—idiot grins on their faces, as she went under.

She stood up on the embankment, her buckskins heavy, her hair plastered miserably to her face and neck, and looked down the stream in time to see a boy swim out and grab the bucket. Kristen felt enormous relief as she climbed the embankment to fetch it from him. She hurried along, her moccasins squirting water comically with each step she took. By this time all the women of the band had lined up to watch her, grinning and laughing wildly, slapping their thighs at the Golden-Haired One's sorry appearance.

Walking Shadow Woman, her white hair flying, her face twisted into a malevolent mask, broke though the ranks of watching women and fell upon Kristen, fresh willow switches whistling as they cut into Kristen's back and neck. The unexpected force of the old woman's attack drove Kristen to the ground. Rolling over onto her back, her arm held up to protect her face, Kristen peered through narrowed eyes at the old woman's panting, convoluted face as she whaled away at Kristen. Suddenly an icy calm, bone-deep rage trembled through her. Though she might die among these savages and have her broken limbs tossed aside for the dogs to fight over, it did not matter. She would take care of this old harpy first.

Jumping to her feet, Kristen bore relentlessly through the storm of slashing willows, reached out, and grabbed both of the old woman's wrists. She stilled, then turned them. The old woman howled in pain and dropped the switches. Snatching them up, Kristen whaled the old woman around the face and shoulders until she stumbled back and fell to the ground. Kristen continued her punishment without letup. Only when her arms were heavy from the exertion did Kristen step back from the pitiful, whimpering old woman sprawled on the ground before her.

Then she turned to face the other Comanche women, expecting the worst. They had been closing in around her, howling out gleefully as she punished Walking Shadow Woman. But now they moved away from Kristen, their eyes averted. Surprised, Kristen turned to look back at Walking Shadow Woman. Her face and shoulders a mass of welts, the old woman raised her bloodied arms piteously to ward off any further blows.

At that moment Kristen realized that she was not going to be punished. She simply had asserted herself, and in the process the pecking order had been readjusted. Leaving Walking Shadow Woman sprawled on the ground, Kristen tossed aside the willow switches, retrieved her second bucket, and went back to her labors.

Though Kristen was no longer the butt of every woman's spite as she moved around the camp in the pursuit of her numberless chores, she was still not accepted by any of them. She had slashed off her long hair, and it had long since lost its sheen and become only a straggly, vermin-infested nuisance. Nevertheless, she was still called the Golden-Haired One, and for this reason she remained a threat to the wives of every warrior in the band.

The wicky, or "squaw cooler," was a kind of arbor made of leafy boughs laid across a crude pole frame elevated on four posts. This gave the women a cool shelter during the hottest spells of the summer. Kristen tried twice to rest there in order to find some relief from the blistering sun. But each time her appearance raised a howl of protest, and the women inside pushed her back out into the sun. The second time it happened, Kristen realized that there never would be room within that leafy shelter for her.

But she did not break. She grew thinner, all softness burned out of her under the relentless schedule of the work Standing Willow laid out for her. As the days and weeks passed, Kristen grew steadily stronger. Her light skin was burnished a deep brown, and she found herself able to do twice the work she had managed at first. Losing herself in her constant, unremitting labor, she was almost content.

The chore easiest to endure was berry picking. Standing Willow was always astonished at the heavy buckets of fragrant wild berries she brought in at nightfall. Kristen was content to move for hours by herself along the river's sandy banks. There, under the cool shade of the cottonwoods, she picked wild plums, chokecherries, pecans, and walnuts. Often she was so intent on her swift-fingered task, a mule deer or antelope stepping out of the willows to drink would catch her unaware.

It was during such solitary hours that she first began seriously to consider the possibility of escape.

Late in the time of the Yellow Leaf Moon, a recently departed war party, their faces still black with war paint, returned to the village in great haste. A hurried council was called as excitement and visible fear spread among the women, who gathered their children, ponies, mules, and even their dogs close about them.

When the council broke up, the order came to move out. Though Kristen rarely spoke to any Comanche, she had been able to pick up much of their language. What she now heard was that the Comanche feared an attack by a large Arapaho war party. Two days after they set out, the Comanche war party led by Iron Cheek had stumbled upon the Arapaho. A brief skirmish followed during which two Arapaho warriors were struck down. Even so, Iron Cheek's warriors had been forced to flee from the large number of Arapaho warriors.

With remarkable speed the women broke camp. Kristen was rudely admonished to stay out of their way. But she watched closely as the women worked, amazed at their proficiency. With incredible speed the tipis came down and less than ten minutes after the command to break camp had been given, the entire village was on the move. Dogs and horses and mules were all pressed into service, pulling travois of all sizes piled high with household goods, tools, and food. Some of the larger, horse-drawn travois were even carrying children and old women.

Throughout that day the long line of fleeing men, women, and children kept going while scouts raced out ahead of the column or followed behind it, their black-painted faces grim. Walking close beside Standing Willow and her mother, Kristen realized that now, during the confusion of this flight from the Arapaho war party, was her chance to escape.

On the second day of their flight, as the sun climbed into the sky, she began to trip occasionally, immediately getting to her feet and hurrying to catch up with Standing Willow and her mother and sister. But they did not seem to care if she kept up or not, and they paid little attention when she fell back. Every now and then they would glimpse her behind them, trudging wearily alongside another family. They gave it no thought when Kristen's stumbling inability caused her to be swallowed up at last in the curtain of dust raised by the hurrying column.

When the group came to a wide, meandering stream, an oasis of cottonwoods and bushes, the Comanche halted to make camp and fill their water jugs. Kristen remained at the rear of the column. Ducking into a thicket, she ran swiftly back upstream, keeping to the cottonwoods and willows, moving with the silent speed of an antelope. She brushed past brambles and splashed through shallows with increasing speed until night fell. Even then she continued on. It was well past midnight when she crawled into a thorny patch of brush close beside the river and allowed total exhaustion to claim her.

She awoke the next morning to the pounding of unshod hooves and saw the grim, painted Arapaho surging past her along the high ground above the river. Judging from their speed, Kristen was sure they would overtake the Comanche column by midday.

It was curious and totally unexpected, but watching the Arapaho war party disappear upstream, Kristen felt an odd sinking feeling in the pit of her stomach. Though she had come to know few of her Comanche captors, she had lived among them for better than six months. In that time, despite their casual cruelty, she had come to enjoy a certain freedom and was able to observe how close the Comanche families were. Brothers, sisters, cousins, aunts, and uncles were always fussing over each other. Acts of kindness and affection abounded. And it was clear that these savages, for all their brutality, could love each other deeply—not once had she seen any of them raise their hands to noisy or disobedient children.

In addition, the village had been her home, her source of life, feeding her, providing her with a warm tipi at night. Though Kristen had made no attempt to befriend any of the women, some of them had nevertheless smiled shyly at her in passing, some even giving her small gifts. Standing Willow's sister gave her a bone-handled knife so Kristen could slice the meat she was stringing up for drying. Another woman had passed her a comb fashioned out of greasewood. And one very old granny, whose tent Kristen had passed every day on her way to the river, had noticed early on how worn and nearly useless Kristen's moccasins were. For many months, despite her failing vision and fingers crooked with arthritis, she had labored over a new pair of doeskin moccasins for Kristen and had presented them to her without ceremony only a few days earlier.

These acts of kindness could not make up for the loneliness and despair she felt at her abduction. Nevertheless, they were enough to trouble her as she contemplated the fate of Iron Cheek's people when that fierce whirlwind of Arapaho warriors descended upon them.

Watching the path of the sun, Kristen continued on up the stream. When she was certain which way south—and Texas—lay, she left the protection of the water and struck out across the prairie. She had planned her escape meticulously and carried a large supply of jerky and one large water bag. Every pocket in her skirt was crammed with berries, and she had a fishhook and a line, something one of the young Mexican slaves had given her for cleaning and mending his tattered shirt. She also had six sulfur matches in a tin case. Stolen weeks before from Walking Shadow Woman, these matches, along with her bone-handled knife, were her most valuable items. She needed both to survive.

Two days later, as she headed toward a line of cottonwoods on the horizon, she crested a slight

THE TEXAN

knoll and saw before her, less than a mile in the distance, a long line of carts moving south. She dropped to the ground, then pulled herself through the tall grass until she could peer down at the wagons. She knew at once that they were Comancheros. Some were on horseback; others walked beside their mule-driven carts.

In Kristen's eyes, the only thing worse than Comanche were the Comancheros—New Mexican traders who encouraged the Comanche to raid Texas, enabling the savages to profit from their bloody pillaging. Most of the horse ranches in northern New Mexico and Colorado were stocked by cattlemen who got their horseflesh and other stock from the Comancheros. And every Texan knew where the Comancheros got the stock they sold to the ranchers—and what it had cost in Texan blood and tears.

If these Comancheros discovered her, Kristen realized, they would promptly sell her back to Iron Cheek or to some other chief's band.

Kristen kept down until the Comancheros vanished toward the southwest, then continued on toward the line of cottonwoods where she knew she would find water. Close to nightfall she reached the trees and slumped down onto a small grassy clearing beside a large pool.

Though Kristen had rationed her berries and meat, after three days her provisions were low. Now, gazing into the pool under the bank, she saw that she had an excellent chance to vary her diet. Taking out her fishhook and tackle, she caught a grasshopper for bait, cut a birch pole for a rod, and in no time at all hooked a shiner. Using only one of her precious matches, she built a fire. While it burned down to a glowing bed of coals she dressed the fish with her bone-handle knife, then placed green pine boughs over the coals.

The aroma of the cooking fish was delicious. It was an effort to wait for her meal to cook thoroughly. She ate proudly and with gusto. Alone in this vast, open steppeland, she was surviving. If she could make it south to Texas before winter's arrival, she would be safe at last.

She had no intention of returning to the Brazos River valley. She had been gone too long for that. She knew only too well what her reception would be after all this time. Throwing a few sticks of wood on the fire, she inched closer to its warmth and prepared to go to sleep.

A whip cracked in the distance.

She jumped up, her heart pounding. Her hand reached for her knife. The bullwhip's crack had sounded like a gunshot. She thought immediately of the Comancheros she had seen earlier. Could they be camped in these cottonwoods?

She kicked sand onto her fire. The whip's sharp crack came again. She stole through the cottonwoods toward the sound. At least a quarter of a mile ahead, she saw the glow of a camp fire through the cottonwoods. Moving closer, she peered at the Mexicans lounging about. The crack of the bullwhip came again, and she saw the Mexican who was wielding it. He appeared to be mending the handle. Every now and then, to test the grip, he would crack the whip.

There was some grumbling, and Kristen caught a few of the words. The men wished the fellow would quit fooling with his whip. It was already loud enough, they told him. After a while the Mexican shrugged, coiled the whip, and dropped it into one of the wagons. Then he squatted before the fire and poured himself some coffee.

Carefully Kristen headed back into the cottonwoods, then ran back to her camp. She could smell the smoke from her fire long before she reached it. She doused the fire with river water and then huddled close against a large cottonwood. She had to sleep, and she would have to stay hidden the next day until the Comancheros cleared out.

She was almost asleep when she heard a light footfall beside her. She glanced up to see a tall, shadowy figure looking down at her. He was wearing not a sombrero but a Stetson. Against the night sky she could see its outline clearly.

"Well, now," the man said softly, "Rest easy, *señorita*. I did not mean to frighten you. It was the smell of your fire and the aroma of fresh-cooked fish that drew me on through the trees."

From his accent Kristen knew at once that he was one of the Comancheros, most likely its leader. If he had come through the trees alone and had not told anyone where he was going, she still had a chance for her freedom. With her knife clutched firmly in her hand she flung herself up at him, driving him back with the suddenness of her attack.

As he fought back, she slashed through the sleeve of his frock coat. Chuckling, he ducked away before she could stab again, then grabbed her right wrist with both hands and twisted. With a sharp cry of pain Kristen dropped the knife. She began to kick furiously, hysterical at the thought of capture. At last the Comanchero flung her brutally to the ground.

"Enough, woman!" he told her. "I do not intend to hurt you!"

"You are a Comanchero?"

"Yes."

She spat at him with all the venom of a Comanche squaw. "I will not let you take me back to the Comanche!"

"*Señorita,* I assure you, I have no such intention."

"I do not believe you."

"You must!"

"Why must I?"

He smiled. "Because, Kristen, your mother has

offered a five-hundred-dollar reward for your return. And I intend to collect it."

She was so astonished at this reply, Kristen allowed the Comanchero to reach down and pull her gently to her feet.

Chapter Six

The following spring a dust-laden Mexican rider approached the Circle N from the west. Carl saw him first and called to Frank, who was in the blacksmith shop. Frank stepped out into the yard, watched for a minute, then moved back into the shop for his rifle. A moment later Cullen Barker left the horse barn to join them.

The Mexican rode slowly through the gate and kept on across the yard, pulling up before the hitch rack in front of the ranch house. The horse he rode—a gray, swaybacked gelding—had seen far better days. Since no one invited the Mexican to alight, he remained in his saddle. He had a handlebar mustache and eyes as black as buttons. His poncho was crudely patched, his boots showing through in places—a sorry caballero indeed.

Lifting his battered sombrero to Kilrain and the two men, he showed very white teeth in a careful smile. Then he turned his attention to Kate Nordstrom, who had just stepped out onto the porch.

"*Buenas tardes, Señora* Nordstrom," he said, touching his hat brim to her.

"Speak English, greaseball," snapped Frank, joining Kate on the porch. "This here's Texas."

"That's enough, Frank," Kate said calmly. Then she addressed the Mexican. "How is it you know my name?"

He shrugged. "I have come a great distance to speak with the *señora*."

Kate's eyes narrowed. "About what?"

"You have daughter?"

"Kristen?" Kate asked sharply. "You mean Kristen?"

"*Si*."

"You've found her?"

"I hear many things. I am not so sure. But maybe I help you find her. I have heard you offer many pesos in reward."

"Five hundred dollars," Kate told him.

"But only if you bring her here," Frank broke in.

The Mexican looked at Frank and shrugged.

"*Por favor, señora, tengo sed.* Please, *señora,* I am thirsty. I may dismount?"

"Of course," Kate said hastily, chagrined for having forgotten her manners. "Light and come inside. There's coffee on the stove. And fresh doughnuts too. You come right on in here."

"Hey, Kate," Frank protested. "You can't trust this here saddle tramp."

"Why not?"

"This is the third one this spring. Look at him! He's just tryin' to get a free meal like them others. He don't know nothin' about Kristen! Hell, Kate, we know where she is. The Comanches've got her."

"You know that for sure, do you?"

"It's all we been hearing—and you know what that girl we rescued told us. Iron Cheek took her."

"She may have escaped."

"That's wishful thinking and you know it."

"I'll handle this, Frank," Kate said, her voice turning to steel. "Get back to work. If I want you, I'll call you."

His face darkening with anger, Frank turned and jumped down off the porch, the two hands trailing after him.

The Mexican dismounted, slapped the dust off his sombrero, and mounted the porch steps.

* * *

Bart and Tim O'Hare were busy breaking broncs when they caught sight of an approaching wagon. They jumped down from the corral, brushed off their clothes, and walked over to the house to await its arrival. Ellen O'Hare was already out on the porch, shading her eyes to see who was driving the wagon. Scott Tyrell came out of the bunkhouse and climbed the porch steps to join Bart and the others.

It was Kate Nordstrom. Without slowing, she rattled on through the gates, pulling to a scrambling halt in front of the porch.

"I'd like to speak to you, Bart," Kate told him, the ribbons still trembling in her hands. She was wearing her black dress and Stetson, an outfit as grim as her expression.

"Afternoon, Kate," Ellen said quickly. "Light and set a spell."

"It's Bart I come to see, Ellen."

The welcome smile on Ellen's face did not falter.

"Then come in out of the heat," Ellen suggested. "I'll make some fresh lemonade."

Bart smiled at Kate. "You better come in," he said.

"I'll see to the horses," said Tyrell, taking hold of the swing horse's bridle.

Kate got down and followed Ellen inside as Scott led the team away. It was clear that Kate could barely contain her excitement. Bart was excited too. He was almost certain Kate had news of Kristen and felt hope stirring within him.

"Another rider came in today," Kate said, sitting down at the table. "A Mexican."

Ellen, while pouring lemonade, paused to look over at Kate. "News about Kristen?" she asked hopefully.

"Yes."

"Good news?"

"Maybe. But I'd prefer to let Bart decide."

Scott entered and joined them at the table. Ellen placed glasses of lemonade down before them and sat down also. Ignoring her lemonade, Kate told them the news the Mexican had brought her.

When she finished, Scott Tyrell leaned back in his chair. "You pay this Mex anything yet?" he asked.

"No. Not yet."

"Well, maybe you should. Looks to me like he's given you a bona fidy lead this time."

"You know this Comanchero leader—the one they call de Santos?"

"I heard about him."

"Do you know where to find him?"

"There's a Comanchero outpost deep in New Mexico, place called Tule. That's where he'd most likely be when he's not out tradin' with the Comanche."

"You ever been to Tule?" Bart asked him.

"Nope. But it's out there, deep in the mountains somewhere."

Kate looked at Bart. "I want you to go after Kristen."

"Why me, Kate?"

"Because there was a time when you thought a lot of Kristen. And I don't think that's changed. Am I right?"

"You are."

"Then you'll go after her?"

Bart thought a moment, then glanced questioningly at Scott. "You want to come along?"

With a casual shrug Scott indicated his willingness.

Bart looked back at Kate. "Scott'll be coming with me, then."

For a moment Kate's face almost softened.

Scott leaned closer. "Miss Kate, am I right? Did this Mex say this Comanchero leader holding Kristen had taken her from the Buffalo-Eater Comanche?"

"Yes."

Scott looked at Kate. "That makes it pretty certain, then. This sure ain't the first report we got she was with the Kotsoteka Comanche."

Kate spoke up. "The Mex says de Santos heard of the reward I offered and went after Iron Cheek, the chief of the Buffalo Eaters, to trade for Kristen.

Only now the Comanchero is keeping her with him at his base."

"Against her will?"

"Of course," Kate snapped. "How could there be any other explanation?"

Ellen had been listening intently. "Kate, did this Mexican say he saw Kristen?"

"Yes. And what's more, he described her perfectly."

"How much does he want you to give him for this information?" asked Bart.

"Since he is only bringing me information, not Kristen, all he wants is a hundred dollars."

"That's it?"

"Yes, and for that reason I trust him."

"Maybe he can take us to de Santos."

"I doubt it," Kate told him. "He wants the money for a ranch of his in Mexico. It is all he wants. He will not go back to New Mexico. He says the Comancheros are crazy for his blood."

"Then I'm bettin' he's already crossed the Comancheros."

Scott nodded. "That's what it sounds like."

"I say give him the hundred, Kate," Bart said. "This sounds solid. If anyone could get Kristen away from a Comanche chief, it would be a Comanchero."

"After you pay the Mex," suggested Scott, "send him over here to us. We'll give him a good feed

THE TEXAN

and maybe, just maybe, we'll be able to convince him to take us to the de Santos fellow."

Kate got up, evidently pleased. "All right. I'll do it."

Scott went back across the yard to get her team, and a few moments later they watched her ride out.

After promising Kate that he would stop at Anchor to talk to Bart, the Mexican left the Circle N. He was not gone long when a band of at least a dozen Comancheros rode through the Nordstrom gate. Kate was on the porch before their leader reached the hitch rack, while Frank and the others hastily took up positions around the yard, rifles in their hands. If they could not fight off the entire contingent, they could sure as hell make things hot for them.

Seeing the armed men peering at him, the leader held up his hand. He was a young man with a handsome, sun-bronzed face.

"*Por favor, señora*," he said, his teeth flashing. "We want no trouble in your country. It is a dog of a thief we seek. We think maybe he come here."

"What makes you think that?"

"His tracks, they lead to your hacienda."

"Why do you want him?"

The young Mexican shrugged. "We sell many horses to the *norteamericanos* in Nevada. Our poor saddlebags, they are heavy with gold. This son of a whore, he rob us. He take our gold and ride off."

"And you trailed him here?"

"He has a very sad horse, *señora*," the Mexican said. "It is easy to track. One shoe, she is crooked. This thief is one big fool. He push his horse very hard."

"Then you won't have no trouble catching him," Kilrain said, stepping into full view from behind the house. "He rode out an hour ago."

"*Por favor, señor,* which way does he go?"

"East," Frank said, pointing.

"*Gracias, señor!*" the young Comanchero cried.

Wheeling his horse, he galloped through the ranks of his fellow Comancheros and led them at a hard gallop out through the gate.

"Damnit, Frank!" Kate said angrily. "Did you have to be that helpful?"

"What's the matter, Kate? There's no reason for us to protect that chili."

"Frank, I wanted him to reach Anchor safely."

"Why?"

"That's my business," she snapped. Then she looked across the yard at Carl. "Get after them, Carl. I want to know what happens. If those riders catch up to that Mex before he reaches Anchor, keep riding and get word to Bart Hardison."

Carl vanished into the barn for a horse. With a

withering glance at Frank, Kate turned and slammed back into the house.

Kate's fears were not unfounded. Trailing the Comancheros from a distance, Carl saw what happened. A few miles from Anchor, the Mexican caught sight of the dust cloud his pursuers were raising. He turned his horse and, using his quirt liberally, took off due south.

Unfortunately his horse was not up to anything that sudden or that urgent and promptly pulled up lame. Halting on a bluff, Carl watched the Comancheros catch up to the Mexican. They circled him, then cut him down with gunfire. The Comancheros took the Mexican's saddlebags, left him where he fell, and rode off to the west.

On Kate's orders Carl rode to Anchor and told Bart what had happened.

When Carl finished, Scott shook his head. "That poor son of a bitch was trying to break the bank, set himself up for life, looks like."

"And he did," said Bart. "Only it was a short life."

"Thanks, Carl," said Tim O'Hare. "You better get back and tell Kate."

"And tell her it don't matter," Bart said. "We're leaving before dawn tomorrow."

With a curt nod Carl mounted up and rode out.

* * *

After a long wait to make sure the move would not upset his mother, Bart had planned to bring Amanda out to Anchor later that week. Ellen had long since prepared her bedroom, and Bart knew it would be a relief for the O'Hares to see her safely back with her son. Now, however, Bart decided that it would be best if she remained in town with the O'Hares for a few more weeks, at least until he and Scott returned.

There was no telling how long it would take them to find Kristen and arrange for her release from the Comanchero chief. Hated by all Texans, the Comancheros were New Mexican descendants of Juan de Anza, who a century before, as an officer of the Mexican governor, concluded a treaty with the Comanche allowing his people and their descendants to trade with the Indians. Honored scrupulously by both parties ever since, the treaty had enabled the Comancheros to act as go-betweens in the ransoming of Indian captives from the Comanche.

As Bart and Scott moved out the next morning before dawn, they came upon the dead Mexican, his bullet-riddled torso already feeding a flock of hunchbacked buzzards. They searched the ground nearby for tracks and followed them through the remainder of that day. The next day, about noon, a hot wind sprang up, sifting sand over the tracks, obliterating them completely. But they kept going and crossed the border into New Mexico two days later.

The land appeared barren of people. Trails they followed for days, even weeks, petered out into white, blazing sands that reached as far as the eye could see. A few Apache bands, lances gleaming, appeared on distant ridges, and at times they saw smoke, but nothing came of these sightings as they rode deeper and deeper into this dry, desolate land.

They finally came to a village, and then another, asking the Mexican inhabitants each time for directions to Tule. Their questions were met with quizzical smiles and sorry shrugs.

These villagers, Bart noticed, did not resemble the fierce Comanchero traders they were hoping to find. For the most part they appeared to be a lazy, happy lot, content to bask in the sun or remain in their one-room *jacales* during the hot noon hours and peer curiously out at the two gringo riders. Each single-room hut was alive with brown children, wearing shirts or tattered straw hats at most.

Weary, saddle-sore, their horses stretched close to their limit, they finally arrived at a village somewhat larger than any they had yet visited. There they spent almost a week recuperating. At the end of their stay, during which they had asked continually for directions to Tule, a toothless, nearly deaf, white-haired Mexican approached them.

For Scott's flamboyant cavalryman's hat, he announced solemnly, he would show them the way to Tule.

With a sigh Scott handed it over.

The old man's eyes gleamed with pleasure as he carefully placed the felt hat upon his white head. Then, smiling happily, he told them that they must go northwest. As he spoke, he pointed toward a mountain range so low on the horizon, it was barely visible. The elder said the Comanchero base they sought was deep inside one of those mountains and situated at the far end of a lush, grass-carpeted valley. To find this valley they had only to keep one of the range's tallest peaks in front of them as they rode.

The old man pointed a bony finger at the peak. They thanked the elder, and he moved off with amazing agility for one his age. Thanks to Scott's felt cavalryman's hat, he was easily the handsomest man in the village.

The next morning they rode out, Scott wearing a black sombrero he had traded for his pocketknife. Keeping the peak in sight was not easy. Four days into the journey, they left the dusty villages behind and rode into higher country, the sand and mesquite giving way to rolling swells of short grass. At noon on the fifth day Scott suddenly pulled his horse to a halt.

"Goddamm it, it's gone!"

"I been noticing," grumbled Bart.

The mountain range was still in front of them, a formidable barrier looming above them. But the peak they had been following had simply dipped below the horizon as they rode closer.

"Now what?" Bart asked.

"We keep going. Look for a valley."

"That old son of a bitch. You think he knew that peak would duck out of sight when we got this close?"

Scott grinned. "Sure."

They continued northwest, and two days later they were stopped by a rampart of rock rising out of the plains, part of a vaulting escarpment that extended in both directions as far as the eye could see.

And there was no sign of a valley.

They split up, each man riding along the base of the escarpment, searching for a way through it. Three days later Bart saw a line of cottonwoods on the horizon indicating water—and beyond that a break in the solid phalanx of rock. He reached the cottonwoods, lit a fire, and kept it going with green pine boughs, dropping a saddle blanket over it every now and then. That night he bathed in a stream.

Two days later, near sundown, Scott rode into Bart's camp. The next day they followed the stream into the mountains and, before long, reached the valley the old man had described to them. At the end of it they found Tule, a settlement of adobe huts and wooden buildings facing the usual plaza, its church at the far end. An hour or so before sundown they dismounted in a clump of spruce on a ridge overlooking Tule.

Scott cut a wedge of chewing tobacco and stuck it in his cheek. "We better not ride in together."

"Why not?"

"When two *tejanos* ride into a New Mexican town that ain't on any map, they're asking for trouble. And these here Comancheros will be glad to trouble us. We ride in together and they'll cut us down in two minutes."

"You got any ideas?"

"Been thinkin' on it."

"I'm listening."

Scott spat out a long dagger of tobacco juice. "I'll ride in alone, leading a lame horse. That'll make me look pretty damn foolish and not at all dangerous. I'll get drunk as soon as I can, then look for a place to flop. I'm just a drifter, see? I'm only there 'cause my horse went lame. And I ain't after no one. All I'm lookin' for is a place to hole up."

"What about me?"

"You stay here until noon tomorrow. If I don't come out to warn you away, why, you just ride on in."

"Big as life and twice as ugly."

"Thing is, no one lookin' for trouble comes ridin' into a Comanchero base alone. Besides, I'll see you and you'll see me, and I'll be covering you all the way. If we don't start another war with Mexico, dismount and I'll buy you a drink."

Bart thought Scott's plan over for a few minutes. It was chancy, but he couldn't see any better way to get into Tule without trouble. He shrugged, loosened the cinch on his mount, and lifted off the saddle.

"All right," he said, "sounds good enough to me." He dropped his saddle at the foot of a tree. "How you gonna lame your horse?"

"I'll put a pebble in under his shoe just before I ride in. He'll be limpin' somethin' fierce by the time I find a livery. There'll be lots of grinning Comancheros watchin' this poor fool gringo—but no guns blazin'. Ain't hardly possible for anyone to see danger in a man leadin' a crippled-up horse, especially if he's wearin' a sombrero."

"You sure of that, are you?"

"I ain't sure of nothin'," Scott said, mounting up.

He rode out of the spruce. Bart watched him angling down the slope for a moment or two, then slumped down on the grass, his head resting back against his saddle.

He was thinking of Kristen.

That Mexican could have been lying to get a part of the five-hundred-dollar reward Kate had posted. And even if Kristen had been here for a while, there was no guarantee that she was still here. It could well be that his and Scott's search for Kristen could go on for months—years, even.

But that didn't matter. They were going to find Kristen and bring her back to her people. He closed his eyes and let himself sleep.

Riding into Tule the next day, a little past noon, Bart noticed the prosperity of the village. The men wore long cotton shirts and baggy, white cotton pants, straw sandals, and broad-brimmed sombreros and stood around in small groups, talking idly. Seven-foot shawls shrouded the women, who hurried about with heads down, keeping out of the men's way.

Next to the church, two large adobe warehouses faced the plaza, both surrounded by fortified walls equipped with gunports and firing slits. There was no doubt about it. This was a major Comanchero base. In front of the warehouses, their backs against the wall, small shops and stalls for trading had been constructed. They were shuttered up now, and as Bart rode closer he noticed living quarters on the top floor of the largest warehouse.

He had no trouble finding Scott. He was sitting on the cantina's porch across from the two warehouses, his back resting against the wall, his legs propped up on the railing. A jug of tequila sat beside him on the porch floor. Bart turned his horse into the cantina's hitch rack and dismounted.

"Howdy, stranger," Scott said, grinning at him. "What in hell're you doin' in this godforsaken place?"

"Lookin' for a place to lubricate my tonsils," Bart replied, mounting the porch.

"Mister, you came to the right place."

Scott picked up his jug and entered the cantina ahead of Bart. They found a table in a corner and sat down. A Mexican woman not much over five feet, with huge eyes and gleaming teeth, hurried over. She had a full bosom and long black hair running down her back, clear to her waist. As she bent over them, Scott tickled one of her chins and ordered tequila for his friend. Then he pinched her ample behind and sent her shrieking with delight back to the bar.

"You've got a friend there," remarked Bart.

Scott smiled. "She is all woman, that one. I did not get much sleep last night. Even so, I don't feel tired today."

"What've you found out?"

"That Kristen saved my life."

"You want to explain that?"

Scott nodded. "Despite my clever ruse, the local Comancheros fell on me like vultures on a dead hog. They would have finished me if I hadn't told them what I was doing here."

"And that saved you?"

"It worked like magic. Mention of Kristen was all it took. They pulled back and let me be. Bart, I don't know how to say this, but I don't think Kristen's staying here against her will."

Bart shook his head emphatically. "No, Scott. I can't believe that. It doesn't make any sense. Have you seen her?"

"She's gone off with de Santos. To Mexico, I hear."

"Goddamn! Maybe he's tryin' to peddle her!"

"I swear, Bart. That ain't the way it looks, not according to Constanza."

"Constanza?"

Scott grinned. "My good friend. Here she comes now."

Constanza brought Bart a jug of tequila and water. She poured the liquor into an earthen mug for him and placed the water next to it. Bart took up the tequila and threw it down his throat, then chased it quickly with the water. He didn't like the tequila's smoky taste, but it had plenty of body to it.

"That's really good stuff, Bart," Scott told him. "You'll appreciate it soon enough."

"I already do."

Two Mexicans shouldered through the batwings, stood for a moment in the doorway, then took a table near the door. Mugs of tequila were brought

THE TEXAN

to them at once. As they sipped their drinks they seemed unusually interested in Bart and Scott.

"Them two gents over there," Bart said, indicating the two Mexicans with a nod. "They the ones rousted you?"

"They're part of the team," Scott said. "It took more'n a few."

"Did you tell 'em about me?"

"Nope. Figured I wouldn't need to."

Bart settled back in his chair. "How long do you figure we'll have to wait for de Santos to get back?"

Scott shrugged. "From what I gathered, not long."

"You got a room?"

Scott grinned. "I don't need one. Constanza's taking good care of me. She says she likes big *tejanos*. I told her I like big women. We get along fine."

Bart threw down another glass of the tequila and this time sipped at the water chaser. He was helping himself to more when a beautiful, dark-eyed girl entered the place. Bart instantly came alert.

Glancing over at her, Scott waved. The girl smiled brilliantly and started for their table.

"You know her?" Bart asked.

Scott chuckled. "Her name's Estrellita. She's yours if you want. She ain't my type. All skin and bones. Might as well make love to a rack of jerky. Constanza's more my type, plenty to hang on to."

"Every man to his own poison."

Watching Estrellita approach, Bart felt warm all over. He didn't know if it was the sight of the Mexican girl or the tequila—and he didn't much care. The girl stopped at the table, looked straight into Bart's eyes, and waited for an invitation to sit down. Bart smiled and pointed to an empty chair beside him.

"I am Estrellita," she told him.

"I'm Bart," he replied.

"You come for the woman with the gold hair. That so, *tejano*?"

"Uh-oh," said Scott, sitting back in mock alarm. "Watch out. She knows you're a Texan."

"So what?"

"These people don't like Texans. Not that I blame them."

"What the hell are *you*?"

"The thing is, I don't advertise it."

"What'd I say?"

"It's the way you speak, I guess—and your britches, the leather vest, the hat—and on top of all that, you're too damn tall and rawboned."

"Hell, I can't help that. And I don't intend to."

"See what I mean? Talkin' just like a Texan."

Bart looked back at the girl. Most of the other bargirls were squat, flat-nosed squaws, some as round as rain barrels and not much taller. But this girl was different, sure enough—a damn sight taller, for one thing, and slender. Her white blouse had a high, chaste neckline, her sleeves were tied at the elbows, and her bright green-and-red skirt was long enough to reach her ankles. But her thin dress was all that covered her warm, sensuous body, and the gleam in her eye was a direct, bold challenge.

"You want a drink?" Bart asked her.

She shrugged. "I don't mind, *tejano*."

"Stop calling me that. I told you, my name's Bart."

She shrugged and flashed a smile at him. "Okay, I call you Bart."

She turned then and waved to Constanza. Bart knew her tequila would be watered but paid no heed as he paid for her drink and tossed down his own. The buzzing from the tequila increased. Feeling acutely Estrellita's nearness he found his need for her becoming urgent.

Scott had noticed.

"Stay here," he told Bart. "I'll take care of your horse and check your gear into Constanza's place. It'll be safe there."

As Scott left the cantina Estrellita smiled, then leaned into Bart. "It is early, but maybe you come to my place now."

"Why?"

"You drink much more, you will not be able to please Estrellita."

She was right. Bart suddenly felt very foolish for letting himself get this drunk in the middle of the afternoon. He took a deep breath and leaned back in his chair, doing what he could to steady himself.

"You are right, Estrellita. Maybe you better take me to your place."

As Bart got up with Estrellita, one of the two Mexicans near the door walked over to his table. Pushing his huge, ugly face close to Bart's, he grabbed Bart's right arm.

"Hey, *tejano*," he said, his peppery breath enveloping Bart, "where you go with Estrellita?"

Bart flung the Mexican back against the wall, and before the fellow could draw his knife, he found himself staring into the yawning muzzle of Bart's Colt.

Bart smiled happily at the Comanchero's sudden confusion.

"Stand easy, you son of a bitch," Bart told him. "If you know I'm a Texan, you know damn well I'll pull this trigger."

The tequila had done its work. A reckless elation was building deep inside Bart. He was eager to cut loose. He got to his feet and waited for the Mexican to do something foolish. Instead the Mexican raised his hands and straightened his back against the wall.

"I jus' wanna know where you goin'," he said carefully, his big yellow teeth showing in a grin.

Bart dropped his Colt back into his holster. "Out!" he told him.

"*Si, señor,*" the Mexican said placatingly. "That ees fine!"

Then he moved carefully along the wall to his chair and slipped back down into it. Bart turned to Estrellita. She stood up. With a low bow he took her by the arm and escorted her from the cantina.

Estrellita's place was a one-room adobe hut just down the street, in a huddled quarter of narrow streets and tiny, one-room adobe *jacales*. When Estrellita lit the single candle by her couch, he saw that the place was surprisingly tidy and clean. There was a small, cleanly swept fireplace where she did all her cooking. Cut out of the wall in one corner was a small shrine on which stood a plaster statue of Mary and the Child. After lighting the devotional candle Estrellita knelt briefly before it.

But Bart hardly noticed. Estrellita laughed as he collapsed facedown upon the faded couch, then rolled over to look up at her, grinning, his head spinning woozily from the tequila.

She sat down on the edge of the couch and began to unbutton his shirt. "You have made bad enemy of Raoul," she told him. "He will not forget."

"Raoul?"

"That man you draw on. He is very important Comanchero."

"Will he be angry with you?"

"Why?"

"For coming with me."

She laughed. "It is not his business who I sleep with."

"Business?"

"Yes. You will be generous, will you not?"

"Yes," he told her. "I will be generous."

He lay back and let her swift fingers finish peeling off his shirt. Then they dropped to his belt buckle....

It was morning. Somewhere a cock crowed. Estrellita lifted her head and propped her cheek on her hand as she gazed at him. Bart turned his head to look at her. She ran her forefinger lightly down his nose, then across his lips, all the way to his chin. The sheet she had thrown over her while she slept fell away, revealing the curve of her slim brown shoulder and the provocative thrust of her breasts. In the dim, early-morning light she seemed to be covered with a faint, lustrous sheen.

"Next time," she said, her dark eyes gleaming, "maybe you shave, huh?"

"I promise."

"I give you bath and shave you myself."

"I can hardly wait."

"You will see. I am more woman than this golden-haired one. I feel sorry for you—almost as much as for poor Salvador."

"What do you mean, Estrellita?"

She shrugged. "This Kristen is not all woman. I tell you, she has no feeling. Salvador take her everywhere with him—even to his *estancia* in Mexico and to his fine house in Mexico City—to such places where he never take me. Still, it does no good. I see it. In his eyes and in hers. It is very sad."

"You mean Kristen is not happy."

"Yes."

"Well, why should she be? This Salvador is keeping her against her will."

Estrellita looked at him in some astonishment, then smiled. "You do not understand. But that is all right. You will take the golden-haired one back to Texas. Then Estrellita will be happy again."

Bart thought he understood. Estrellita was jealous. She wanted Salvador de Santos for herself. So she blamed Kristen and wanted her gone.

The door opened. A bright shaft of sunlight cut through the cool shadows. "Let's go, Bart," Scott said, stepping into the doorway, his sombrero in his hand.

"What's the hurry?"

"The big boy's on his way into Tule."

Estrellita sat up quickly, making no effort to cover her nakedness. "Salvador is return?"

"Yup."

Estrellita turned to Bart, her teeth gleaming. "How you feel, *tejano*? You lighter now?"

Bart grinned at her. "A strong breeze could blow me away."

"Good. Now see if that golden-haired one can do same for you. When you take her, you will want Estrellita."

"Cut it out," Bart snapped.

She shrugged and left the cot, padding on naked feet across the floor to where she had hung her clothes. She pulled on her skirt. Then, before she dropped her blouse over her head, she turned to give him one last glimpse of her breasts.

"Remember," she told him. "You said you would treat Estrellita well."

"Scott," Bart said. "Bring my saddlebags, will you?"

"Just hurry up," Scott said, vanishing from the doorway.

He returned a moment later and tossed the saddlebags at Bart. Fully dressed by this time, Bart took out three cartwheels from one of them. Estrellita ran over to him, and Bart dropped the gold coins into her waiting hands.

"Three dollar!" she cried, embracing Bart and kissing him warmly on the lips. Then she stepped

THE TEXAN

back, grinning. "You not lie. You treat Estrellita well!"

He slung the saddlebags over his shoulder and reached for his hat. "What's the matter, Estrellita? Didn't you think I would?"

"No. After all, you are *tejano*."

"Well, then, let this be a lesson to you. Texans always pay their debts."

Chapter Seven

Bart and Scott found chairs on the cantina's porch and waited for de Santos to arrive. There seemed to be a small increase in the town's population. About ten or fifteen Mexicans had gathered around the gate leading into the larger warehouses, a considerable number of them wearing clean sombreros and trousers. One or two had even shaved.

"Heard you had some trouble with Raoul yesterday," Scott remarked.

"A little."

"And you're still alive?"

"Why shouldn't I be?"

"Raoul's one of de Santos's chief lieutenants. It

only proves what I told you yesterday. These chilis are afraid to kill us."

"Afraid?"

"That's right. The fact that we know Kristen—that we've come for her—means that no one can hurt us. Not permantly, anyway. Like I told you yesterday, Kristen carries a lot of weight around here—almost as much as her lord and master, de Santos."

Before Bart could reply, he heard the heavy rattle of wooden wheels and looked up to see a long line of high-backed ox-drawn carts rumble onto the plaza.

"Speak of the devil," said Scott.

From the sound of the wooden wheels as they rumbled over the hard-packed ground, it was obvious that each one was heavily laden with goods for trading. De Santos's trip to Mexico had been a shopping trip. Most likely he had returned with trinkets and guns, goods for trading with the Comanche.

Not long after the last cart disappeared through the warehouse gate, de Santos's personal stagecoach rattled onto the plaza. Flanked by six outriders, the coach body was gleaming red with a black leather top. It was drawn by four powerful black horses. They were probably the best the Comanche could find in all of Texas, Bart reflected grimly. A guard sat beside the driver, a gleaming double-barreled greener resting across his knees.

It must be nice, Bart thought, to have your own stagecoach and a private army to see you to your destination.

The stagecoach halted in front of the largest gate in the wall where the small crowd of Comancheros had been waiting. As the coach door opened, those waiting to greet de Santos doffed their hats and shouted greetings to the tall, slender man who stepped down. De Santos returned his men's greetings, then reached back into the coach to help Kristen out.

Bart had not seen Kristen for four years. During those years he had spent many hours trying to imagine how she would look when he finally gazed upon her once again.

But he had not been prepared for the tall, slim woman he now saw stepping out of the coach. She, too, greeted the waiting Comancheros, then paused beside de Santos as he spoke to his waiting lieutenants. Her blond hair was piled up under a fashionable wide-brimmed hat, which sported a lilac ostrich feather that arched over her back. Even from this distance Bart thought he could catch the brilliant flash of her eyes as she glanced around. Under her short green jacket she was wearing a white silk blouse. A pleated black silk skirt brushed the instep of her high-button shoes.

"It don't look like she's suffering all that much under the heel of her master," remarked Scott.

Bart was no longer able to argue the point. It was clear that Scott had been right all along. And now Bart understood what Estrellita had been talking about too.

Raoul stepped closer to de Santos and, pointing toward the cantina, said something to him. Both de Santos and Kristen looked across the plaza, directly at Bart and Scott. A brief word or two passed between de Santos and Raoul, and then de Santos escorted Kristen through the gate.

"Well, now, how do you like them apples?" Scott remarked. "She knows we're here. Raoul just told her. And she's so damned eager to see us, she turns her back and walks off with de Santos. I got a feeling we came a long way for nothing, Bart."

Bart was too upset to respond. Besides, he was watching Raoul. The big, swarthy Mexican was heading across the plaza toward them, the brim of his big, freshly brushed sombrero tugging in the hot wind.

"Why, lookee here," Scott said. "Looks like we're gonna get a special invite."

Raoul did not doff his hat when he pulled up in front of them. "Hey, gringos," he said. "You come with me now."

"Where to?" Bart asked.

"You want to see Señor de Santos?"

"Yes."

"And hees woman?"

Bart didn't like the way that sounded, but all he could do was nod.

"*Bueno*. You gringos come with me."

Raoul led them across the plaza and through the main gate in the wall. Outside wooden steps led to the top-floor apartment Bart had noticed earlier. As Bart followed Raoul up the steps he was able to see down into the loading areas behind the two warehouses.

A swarm of Mexicans were busy unloading the carts that had preceded de Santos into Tule. Piled on the ground beside each one were boxes, most of which had been opened for inspection. Bart was astonished at the range of goods. He saw knives and hatchets, arrowheads, beads, cooking utensils, blankets, bolts of calico, kegs of lead for bullet-making, cartridges, and long boxes that probably contained new repeating rifles—Spencers, more than likely.

He looked away just as they reached the landing. The door opened, and Bart saw de Santos standing in the hallway.

"Welcome, *señors*," he said, smiling.

As Bart and Scott moved past him through the doorway, de Santos dismissed Raoul with a curt nod. Shutting the door, de Santos turned to Bart. He smiled. "You must be Bart Hardison. I am Salvador de Santos."

Bart shook de Santos's hand and introduced him to Scott Tyrell, after which de Santos led them down a long, cool corridor into his apartment. The living room was wide and spacious with four large windows along one wall. Heavy, brocaded drapes hung at the windows to keep out the midday heat. The sunlight was strong enough, however, to push its way through them, flooding the room with a warm, luminous glow.

De Santos sat down in a high-backed armchair and told Bart and Scott to make themselves comfortable. They sat on a leather sofa facing him. An old Indian woman appeared carrying a serving tray. On it sat a coffeepot, cups and saucers, spoons, and a sugar bowl—all in highly burnished silver.

As the Indian woman poured the coffee de Santos said, "Kristen wanted me to tell you that she will be out presently. It has been a long, dusty journey for her, and she wanted time to freshen up. I am sure you understand."

"Sure," said Bart woodenly. "We understand."

A spare, graceful man, de Santos was easily six feet tall. Dressed in a white shirt and immaculate, tapering pants, his stylishly pointed boots a gleaming black, he did not resemble the leader of a Comanchero band. His dark, almost black hair was slicked back, and his mustache was meticulously trimmed. His olive skin was stretched tightly over his high cheekbones, and his large, dark eyes had the impenetrable depths of a Comanche warrior.

As the Indian woman poured his coffee de Santos addressed Bart. "I understand you had some trouble with one of my lieutenants yesterday."

"Yeah. That fellow Raoul."

"You would be well advised not to anger Raoul unduly."

"Then tell him to keep his nose out of my business."

"You mean Estrellita?"

"That's right."

"But you see, this *is* his business."

"Not according to her."

De Santos shrugged. "That is always the way, I am afraid. Men fight over women. And women love it. But you must be careful of Raoul. He is now your enemy and has a long memory."

Bart met de Santos's gaze coldly. "We Texans have long memories too. Memories of murdering savages who loot our lands and carry off our women and children. And of your Comancheros taking the bloody plunder off their hands. I had a sister when I left Texas four years ago. I don't have one now. I wonder how much her necklace brought the Comanche who killed her."

"More than likely the brave has it still. I deal only in livestock."

"And rifles and bullets and arrowheads. Don't try to make your blood trade any less filthy than it is."

De Santos shrugged. He seemed impervious to

Bart's charges. He had heard this all many times before, Bart realized. "Is this why you two have journeyed so far?" de Santos asked softly. "To tell me what you think of my filthy trade? Or did you come to see Kristen?"

"You know the answer to that."

"Did you know we were coming?" Scott asked.

De Santos nodded. "One of my men went a little mad. He had a notion of owning his own ranch in Mexico. The idea became an obsession. He tried to abduct Kristen for the five-hundred-dollar reward her mother had offered. When he found this impossible, he robbed my men and headed for Texas. He was not only foolish, he was greedy. My men followed him to Kate Nordstrom's ranch before they ended his foolish odyssey and took back the gold he had stolen."

"He was on his way to my ranch when they caught up to him," Bart acknowledged.

"I was certain he had told Kristen's mother she was with me in hopes of prying loose some of the reward. And that meant Kate Nordstrom would most certainly send someone here to find Kristen. I told Raoul and his men to watch out for whoever came but not to hinder them in any way." He smiled. "And here you are. Kristen's mother is fortunate to have two such brave men. But may I ask why it took you so long?"

"This place ain't so easy to find," Scott told him.

De Santos smiled. "I am pleased to hear that."

At that moment Kristen stepped into the room. She had changed into a long white dress and had unfastened her gleaming blond hair. In the soft glow of the light filtering in through the curtains she looked scarcely real.

Bart put down his coffee and stood up. "Kristen!"

"Hello, Bart."

Kristen quickly walked over to de Santos's chair and stood behind it, her hand resting on its high back.

"Kristen, we've come for you," Bart said eagerly.

"Mother sent you?"

"That she did," said Scott.

"You've come a long way, then," Kristen acknowledged. "And I appreciate it. But I'm sorry. I am afraid you will have to go back without me."

Bart did not want to believe what he was hearing. "But, Kristen, how can you stay here with this man? You know what he is."

"Yes, I do. But I am afraid that you do not."

"He's a Comanchero!"

"Please, Bart. You are making this very difficult for me."

"But your mother! Kate! What can we tell her?"

"Tell her this is what I want."

"To stay here?"

"Yes."

"You can't mean that!"

"Please, Bart. Go back. Tell my mother I am fine. But tell her I cannot go back home."

"But why...?"

"I have my reasons."

"Gentlemen," de Santos broke in gently, "do not fear for Kristen's well-being. She has consented to stay with me. I assure you, she will always be treated with the respect and affection a woman of her beauty and courage deserves. She alone escaped from Iron Cheek's Comanche band—without any help from me. I found her heading south. She accepted my help in putting the Kotsotekas behind her, but I believe she would have made it on her own."

Bart looked back at Kristen. Her face was somber and incredibly beautiful. He took a deep breath. He and Scott had come a long way to bring her back, and the thought of leaving her here with this Mexican dandy was intolerable. But there was nothing else to do, he realized numbly. Returning or not returning to the Brazos was a decision Kristen had to make for herself. No matter how difficult it was to accept, he had to respect her wishes.

Or did he?

Bart and Scott left later that same day. But they did not go far. When night came, they rode back, keeping to the timber high above Tule. Bart left Scott to guard the horses, then scrambled down the steep slope behind the warehouses and slipped through a gate in the rear. Staying in the shadows, he came upon the Mexicans still unloading the wagons de Santos had brought up from Mexico.

De Santos and Raoul were busy making an item-by-item count. Dressed like his fellow Comancheros—in rough leather pants and vest and rolled-up sleeves—de Santos no longer resembled a smooth Mexican gentleman.

Slipping up the outside steps leading to de Santos's lodging, Bart found the door unlocked. He opened it and stepped inside. His Colt out, he moved swiftly down the corridor. The door to de Santos' apartment was ajar. He pushed it open and entered.

The Indian servant appeared in the far doorway. Before she could cry out, Bart leveled his Colt at her and placed his finger to his lips. The woman backed hastily out of the room.

"Kristen!" Bart called sharply.

Almost at once she appeared in the living-room doorway. She was wearing a long, blue silken robe. Never had Kristen looked more beautiful.

"Bart! What on earth—!"

"I've come back for you, Kristen."

"Oh, Bart! We've already been over this! You must go!"

"Not until I get an explanation."

"But I've already given it to you."

"I know you couldn't talk freely with de Santos in the same room. But we're alone now. You can tell me the truth. Hell, Kristen, we never had any secrets from each other."

Kristen looked for a long, weary moment at Bart, then sighed. "Come into my room. It has a balcony. It's cooler there."

As Kristen led Bart through the apartment she reassured the Indian woman that it was all right, then asked her to bring them something cool to drink.

Following her through the bedroom, Bart stepped out onto the balcony. It looked out over Tule and the valley beyond. The mountains that towered over the town were like vast velvety wings holding back the night.

"You're right, Bart," Kristen began. "I couldn't tell you everything this morning."

"So tell me now."

Kristen sighed. "You men, you really have no idea why I'm staying?"

"No riddles, Kristen. I wouldn't be asking if I knew."

"Bart, I've lived with the Comanche! I was Iron Cheek's woman. I slept with him, Bart. Whenever he wanted me, he took me—and I let him."

Bart found himself wincing. "All right," he said. "All right. I know all about it. What's that got to do with anything?"

The Indian woman stepped out onto the balcony. She handed Kristen a tall glass of lemonade, and to Bart a small earthen cup containing tequila.

Kristen thanked the Indian in Spanish. As she hurried off, Kristen studied Bart carefully. "You didn't like me mentioning that I slept with Iron Cheek, did you?"

"What did you expect?"

"It disgusted you, didn't it?"

"I didn't say that. Don't put words into my mouth, Kristen. I just don't see why you have to talk about it, that's all."

"I see." Her eyes glinted angrily.

"No, you don't see. It doesn't take much imagination to figure out what happened. But what's the sense dwelling on it? Why think about it at all? It's all in the past. It's over now."

"You mean, you're willing to forget it happened —to forgive me."

"Of course!"

"Thank you," she said ironically.

"Dammit, Kristen! Why are you making it so hard for me?"

"I just wanted to know. I just want to be sure you didn't think I should have killed myself rather than let that savage take me."

He did not hesitate for a moment. "Of course not."

She smiled sadly. "But don't you see, Bart? That is precisely what the others think I should

THE TEXAN

have done. I am damned in the eyes of all who know my past. My virginity was lost—not to a white man but to a Comanche savage."

"Stop it, Kristen."

"You and I talked of marriage once. Do you still want to marry me? Will you stand by me and be damned to perdition by everyone we know, by all our neighbors and acquaintances, for consorting with a woman who was used by a filthy Comanche savage? Can you imagine what it would be like for you? And for our children?"

"You're making it sound worse than it is."

"Am I? Bart, do you know of any women who returned from captivity and were welcomed back to their community and allowed to resume a normal life? Name one."

Bart couldn't. He was aware of at least four women who had returned from living with the Comanche or the Kiowa. One had been fearfully scarred and headed east and was never heard of again. Two had committed suicide. One had come back to find her husband remarried, and he had refused to let her see her children. Though her own people took her in, she died within a year.

Bart felt suddenly drained. He realized the terrible truth of Kristen's words. "Kristen, it could be different for us."

"How?"

"I'll sell Anchor. We could move someplace else."

"Where no one would know my shame."

"Yes."

She smiled again. "You see? You admit it is my shame."

"Damn, Kristen. I didn't mean that. You're twisting my words. I told you, it doesn't matter."

"Not now, perhaps. But it will—later."

"How can you know that?"

"Because I know how you feel about Anchor—and what it would mean to you if you had to give it up—for any woman. And how terrible it would be for you to have to move away forever from your own people. From the land you love."

"I would do it. And I wouldn't look back."

"Brave words, Bart. And I think right now you believe them. But that's not the kind of dowry I want to bring to you on my wedding night—or to any man."

"Damnit, Kristen. We can find a way!"

"There's something else."

Bart felt his heart sink. How could there be anything more after this?

"I'm listening," he said wearily.

"After what happened to me I changed... inside. I don't fully understand it myself. But I'm... not much of a woman anymore. I can't feel anything. No warmth. No affection. No love. There is something missing. Do you understand?"

"You mean, you feel nothing for me?"

"Not just you. It... goes deeper than that."

"What about this de Santos?"

"He is very kind. And like all men, he hopes he can find the key that will unlock my heart and make it all right for me again."

Bart looked at her. She was so incredibly lovely, so beautiful and yet so distant. He saw the lack of any real emotion in her eyes. She was right. There *was* something missing.

Those damned savages had destroyed her.

He put down his tequila and pulled her closer. Without protest she moved against him and placed her cool cheek against his. Then he gently turned her face to his and kissed her on the lips. She kissed him back. But there was nothing there—nothing at all. No pliant warmth, no sudden eagerness.

Gently he stepped back from her.

"You see?" she said.

In the dim starlight he watched a single tear move down her cheek.

It was close to sundown when Bart and Scott rode up to Kate's ranch two weeks later. Kate was standing on the front porch waiting for them. She had seen them coming from a mile away. Beside her on the porch sat Frank Kilrain, his chair tipped back against the wall.

The two riders reined in before the porch.

"I see you lost your Confederate hat, Scott," Kate remarked.

"Traded it away," Scott replied, smiling faintly. The small talk was over.

"Where's Kristen?" she asked.

"She's alive and well, Kate."

The relief on Kate's face was touching to see. To the world she was a hard woman. But in that instant Bart could see that she was only flesh and blood.

"You mean she's still with that Comanchero chief?"

"Yes."

"What ransom is he asking?"

"Kristen can leave him anytime she wants, Kate."

"Why, what do you mean?"

"I mean she is not being held against her will."

A gray hue came over Kate's face. Frank Kilrain eased his chair forward.

"I don't understand," Kate said. "If she is not being held against her will, why didn't she return with you?"

"All I know is she doesn't want to come back, Kate."

Kate struggled to keep her composure. "I see. She has no interest in returning to her home. Did she tell you why?"

"She knew what kind of a reception she'd get from the people in this valley, Kate—her living with the Comanche and all."

"But you told her that was nonsense, didn't you?"

"Yes, I did, Kate."

Scott spoke up then. "I wouldn't worry about her none, Kate. This fellow she's with is treating her just fine."

"You mean that Mexican! That filthy Comanchero?" she shot back, her voice heavy with shame.

"Yes, Kate," said Bart.

A hard, bitter resolve settled over Kate's face. She had heard the worst and would now simply have to live with it.

"I thank you, Bart," she said, her eyes bleak. "You, too, Scott. You men went a long ways to get Kristen back, and I'm sure grateful to you. I'm sorry you had to go so far for nothing."

"That's all right, Kate," Bart told her. "We were glad to do it."

As Bart rode out of the compound a moment later, he glanced back to see Kate slowly entering the ranch house, Frank Kilrain following in behind her. It was dusk, and darkness was falling over the land.

Bart turned back around in his saddle, recalling vividly the bleak despair he had seen in Kate Nordstrom's eyes.

PART TWO
Kate

Chapter Eight

Soon after Bart and Scott returned from New Mexico, Amanda Hardison was brought out to Anchor. At first it did not appear to have been a wise move. There was no improvement in her condition. Nevertheless, Bart wanted his mother near him, and he believed that she wanted to be close by as well. At times he found himself able to carry on a limited conversation with her. During these brief periods, when the veil of madness seemed to have lifted for a while, she was her old self: cheerful, wise, observant. And as the days and weeks flowed by, the periods of lucidity seemed to occur more often. Scott handled her best. He fussed over her, insisting that she was still the prettiest girl in the county—

as he had in the days when both he and Bart's father had been courting her.

Yet overall, to those who knew and loved her, Amanda's progress was heartbreakingly slow.

Meanwhile, not just along the Brazos but all through Texas clear down to the Gulf Coast, the brushlands and grasslands swarmed with fat, unbranded cattle that had multiplied during the war years. A glut on the markets, these longhorns were worth only three to five dollars a head. It was hardly worth slaughtering them for their hides and tallow.

It was during the following winter when news came of a town in Kansas, a place called Abilene, where someone named Joe McCoy had built vast holding pens and loading platforms alongside the Kansas Pacific Railroad. From all accounts, during its first season in operation, Abilene had shipped one thousand carloads of cattle to the stockyards in St. Louis and Chicago.

Overnight, this news transformed Anchor's prospects—and those of every other rancher in Texas. As the range began to turn green, Bart, Tim, and Scott set about rounding up and branding their calf crop—and whatever mavericks they found feeding off their rangeland. Excited talk of trail herds and Kansas stockyards filled every saloon in Burnt Creek. In fact, it was rumored that Kate Nordstrom had ridden down to San

Antonio with her foreman and returned with a small army of hired hands to help her round up her immense stock.

On a Friday afternoon toward the middle of April, the local ranchers and their foremen began drifting into Sam Bronson's general store. They were meeting to decide on the trail boss for the herd the ranchers were sending north within a fortnight.

On Bart's advice Don O'Hare had called the meeting. Molly O'Hare and Bronson's wife provided coffee and platters of doughnuts, but as soon as the womenfolk left, whiskey flasks appeared as the voices grew louder and the laughter heartier.

Bart sat up front with Tim and Scott. Scott had grumbled most of the afternoon at the prospect of having to sit through this palaver, but he had come, anyway. Now he sat with folded arms, one cheek bulging with tobacco. Glancing idly over the ranchers still filing into the back room, Bart realized that Kate Nordstrom was missing.

When he saw Dan getting ready to call the meeting to order, he stood up to get his attention.

"Dan, where's Kate Nordstrom?"

Dan shrugged. "I sent news of this meeting out to her last week."

"Maybe we should wait for her, then."

There was some grumbling at that suggestion.

Someone remarked that she didn't need them, that she'd bought her own army and probably was going to send her own herd up to Kansas. But Dan saw the wisdom in waiting a while longer for Kate, just in case.

About ten minutes later the rumble of voices faded. A restlessness came over the men, and several ranchers demanded that Dan get the meeting under way.

Dan struck the wooden bench in front of him with a large wooden mallet. The place quieted instantly. Dan cleared his throat and announced what a few men already knew. A single head of beef in Chicago was bringing three more dollars than at the beginning of the month. A cheer went up at this news.

Grinning, Dan gaveled the meeting to silence, then promptly asked for a show of hands to see how many ranchers were sending their cattle to Kansas. Six hands shot up. Every rancher at the meeting. Dan smiled broadly, pleased.

"We got the critters, then. What we need is a trail boss."

Tolliver Adams got to his feet. "I'd like to nominate my foreman, Ned Perkins."

Everyone liked Ned. There was quick applause and shouts of approval.

"Any more nominations?" Dan asked.

John Tanner shot to his feet. "Bart Hardison!" he said. "I seen him fight at the Canyon. Seems to me we're gonna need that kind of experience if we got to go through the Indian nations."

"Close the nominations!" someone shouted.

"Any seconds?"

Both nominations were seconded by a thunderous shout, followed by a great roar of laughter. Dan slammed his mallet down on the bench.

"All right," he said, "all those who want Ned Perkins, raise your hand."

Tolliver Adams and one other rancher held up their hands. There was no need for any more voting. Bart was the trail boss.

Bart got quickly to his feet. "I'd like for Ned Perkins to be my *segundo*," he said.

Ned grinned his acceptance. There were shouts of approval as Dan asked Bart to step up beside him and conduct the rest of the meeting. They had yet to settle on a route, Dan reminded Bart, and there was already some worry about having to take the trail drive through the Indian nations.

Bart took the mallet from Dan and turned to the ranchers.

"I say we go northeast," he began without preamble. "The Shawnee Trail won't do us any good. But after we cross the Cimarron, there's a trail that goes north to Abilene called the Chisholm. If we can find it, I say we take it."

There was general agreement, after which the place quieted down so that Bart could continue.

"Looks to me like our best bet after we cross

the Red River is to skirt the Washita, cross the two Canadians, then the Cimarron. After that we keep northeast until we hit the Chisolm. If we miss it, we'll just keep on going until we hit the railroad tracks."

"Won't be nothin' to it!" someone in back shouted. "We'll just follow them tracks right into Abilene!"

"We might even get a brass band!"

Bart smiled and nodded.

"Bart, when we startin'?" Tolliver asked.

"I figure around the first of May, if we can make it. The sooner the better. The first herds into Abilene should get the best price—and we'll have a good jump on them drovers south of us."

There was a general mutter of agreement to that. The meeting progressed swiftly as the ranchers settled on a trail brand and a place to bring all their herds together for the roundup and branding. At the close of the meeting Dan O'Hare was the unanimous selection as the tally man.

Bart was giving the mallet back to Dan so he could close the meeting when the sound of heavy boots came from the front of the store. Every man turned to see who was coming.

Kate Nordstrom was the first to move into the light. Frank Kilrain was at her side. Six more men followed, all of them strangers to Bart. Evidently these were the men Kate had brought back with her from San Antonio. They wore dark, floppy-brimmed hats and linen dusters. They looked grim enough. Evidently Kate had selected them from that tribe of bitter, lawless men who had been drifting into Texas since the war's end.

As Kate came to a halt at the rear of the seated ranchers Dan cleared his throat. "Howdy, Kate."

"Howdy, Dan."

Kate looked around at the ranchers and their foremen, nodding to each of them in turn. When she had finished, she said, "Looks like you men weren't so anxious to have me at this meeting. But here I am, anyway."

"That ain't true, Kate," Dan protested. "I sent word out to your ranch last week."

Kate looked surprised. "You did?"

"Yes, I did, Kate."

"And just who did you send?"

"That peddler, Jacob Kravatt. He said he was passing by your place on his way south. I gave him a notice about this meeting and he said he'd be sure to see you got it."

Kate looked at Kilrain.

Her foreman's lean face went pale as he shrugged his shoulders. "My fault, Kate. I should've mentioned it, I suppose. Kravatt never got past them cottonwoods on the south flat. We saw him comin' and shooed him off. His pans were rattlin' somethin' fierce and spookin' that stock we was pushin' across the river."

Kate looked back at Dan. "My apologies, Dan. Maybe the next time you'll send someone who will make it to my place—not some itinerant peddler."

"How'd I know your foreman would drive him off, Kate?"

Kate didn't bother to answer Dan. "I see the meeting is about over," she noted. "What'd you men decide?"

"We're sending a trail herd north to Kansas—right on through the Indian nations."

"How many ranches are involved?"

"Six."

"Who's the trail boss?"

"We settled on Bart Hardison."

She glanced at Bart. "That's a fine choice to my way of thinking. Does he have a *segundo*? I was thinking of Frank here, since my cattle will no doubt be the largest gather."

"We already settled on Ned Perkins, Kate," Bart said.

"That's all right," spoke up Ned. "Let Frank do it, Bart. Ain't no skin off my hide."

Bart did not like Frank Kilrain, not at all. But at this moment his hands were tied. Everyone seemed anxious to mollify Kate. "All right," Bart said. "If no one has any objections."

There was a general murmur of assent. It wasn't hearty, but there was nothing in the tone to make Frank take offense.

THE TEXAN

"All right, Kate," said Dan, obviously relieved. "Frank will be Bart's *segundo*."

Dan gave Kate the other details.

Kate nodded her thanks and left the meeting, her small army tramping after her. As soon as she was gone, the remaining ranchers broke into quiet, agitated conversation. Still buzzing over the new development, they filed out of Bronson's store, heading for the saloon.

Bart decided against joining them. He did not like to leave his mother and Ellen alone at Anchor this late at night. Urging Scott and Tim to stay in town and drink their fill if they wanted, he mounted up and headed out of Burnt Creek.

As he rode, he found himself thinking of Kate Nordstrom's ominous company of hired hands. Like most ranchers at that meeting, Bart understood that it was her sudden, dramatic presence that had forced them into accepting Frank Kilrain as Bart's *segundo*. Back in the saloon talking things over, they were probably wondering if it had been a mistake.

Bart didn't wonder. He knew. It *had* been a mistake.

A week later, around noon, Scott and Tim rode hard into the compound, their faces grim. Ellen had been sweeping the porch. She put aside her broom as the two men dismounted hurriedly and headed toward her.

"Where's Bart?" Scott asked her.

"Inside."

As Scott started up the porch steps Bart stepped out of the kitchen, a cup of coffee in his hand. "What's up?"

"There's riders on our land. Circle N riders. And they all got branding irons, looks like."

"Where, exactly?"

"Twin Creek. Hell, Bart, they got two or three branding fires going. I'd say they've already branded more than fifty mavericks."

Bart flung the rest of his coffee away and hurried back inside. A second later he emerged, his gun belt strapped to his hip.

Glancing over at Ellen, he said, "Keep an eye out, Ellen."

She nodded as he strode off the porch and headed for the stables. Scott and Tim, leading their own horses, had difficulty keeping up with him.

Frowning with concern, Ellen pushed an errant lock of hair off her forehead. Upset at this ominous turn, she thought of Bart's mother, alone inside. Entering the kitchen, she closed the door and moved to the window to look out.

"What's wrong, Ellen?"

Ellen spun around, startled. Bart's mother was standing in the doorway, one hand on the frame.

"Why, Amanda!" Ellen cried. "What are you doing in the kitchen?"

"Can't I come in here?"

"Of course, you can. I'm just surprised, is all."

"I'm sick of sitting in there. It's time I got up, don't you think?"

"Of course, Amanda."

"Besides, I'm frightened. There's trouble, isn't there?"

Ellen nodded. "I'm afraid so."

A sudden drumbeat of hooves filled the yard. Ellen looked out through the window and watched Bart and the others ride out.

An hour of hard riding brought the three riders to a slight rise that gave them a clear view of the creek and the branding party alongside it. So intent was the branding party on the business at hand, none of them noticed that they were being watched. Kilrain, forking a big chestnut, was about ten yards to one side of the branding fires; Carl and Cullen Barker were seated on their mounts alongside him. Under their intent gaze the six new ranch hands were branding the downed calves with commendable speed and efficiency. The sound of bawling cattle filled the air.

"Son of a bitch," Bart muttered angrily.

Scott popped a plug of tobacco into his cheek and said nothing. Then he glanced at Bart and nodded. Bart nudged his mount forward; Tim and Scott followed. As he neared the creek a gust of wind carried the acrid stench of scorched hide to his nostrils.

At that moment Kilrain and his two sidekicks caught sight of them. They shouted something to the six hands, then spurred their horses across the clearing to intercept Bart and his two companions. Bart slowed down as Kilrain and his two sidekicks pulled up in front of him.

"What the hell is going on here, Frank?" Bart demanded.

Kilrain shrugged. "You ain't blind, are you? I'm brandin' mavericks."

"On Anchor range?"

"Who says this is Anchor range? It's open range."

"I got advertisements in for all this land, on both sides of this creek and for ten miles in each direction. I'm tellin' you again. This is Anchor land."

"Hell, I can't just rely on your word. How do I know you're tellin' the truth?"

"You callin' me a liar?"

"You can say that if you want—but all I'm sayin' is, I need proof. We ain't got much time. The trail herd'll be pullin' out next week."

Suddenly Bart saw something in one of the men's hands—a running iron. He roweled his mount past Kilrain, and when he came alongside the nearest branding fire, he flung himself from his saddle. A calf, bleating miserably from its recent branding, was struggling to its feet.

Brushing past the man wielding the running iron, Bart caught the calf by the ear, wrapped his forearm around its neck, and flung it around so he could read the brand. With an enviable skill the Circle N's new hand had changed Bart's brand so that Anchor's A was now an N, and the A's tail had become part of the circle burned around it.

Kilrain's new men weren't branding mavericks. They were branding Anchor cattle.

Bart let the calf go and looked back at Kilrain. By this time the rest of Kilrain's crew had thrown down their branding irons and were drawing close around Bart. His face cold with resolve, Frank Kilrain rode through the ranks of his men toward Bart. Behind Frank rode Scott and Tim; Kilrain's two partners, Carl and Barker, brought up the rear.

Kilrain reined in his mount and looked down at Bart. The look on his face was defiant. "Find out what you wanted, did you?"

"Does Kate know what you're up to?"

"She knows she's goin' to get rich when her cattle make it to Abilene. That's all she needs to know."

"She doesn't know, then."

"And you ain't goin' to tell her."

"We'll see about that."

"No. I'll see about it."

As he spoke, Kilrain drew his gun. But Bart's Walker was already drawn. Before Kilrain could fire, Bart's weapon detonated, knocking Frank back off his horse. Instantly Frank's men unlimbered their irons and returned Bart's fire.

A slug caught Bart in his left shoulder. At the same time he saw Tim spin off his horse, while Scott—ducking low in his saddle—was busy returning fire coming at him from all sides. Bart swung his own gun around, firing the huge Walker as fast as he could cock it. A round hammered into his hip. Then a third slug knocked his left leg out from under him.

Bart spun to the ground. A swarm of bees entered his skull, buzzing like crazy. A calf Kilrain's crew had tied down broke loose and ran bleating over Bart's back, its sharp hooves driving him further into the ground.

And that was all Bart remembered.

The first volley caught Scott in his side, inches above his right hip. Slipping back off his horse, he pulled it down beside him. Using the frantic, thrashing beast for cover, he kept up a steady return fire. He had no idea how many Circle N riders he hit, if any. But after his horse took two slugs in its chest, the Circle N crew rode off with the wounded Frank Kilrain—and all the Anchor cattle they could keep in front of them.

THE TEXAN

The bullet that hit Scott had gone right on through his side, and he could feel the warm blood pouring down his thigh. He thought maybe he could smell it too. Tim O'Hare was lying about ten feet away, his head facedown in the grass.

Scott dragged himself to Tim's side, grabbed his hip, and rolled him over—then wished he hadn't. The bullet from a .44 had destroyed his face. Entering through his nose, it had ranged upward into his skull before crashing out just above his right ear.

Scott rolled Tim back over onto his face and crawled past him to examine Bart. Resting his hand on Bart's back, he felt the steady rise and fall of his chest and relaxed. He counted three wounds in all, steady rivulets of blood flowing from each one. Working rapidly, he managed to staunch the flow in Bart's shoulder and leg wounds by wrapping strips of torn shirt around them. But Bart's hip wound was a more difficult matter. He tightened Bart's gun belt around it, slowing the seepage of blood only a little.

Bart's horse was grazing placidly nearby. Scott went after it and brought it close to Bart. But when he attempted to lift Bart up over the pommel, a dark cloud seemed to pass over the sun. Scott realized that he had lost a lot of blood.

He passed out.

* * *

It was night when Scott awoke.

He was on his back, staring up at the Big Dipper stretched across the black sky, its gleaming pinpricks of light winking cheerfully down at him. Each star held the soul of a white man or Indian he had killed; but all was forgiven if he would fly up to join them. The prospect was exceedingly pleasant, and Scott felt himself sinking back into the dreamless sleep from which he had just emerged, the soft grass holding him as gently as a woman's arms.

Beside him in the grass, Bart groaned and moved slightly.

Scott forced himself to sit up. Shaking his head, he peered over at Bart's horse, still cropping the grass nearby. With a deep, weary sigh, Scott staggered back up onto his feet. This time he managed to slip Bart's body over the pommel and climb up into the saddle behind him. He clucked softly. The horse started up eagerly, anxious to reach the oats and water he knew were waiting for him in his Anchor stall.

Without waiting for Ellen to greet her, Kate dismounted and headed for the porch. Ellen, her mouth a grim, unforgiving line, kept herself squarely in front of the door. Sitting in a wicker chair on the porch beside her was a startlingly pale Scott Tyrell, a blanket over his lap. Ellen's implacable stance, however, did not daunt Kate.

THE TEXAN

She mounted the porch and stopped in front of Ellen.

"Ellen, I'm sorry about Tim," she said. "I can understand how you feel."

"No, you can't understand how I feel, Kate. It's indecent for you to say you can. I don't think you can understand or feel anything—not anymore. Not you or a single one of your hired guns were at the funeral."

Kate looked at Scott. "How's Bart?"

"About the way your men left him," he replied. "He ain't come around yet."

"I'd like to see him."

"Why?" Ellen asked bitterly. "To gloat?"

"I ought to slap you for that."

"Lay a hand on her and I'll knock you off this porch," Scott told her quietly. As he spoke, he rose carefully from his chair.

Kate looked back at Ellen. "Please," she said, her tone softening. "Let me see Bart. I won't be long. I just want to see him."

Ellen hesitated a moment, then stepped aside to let Kate pass.

Bart lay in Ellen's bed. His mother was sitting beside him, holding his hand. She glanced up as Kate entered and frowned. Her face turned white when she recognized Kate.

"Kate just wants to see Bart," Ellen explained.

"I heard you was better, Amanda," Kate said, addressing Bart's mother. "I'm glad."

Amanda was too confused to respond. Her son was lying unconscious, thanks to Kate's foreman. Ellen moved protectively behind her and rested her hand on Amanda's shoulder.

Kate peered down at Bart. He was breathing regularly, but his face was sunken, his complexion as pale as the pillowcase under his head. He was clean-shaven, but whoever had shaved him had let the razor slip. There was a nick just under his chin, the scab fresh. From what Kate heard, he had been in this condition for almost a week.

He was in a coma. She had heard of such cases. Bart would not live, she concluded.

Stepping back from the bed, she turned to face Ellen. "I came here to tell you we've finished the roundup and the trail herd is leaving tomorrow morning. We have your Anchor stock. The cattle my foreman branded by mistake and the mavericks taken from your ranges—as many as we could determine—have been tallied and assigned to Anchor. When we sell the herd in Kansas, you will be paid in full."

Behind her, leaning for support against the doorway, Scott asked, "How many head you reckon that'll be?"

She turned to face him. "At least six hundred, maybe six hundred fifty."

Scott said nothing, but he was impressed. That

was just about the figure he had in mind when he asked her. He smiled. "How's Frank?"

"Well enough."

"He goin' to be the trail boss in place of Bart?"

"Yes."

"Still trust him, do you?"

"I came here today to tell you that I'm sorry for what happened. For both of us. One of our men was killed also, you know, and Frank's shoulder is still bothering him."

"He was lucky Bart didn't kill him."

"Frank has explained everything to my satisfaction. It was all a terrible mistake."

"Is that what you think?"

She took a deep, unhappy breath. "I have no choice. Carl and Cullen Barker backed his story. Frank came upon his men branding the calves and simply assumed they were branding mavericks. I've fired the remaining hands."

"And you think Frank can handle the job of trail boss, that he can nurse them longhorns all the way to Abilene?"

It was obvious Kate did not like Scott's questions. It was also clear she was intent on not taking offense. "Frank will not be alone with the herd," she reminded Scott. "There's still Ned Perkins, and Tolliver Adams of the Lazy T. And I will be going north with the trail herd also, as the drover."

Scott knew what Kate was telling him. During

the drive north, while she handled all the negotiations for provisions and so on, she would keep a tight rein on her foreman. The drive would force her man to extend himself, and before they got to that cow town in Kansas, Kate would discover what she needed to know about Frank Kilrain.

Kate glanced back down at Bart. He had not moved an inch since she entered the room. Her face was pale with concern, but she could not bring herself to say anything. She brushed past Scott and left the ranch house. Scott and Ellen followed her out onto the porch.

Wearing trousers under her long shirt, she swung onto her mount like a man and without a single glance back, rode out of the yard. She was not the kind of woman to look back, Scott figured.

Chapter Nine

Kristen gazed up at the night sky from her bedroom balcony. There was no point in denying it. She still loved Bart. She had hurt him grievously when she refused to return with him. The reasons she had given for not going back were true enough, but there was an even more compelling reason: her mother.

If returning to the valley with Bart was unthinkable, returning to her mother was out of the question. Though Kristen was willing to believe now that her mother had not consciously intended to kill her father, deep down, Kate wanted him dead. And so did Frank Kilrain. Her father's death was inevitable.

If only Nils had not died in the war! On her

father's return Frank would have been sent packing. Whole again, the family could have bound up its wounds. But out of fury at Nils's loss, Kristen's mother had let Frank take her father's place. Kristen understood her mother's rage—and she understood her fierce need to punish Seth.

But that did not mean Kristen could forgive her.

"You look so pensive standing there," Salvador said, stepping out onto the balcony. He was carrying two glasses of wine.

She took the glass he handed to her and sipped the wine. The heat had been unbearable all day. Now, almost too late, came the cool breeze off the peaks. She pulled her black knit shawl up over her shoulders.

"It is getting chilly."

"Yes," he said. "You had best go inside."

"Will you be going out...later?"

He shrugged and sipped his wine. "Perhaps."

"Señora Mendoza?"

"She has a fool and a pig for a husband. I have taken pity on her."

"You are such a kind man."

He said nothing for a moment, then moved closer to her, his hand stroking her hair so gently she barely felt it. "Kristen, if only it were different for us. If only you were not—"

She turned her head to look at him. "But don't you see, Salvador? If I were not what I am, I would not be here with you now."

He laughed. Her unflinching appraisals always pleased him, even when they contradicted him. "That is true," he said with a sigh.

"Salvador, when you return from Señorita Mendoza, I would like to talk to you."

"It is important?"

"I think so."

"It is about us?"

"Yes."

"We can talk now, then."

She shrugged. "As you wish."

He waited.

"I want to leave here. I am not happy. I am sorry, but it is so."

"Where will you go?"

"Anywhere."

"Is my company—my protection—so distasteful to you?"

"Of course not, Salvador. But you said it yourself just now: If only it were different for us. Well, it can never be different for us. For me, anyway. I must play this part that is such a lie. On the outside I am this warm, desirable woman, while on the inside I feel like stone."

He winced. "Do not talk about that. I swear, I think you make too much of it."

"Do you really think so, Salvador? Would you

prefer, then, to stay at home with me tonight—visit *my* bed?"

"You are too unkind!"

"Then let me go."

"No! In spite of what you must think, I love you!"

"But I do not love you."

"Who do you love?"

"Bart Hardison."

"That Texan, the one who came after you?"

"Yes."

He sipped his wine thoughtfully. Then he shrugged. "It does not matter who you love. You belong with me. I am proud to be at your side. Your beauty, it transforms this barren world for me. I will not let you go."

"Then I will run away. Someday you will go off on one of your trading expeditions, and when you return, I will be gone. Even if you chain me up, I will find a way to escape."

"Do not say such things. You know I could never cage you like an animal."

"Then do not stand in my way."

"Your mind is made up?"

"Yes."

"It is for this Hardison you leave me?"

She shrugged. "Perhaps, in a way. But I will not be going to him. Why should I punish one I love as I have punished you? Besides, what does all this talk of love matter, Salvador?"

Salvador smiled gently. "My heart is sad to hear such a beautiful woman talk so of love!"

"So let us talk no more of it. The truth is, I am sick of this valley—and of my empty life here. All of us are hidden away like frightened animals. If you cannot help me to find a better place, at least do not try to stop me from leaving."

He finished his wine. "We will talk of this when I return," he told her.

There was soft urgency in his tone. She could sense his need for the passionate wife of Hector Mendoza. As he left her room a moment later she called after him, "If you come in late, do not wake me."

Kristen was not entirely surprised when Salvador came to her that night. Their earlier discussion had aroused him, as she had suspected it might. She represented a challenge to him—if nothing else.

He made no effort to enter her bedroom quietly. She awakened at once and watched him pause in the moonlight beside her bed to peel off his shirt. She made no effort to stop him as he stepped out of his pants and lifted the covers to slide in beside her.

"You are back early," she said.

"That fool Mendoza. I think he suspects something. He would not leave to join his friends in the cantina."

"My poor Salvador."

"But I am glad. I think of you and I say to myself: Salvador, you do not want to lose such a beautiful woman. Do not be so impatient. She is only human. So maybe this time you bring her to life. Is it not something to hope for, my golden-haired one?"

Kristen sighed. "It is a wish I have made often, Salvador."

"Here," he said, putting his arms around her. "We talk too much of this thing. Let me kiss you."

She let him, then kissed him back, not with love but with affection and hope, as her young body strained eagerly toward his....

Afterwards, naked, he sat on the edge of the bed, his bare feet on the floor, his head resting in his hands. Kristen's back rested against the bedstead. Watching him somberly, she pulled a sheet up over her breasts. She was beyond tears, but deep inside her she felt an ache that was almost intolerable. And also she felt a dull fury, not at Salvador but at those hellish savages that Salvador dealt with so easily.

Abruptly Salvador lifted his face from his hands and looked at her. In the darkness she could see his anguish, and in that moment she almost loved him. It was so difficult for a man to believe he could not arouse a woman.

"Kristen," he told her softly, "in spite of this

night—in spite of everything—I love you. This sad business does not matter to me. I want you to stay here with me."

"And it does not matter that you cannot... awaken me, make me forget how your beloved Comanches used me?"

Salvador shrugged. "Please. They are not my Comanches. Like you, I see them for what they are. They are savages. But someday you will forget. You will think of it no longer. You will become a woman again."

"Never."

"You will see. Salvador knows of such things."

"You have never been taken by the Comanche."

Salvador shrugged unhappily. "You are right. Such a thing has never happened to me. But I understand. Deep inside you are hurt. That part of you is like a clenched fist. I never think till now what it must be for you. You must hunger for love like any other woman."

"I'm tired, Salvador."

She reached out and rested her hand on his shoulder. He took it and kissed her fingers. She pushed herself back under the covers, turned her back to him, and closed her eyes.

Salvador watched her for a moment, then dressed and went out onto the balcony and lit a cheroot. He stood there until he had finished his smoke. Then he left Kristen's bedroom to see if that damn fool Hector had gone to the cantina yet.

If he hadn't, Salvador decided vehemently, he would go to the man's bedroom and boot him the hell out of it.

As soon as Salvador left, Kristen threw off her covers, stepped into her robe, and found the decanter containing Salvador's smokes. She lit one of his cheroots and moved out onto the balcony. She glimpsed Salvador's slim form moving across a corner of the plaza.

At first she had been troubled that Salvador still found her presence desirable. It did not seem natural that he—or any man as passionate as he—should still want her near him, since this night's embarrassment had happened many times in the past.

Only gradually had she come to understand why Salvador wished her to remain with him. To Salvador, like that Comanche chief, Kristen was a great prize to be displayed. She was a scalp on Salvador's scalp pole. When he wanted to make an impression in the villages of his own people—such as a crowded ballroom in Mexico City—he took with him his greatest trophy, his golden-haired Texan.

And when he needed a real woman, he would take his pleasure with the women of his village.

Kristen played his game well. She knew how to wear the clothes Salvador bought for her, how to enter a room with a flourish, and most important, how to converse in passable Spanish with those men and women in the highest circles of the Mexican aristocracy. All this was second-nature to her now. On their last trip to Mexico she had danced with many fine gentlemen, including a very powerful general. She had made an excellent impression on all she'd met. Salvador had been more than pleased, rewarding her with a stunning necklace worth thousands of pesos.

Indeed, considering everything, Salvador was very kind and generous to her, and she wished she could at least return his indulgent affection. But she could not. Their relationship was a charade. Not only for Salvador but for herself as well.

There was nothing to do now but to leave—with or without his help.

With a stifled gasp, Kristen halted in Estrellita's doorway, then stepped back hastily, pulled the door shut, and waited in the alley for Estrellita's customer to leave. When he left, tightening his belt and muttering, Kristen knocked softly and reentered.

Estrellita was standing by her narrow mirror, her flimsy dress already on, combing out her long, dark hair. She turned slightly at Kristen's entrance, an angry scowl on her face.

"That fat bastard, that son of a peeg!" she cried, her voice vibrating with anger. "Again he not pay me! He promise me thees time he pay, and when he finish with me, he just laugh."

"You shouldn't let him get away with that."

"When I try to slap him, he punch me on the chin. Very gently, you see. But it is enough. So now he is gone. That ees the last time weeth him! When he beg me next time, I say no!"

"He'll just punch you on the chin again."

Estrellita sighed and put down her comb. "This is so, *señora*." She walked over to her cot and began to make it. "Why you come here? I see your man ride out this morning with many wagons. He go north—to the Comanche, I think."

"Yes. That's where he's going."

"I see that beeg Comanche ride in last night. He ees one handsome brute."

"His band just came back from Mexico. With captives and horses. Salvador went out to trade for the horses."

"That ees dangerous business."

"Not for him—or the other Comancheros. But it *is* dirty, bloody business. But that is not why I came here to see you, Estrellita."

There was a small wooden rocker in the corner. Kristen sat in it and looked around her. A candle flickered in front of the statue of the Virgin in a corner nook, and another candle sat on the wooden box that served as a nightstand by Estrellita's couch. Estrellita had flung a red, moth-eaten blanket over the nightstand. The earthen floor had been swept clean. Then Kristen saw a large beetle moving across a corner of one of the serapes she used for a rug.

Estrellita sat down on her cot. "I am listening, *señora*."

"I want to get out of here, Estrellita," Kristen said. "And as soon as possible—before Salvador returns."

"You must be crazy. How can you leave this place?"

"I have money. Jewels."

"Gold?"

"Yes, coins and much gold dust. Salvador has given it to me to spend, but I have saved it for this moment. The jewels are very valuable. They are gifts from Salvador."

"He will be very angry."

"He will understand."

"Maybe he understand, sure. But still he will come after you and take you back. Maybe then he will beat you."

"It does not matter. I must go, and you must help me."

"But what can I do?"

"You can hire the men we will need to take us to California."

Estrellita's eyes gleamed suddenly at the mention of California. The thought of escaping to that magic place aroused her interest. She thought for a moment and leaned toward Kristen. "No. California is too far. I have better place."

"Where?"

"A town in Kansas. It is called Abilene."

Kristen frowned. "But why there?"

"I have heard much these past months. The railroad, it comes from the East, and beside the tracks they build this place called Abilene. Many fine caballeros drive their cattle to this place. When they get there, they have much gold and are very hungry for woman and for good time! You see! There we will make our fortunes!"

"You, perhaps. But not I, Estrellita."

"That is no matter. You help Estrellita leave this filthy place, I will take care of you!"

"That's very kind of you."

"Look around you. See this hovel? I tell you, once I live in fine house with my mother and father and many strong brothers—before the Apache came. I know how I live now, and I know what a pigsty this is! We go tomorrow."

"At night?"

"Yes."

"But we will need men to guide us."

"I will find the men. I know of two who would help us—for a price. We need good horses and a fine wagon. But can you pay for them?"

"I will pay them a hundred dollars in gold. But do not tell them we go to Kansas. And listen carefully now. Tell them we go to California."

Estrellita's dark eyes glowed with this news. "Yes. I will tell them that. And don't worry. These men I know are greedy. But when I tell them of the gold you pay, they dare not cheat us."

Kristen got up from the rocker. "I'll be waiting to hear from you."

"When I have made the arrangement, I will visit you later tomorrow in your grand apartment above the square."

Kristen smiled. "Perhaps you will join me for coffee while we plot our freedom?"

"Ah, but yes, *señora*! It will be fine occasion. And soon I will be gone from this hovel of dust and cockroaches—and from stinking men who do not pay!"

Kristen hurried through the night, her heart pounding with excitement. Salvador would be furious, she realized, and would do all he could to bring her back. But having Estrellita tell everyone—including the men she hired—that they were going to California would cause Salvador to spend valuable time covering the trails leading west.

And once she reached this place in Kansas, there was little chance he would ever find her again.

Kristen did not like the two men Estrellita had hired.

Pancho was a small, knobby man with a whining voice and a sidelong glance that never looked directly at her but whose eyes were filled with furtive desire. Whenever he passed close by, he made her skin crawl. He had brought with him an enormous supply of tequila, which he drank from a leather gourd that sweated like a wine sack.

Esteban was taller, thinner, a dark mestizo with a long, ugly white scar down one side of his face. Estrellita had taken pity on the man long before and allowed him to visit her occasionally without payment. She was calling in that debt now. When he was not riding, he trudged alongside the wagon, bent slightly forward, his eyes peering narrowly out from under the brim of his huge straw sombrero. He said little, speaking for the most part to his partner in a low, snarling voice. Both men wore filthy ponchos and stank worse than the horses.

A creaking, two-wheeled wagon, drawn by a span of mules, carried their belongings. Estrellita had a single steamer trunk that contained her things. Kristen had taken less. The gold and jewelry was all she needed, and she kept them in two bulging saddlebags under her night blankets. For provisions Estrellita had procured bags of potatoes, pinto beans, and rice. In addition she had managed to get hold of salt pork, a barrel of flour, sourdough starter, salt, tea and soda, a can of sugar, and plenty of coffee. For her part,

Kristen had not forgotten to bring along her fishhook, tackle, a tin of matches, and her bone-handled knife.

The mules, their ears drooping dejectedly, had seen better days and were as much a disappointment as the men. They were probably a glossy brown once. Now they were gray enough to be called roans. The two Mexicans rode the two horses or walked beside the wagon while the women stayed inside.

As a precaution both women kept loaded derringers in the hollows of their breasts during the day, and under their pillows when they slept. Both guns had been supplied by Kristen and were presents from de Santos. Kristen's derringer was a pearl-handled model, twin barrel, firing a 44-caliber slug. Estrellita's was also a twin barrel, and Kristen had fired it often enough to know that Estrellita's was as good a weapon as hers. It was Salvador who taught Kristen how to shoot, and over the past year she had become quite expert.

Kristen had insisted that the men be told they were going to California. Only when they were well out of the valley and clear of the mountains did Kristen let Estrellita tell the Mexicans where they were headed. They accepted the change of direction without protest. Like Kristen, they saw the wisdom in not giving de Santos a clue as to their real destination—and all that mattered to them was the gold they were promised at the end of their journey.

Once they reached Comancheria, in accordance with Kristen's suggestion, they traveled only at night, holing up in ravines or dense thickets during the day.

A week after they set out, what both women had been expecting took place. They had halted beside a stream, preparing to camp for the night in the high grass. The stream was flowing at a fairly brisk pace, and the women suggested that the men bathe upstream, while Kristen and Estrellita would stay close to the bank a few hundred yards farther down.

There was enough light left in the sky for Kristen to see the two men coming toward them. Pancho was in the lead, grinning. Esteban, his tall figure bobbing comically, was right on his heels. Both men were naked.

Kristen touched Estrellita lightly on the shoulder, then swam to the bank as casually as possible. As she stood boldly and headed up the embankment toward her clothes, she could see the men leering at her. Ignoring them, Kristen grabbed her clothes and reached under her skirt for her derringer. Pulling it out, she released its safety catch and aimed it at Pancho.

Pancho and Esteban halted in confusion. Behind Kristen, Estrellita was splashing hurriedly ashore. Running up behind Kristen, she reached for her own derringer and brought it up as well.

"Keep back, you bastards," said Estrellita, the little gun wavering precariously in her hand. "All you're getting is that gold we promised you."

Pancho smiled, exposing a mouthful of rotten teeth. "But here there is no place to spend all that money."

"That's not my fault," Kristen snapped.

"But we are men, healthy men. We need more than gold."

"Well, you ain't getting it," Estrellita snapped.

"*Por favor*," pleaded Esteban. "Be reasonable, Estrellita. It will be just business. Like always."

"I am no longer in the business."

Esteban smiled. "Ah, and when you get to this Kansas, you will be in the business again?"

"It is possible."

He twisted his head ingratiatingly. "Maybe until you reach Kansas you should practice."

"Hah! Not with you buzzards."

Esteban straightened angrily. "Then we take the gold and go back."

"*Si*," said Pancho. "We will leave you to the Comanche."

Estrellita laughed. "Sure. Go back to Tule and get skinned by de Santos, eh?"

They shifted their feet unhappily.

"But Estrellita," Esteban said. "It is just you we want. Not that pale gringo woman."

"You won't get either of us," Estrellita told him.

The two men looked at each other, shrugged their shoulders, and headed straight for Estrellita. Esteban was in the lead. They did not think Estrellita would shoot. Here she was, standing naked before them, and they needed her. Never before had she refused them—even when they had no money for her. Why should she turn them away now?

"I'm warning you!" said Estrellita, raising the gun.

"You will not shoot us," Pancho explained reasonably. "If you do, you will be alone. There will be no one to guide you to Kansas. Let me tell you something, you do not have any choice."

They kept coming. Estrellita moved back a step. Unwilling to fire, she looked with sudden consternation at Kristen. Kristen raised her weapon, aimed carefully and fired at Esteban, who was closest to her. The round caught him high on his left shoulder. It was only a flesh wound, but it was enough to stop him in his tracks. Aghast, close to panic, he sagged down onto one knee, his hand clapped over his wound, blood oozing through his fingers.

Kristen swung the derringer, this time aiming at Pancho's face.

The man paled and backed away hastily, holding up both hands. "Don' shoot, *señora*! *Por favor*! We only make joke!"

"No," Kristen replied, advancing on him boldly, "I think maybe *you* are jokes. Maybe we should leave you behind and take the gold. It will be easier for us if we do not have to deal with faithless pigs like you."

Crestfallen and thoroughly cowed, the two men turned and plunged back through the grass toward the wagon. Twice they looked over their shoulders like frightened apes. As soon as they were gone, Kristen sank to the ground and took a deep breath. Estrellita grinned down at her proudly, her dark eyes dancing in triumph.

"For so long I want to do such a thing!"

"It's only a flesh wound. Plenty of blood, maybe. But nothing else. I only wanted to scare him."

"If they had pants on, they would have soiled them!"

"I'm glad they don't own guns."

"Why do you think I hire them? They are two poor to own such weapons."

"You think we can handle them the rest of the way?"

"If we are careful."

They dressed and started back to the wagon. The rising sun was already above the horizon. Soon it would be full daylight. They had pushed on over rough ground through a black night, and Kristen was physically exhausted. The ugly business of a few moments before had left her emotionally drained as well. While following Estrellita through the tall grass it occurred to Kristen that there was a good chance they would never reach Kansas. It was so damn far away.

It wasn't just the Indians they had to watch out for, it seemed.

Chapter Ten

The warmth seeped through Bart's hand, flowing up his arm, pulling him from a deep, dreamless sleep. He opened his eyes. The sunlight flooding the room blinded him. He shut his eyes quickly, then slowly reopened them.

His mother sat in her rocker by his bed. She was clasping his right hand in both of hers, and it was the love flowing through those hands that had pulled him back. While she rocked, she looked past the foot of his bed and out the window. Her rocking was a gentle, soothing movement—not the mindless, obsessive motion he remembered from before. Her face had changed too. It was no longer gaunt. Her eyes were keen and alert, though filled with a deep sadness and longing.

Her lips moved steadily, soundlessly. She was praying.

In that instant Bart realized that his mother was well again.

In a voice that sounded faint and strange to his own ears, he said, "You can let go of my hand now, Ma."

He had startled her. She dropped his hand as if she had been scalded.

"Ellen!" she cried. "Ellen!"

As Ellen appeared in the doorway, a dripping ladle in her hand, Amanda snatched up Bart's right hand again, covering it with kisses. Despite a deep, searing pain in his shoulder, Bart pulled his mother closer and hugged her to him. For a blessed moment the two rocked in each other's arms.

Ellen stepped into the room, tears streaming down her cheeks. "How do you feel, Bart?"

"Sore."

"That all?"

"And hungry."

"There's some soup on the stove. I'll get it."

Scott had heard the commotion. Looking tired and leaning on a hickory cane, he appeared in the doorway. He stuck a chaw in his mouth and grinned.

Sitting back in her rocker, Amanda brushed the tears out of her eyes. "My, such a fuss I'm

THE TEXAN

making," she said. "Why, Bart, don't you know? As sure as I'm sittin' here, I knew you was going to be all right."

"How long have I been out?"

Scott spoke up. "You been lyin' there without moving near seven days now."

Bart was astounded. "That long?"

"Looks like maybe you was catching up on some sleep you missed during the war," Scott drawled. "But we knew you'd come out of it, soon's you got around to it."

Bart's mother leaned over to brush a lock of hair off Bart's forehead. "You always was a sound sleeper, Bart."

"You look good, Ma. As sassy as a spring calf. Back to normal, huh?"

She nodded sprightly. "Thanks to Ellen—and Scott here. He just wouldn't let me think on it any longer. He and Pa were such good friends."

"So I understand."

A sudden cloud passed over Amanda's face. "Jill's gone, Bart," she said, her voice suddenly low. "I know that now. She's gone forever."

"I know that, Ma."

"But someday I'll see her again. And your pa too. Someday. If it's God's will."

"That's right, Ma."

She brightened immediately. "But you're here now! You're back! That's what matters."

Beaming, Amanda got up from the rocker and

dragged it over into a corner. Then she straightened her dress and announced that she was going out to help Ellen in the kitchen. She dried her eyes with the heel of her hand and hurried from the room.

Scott walked on into the bedroom and looked down at Bart. "You gave us all a scare," he admitted.

"Was it you brought me back here?"

"Yup."

"You look like you took a round."

"I did."

"I owe you again."

"Just see you return the favor," Scott said, grinning.

Bart hesitated. He hated to ask the next question because he was almost certain what answer he would get. "What about Tim?"

"He's dead, Bart."

Bart looked away, seeing Tim's prostrate form lying facedown in the grass.

"Goddamn," he said softly. "That bastard Kilrain!"

But cursing Frank Kilrain did not help. After going through the war with Tim, Bart had come to think of them both as indestructible. Nothing could touch them, he had thought. So Tim comes home, and with nothing ahead but roses if only he plays his hand right, he gets shot down by

Kate Nordstrom's foreman and his crew of gun slicks.

He realized how Ellen must feel. Then he thought of Dan O'Hare and Molly, and felt an anguish so intense that he almost cried out. Ellen entered the room with a steaming bowl of soup on a tray and placed it on the nightstand beside his bed.

She caught Bart's grim mood at once. "Why, what's wrong, Bart?"

"I told him, Ellen," Scott told her. "About Tim."

"I'm so damn sorry, Ellen," Bart said.

She avoided his eyes. "I know you are," she said tightly, standing back and folding her arms. "Eat now, Bart. Get your strength back. Then maybe you can do something about Tim's death."

Under his mother's and Ellen's care, Bart steadily regained his strength. When he looked at himself in the mirror and saw how much weight he had lost, he realized how close he had come to death. It was his mother's prayers and her love, he felt, that had pulled him back from the abyss. To his mother Bart's recovery was a miracle. But to Bart the *real* miracle was the fact that his mother had regained her senses completely and was once again her old self.

When Bart felt he was ready for the trip, Ellen hitched up the buggy and they drove over to the graveyard at Burnt Creek to visit Tim's grave. Ellen put a bouquet of wildflowers against the modest wooden grave marker. Bart stood off to the side, grimly determined not to break down and embarrass Ellen.

Ellen took a step back, bent her head, and prayed silently for a few minutes. Then she looked over at Bart.

At the sight of him standing there so straight and stiff, trying so hard to keep his composure, she rushed over to him, a single sob breaking from her. He caught her in his arms and held her close, doing his best to comfort her as the pent-up sorrow of these past weeks broke through Ellen's own resolve. At last, when the storm had passed, she stepped away from him. Gently he wiped the tears from her cheeks with his big hands.

Then, still holding her, he looked over at the grave marker.

"We were trapped in a gully once," he told her softly. "The Yankees were coming right for us. Tim stood up and showed himself. Then he fired his rifle and ran off, the Yankees tearing right after him. That's how I got away."

For a moment Bart had difficulty going on. But he forced himself to continue. "Three days later I found Tim asleep against a tree alongside a dirt road. He had his arms wrapped around his rifle like it was his baby. I had thought I'd never see him again. He said the same thing about me. I'm telling you, Ellen. For the rest of that goddamn war, we never lost sight of each other again—except when we slept."

In a small, soft voice she said, "He was very brave, wasn't he?"

"Yes, Ellen. He was. And a good friend. A man you could ride the river with. I'll miss him."

On the way back to Anchor they stopped off at the O'Hares's so Bart could extend his condolences. Dan had thought seriously of making the trip north with the trail herd. But when word got around that Kilrain was taking over as trail boss, he did not even take the tally. Tolliver Adams was the only other cattleman beside Kate to go with the herd. Tolliver's foreman, Ned Perkins, went along as the *segundo,* and each ranch with stock in the herd sent along as many of their ranch hands as they could spare, and they were generous in stocking the remuda. It sounded to Bart as it there would be plenty of men and cow ponies to handle the trail herd.

Bart told Dan that as soon as he could get his gear together, he and Scott were going after the herd. Though no one in the room said anything, they all understood why Bart was joining the ride. The reason was Frank Kilrain.

Ellen suggested that Dan and Molly move out to Anchor while Bart and Scott were gone. Dan agreed at once. On the way back to Anchor, Ellen took the reins and chose a route that brought them through a patch of willows alongside a riverbank. She halted the team and turned to Bart.

"You and Scott are going after Frank Kilrain," she said. "Aren't you?"

"I thought you understood that."

"Yes, I did. And it was what I wanted—what I hoped you and Scott would do—but now... Oh, Bart, I'm not so sure. Suppose you don't come back? Suppose Kilrain kills you, too?"

"Not likely, Ellen."

"You men talk so brave. But look what happens to you!"

He reached out to comfort her but found her in his arms for the second time that day. In a pure, unabashed show of her feelings for him, Ellen covered his face with kisses, clinging to him all the while, crying as if her heart would break.

Bart was sure he understood. First she had lost her brother. Now, if her bad luck continued, she would be losing Bart as well. But as he held her, returning her kisses gently and without passion, he became aware that it was not Ellen he wanted in his arms.

It was still Kristen. And no other woman. Since he first rode up to the Nordstrom ranch as a young man, Kristen Nordstrom was the only woman he had ever desired.

Two days later, out of the rising sun, a lone horseman materialized, heading straight for Anchor. Hanging up the wash, Ellen was the first to spot him. She alerted the others with a sharp call. Bart came rushing from the blacksmith shop to join her. A moment later Scott and Amanda were standing beside them.

By the time the horseman reached the lower pasture, they could see his floppy-brimmed Confederate hat and the faded yellow sash around his waist. A thin stubble of a beard covered his lean face. Something stirred a memory deep inside Bart.

"That's Nils." Ellen gasped softly. "Nils Nordstrom!"

Bart nodded. There was no doubt about it.

"Yes," said Bart's mother, her voice hushed with the wonder of it. "It *is* Nils. He rides just like his father."

Before Nils reached their gate, Scott and Bart were hurrying to greet the man returning from the dead.

After finding no one home at the Circle N, Nils had gone to Burnt Creek. There he had learned of his mother's decision to go north with the trail herd—and also of his father's safe return from the war and his death later, at the hands of the Comanche.

As soon as the ex-soldier had been fed and a pot of coffee placed down in front of him, Nils told his story. Hit by a Yankee minié ball, the conical 58-caliber bullet's soft lead had distorted on impact and torn a gaping wound in his upper chest, shattering his ribs and narrowly missing his heart—but not his left lung. For a day and a night Nils lay in the ravine where he had fallen until he was carried to Yankee surgeons, who took out the minié ball and did their best to clean out his wound before sewing up his chest. Chloroform had been given to him liberally during the operation but only whiskey and laudanum after it.

His troubles began at a place called Andersonville. Almost immediately after his arrival he began coughing up blood. A second operation had to be performed to cut away pieces of his infected lung. This time there was no chloroform, no whiskey, and no laudanum, and the pain of it almost killed him. Though the operation was proclaimed a success, Nils continued to sink and would have died but for his fellow prisoners, who nursed him diligently and gave him what little food and drink they could scrounge.

So bad was his condition at the end of the war,

however, that when the prisoners were set free, Nils was taken to a private hospital in Washington, D.C. There he was slowly nursed back to health. In order to get the money he needed to come home, he took a job as a carpenter. The healthy, outdoor work did his lungs a world of good, and with the money he had saved, he was able to come home at last.

He would have written, he said, but there was no mail delivery to this part of Texas—and besides, he wanted to surprise his family when, completely mended at last, he rode into their yard.

But it hadn't worked out the way he had planned.

When Nils finished his story, he asked for details concerning his father's death. It was Bart who told him what was generally known, that marrauding Comanche had caught his father outside the ranch house, and before he could get inside, they had killed him.

Then Bart told him about Kristen's capture by Iron Cheek, her escape, and now her wish to remain in New Mexico. When Bart finished, Nils shook his head in stunned disbelief, unwilling to comprehend how his sister could choose to remain with a Comanchero chief—until Bart pointed out to him Kristen's reasons. Nils knew—as did Bart—what it would be like for a woman who had once lived with the Comanche to return to her own people.

During all this Nils was fussed over by Bart's mother and an excited, pleased Ellen. As Bart recalled, Nils and Ellen had been pretty thick at church outings, local picnics, and barn raisings, and Ellen was glowing now, her face frozen in a perpetual smile as she hovered around Nils.

She took great pleasure in drawing his bath and telling him it was ready.

"...and you better get in there," she continued, "before the water cools."

"Sounds good," Nils said, pushing his lean figure erect. "Last time I took a bath was in San Antonio." He grinned at Ellen. "Guess maybe its about time for another."

As Nils left the kitchen Bart spoke to Ellen. "Why not wait a decent interval, then go in and help him scrub his back?"

Ellen smiled happily. "You won't mind, Bart?"

He laughed. "Of course not."

A moment later, as Ellen left the kitchen with a long-handled scrub brush, Amanda glanced over at Bart. "Now, what was that all about? Why ever should Ellen ask if you'd mind?"

Bart grinned at her and shrugged. "Beats me, Ma."

And then Amanda understood. "Oh," she said. "I was hoping it meant there was something between you two—an understanding, maybe."

"If you'll remember, Ma, Ellen and Nils have always gotten along pretty well."

"You mean, like you and Kristen."

"That's exactly what I mean, Ma."

Amanda brightened. "Well, now, I'm right happy for Ellen."

Bart glanced at Scott and got to his feet.

"Scott and I will be in the blacksmith shop," Bart told his mother. "When Nils is finished with his bath, tell him we'd like to talk to him."

As Bart and Scott walked toward the blacksmith shop Scott said, "Looks to me like Nils is goin' to want to go after Kristen himself."

"That's the way I see it."

"You think he can convince Kristen to come back here?"

"He can if anybody can."

"And you'd like that?"

Bart smiled at Scott. "Yes, I would."

Entering the shop, Bart checked the forge fire. It was now only a dim, glowing bed of coals. Reaching for the bellows, he pumped the fire back to life.

Watching from the doorway, Scott said, "You think maybe Nils might appreciate some company on that trip to New Mexico? Two men who knew right where to find that valley?"

"Wouldn't be a bit surprised."

"And then afterward," Scott said, "we could

swing north to Kansas. I don't suppose that herd will be movin' all that fast."

Bart reached for his tongs. "Not with that son of a bitch Kilrain as trail boss."

Chapter Eleven

The sight of the trail herd moving north was something Kate knew she would never forget. It crawled over the prairie like an enormous snake, while above it hung a constant pall of dust, making the cowboys who rode drag a weary, hacking lot at the end of each day. There were more than three thousand head all told. The Circle N had a thousand, Anchor more than six hundred, and the cattle from the other outfits totaled almost fifteen hundred.

What the men had come to call the chuck wagon stayed about ten miles ahead of the lead steers, Herman, the cook, keeping company with the remuda. Instead of making each man responsible for his own cooking and provisions, as was customary with previous trail herds, Kate had suggested they hire a full-time cook, outfitting him with a wagon for holding his cooking utensils and provisions. As she explained it to the men, this would make things much simpler for everybody. She didn't tell them that her principal reason for the suggestion was her fear that she would be saddled with the job of trail cook her self, for she had overheard talk that since she was a woman, they might as well let her handle the chore.

Meanwhile, because of the dust and heat generated by so many longhorns—not to mention her craving for privacy—Kate kept her own wagon well away from the trail herd, a mile or so behind of the remuda.

One hot, blistering morning Kate heard the sound of galloping horses coming up on her wagon. She looked back. Waving to her as he passed, Frank Kilrain and his two sidekicks rode on by her—on their way to the Red River to mark safe fords for the herd's crossing. Kate waved back and watched the three riders disappear into the shimmering distance.

In camp the night before, Kate had overheard the old-timers discussing the upcoming river crossing. The Red River, it was pointed out, had its headwaters in the mountains to the west. Distant storms in those mountains could send floodwaters surging downriver so fast that a river six inches deep in the morning might be twenty-five feet deep by nightfall. The trees crowding the bank of the stream were a treacherous tangle of vines and driftwood, and in some spots steep cutbanks made approaching the river with an unruly herd a decidedly tricky business. But most troubling of all was the quicksand lining the banks. This river crossing would be a damn good test of any trail boss.

Not long after Frank had galloped past, Kate saw two riders approaching from the north. At first she thought they might be Frank and one of his men returning. But then she realized that there hadn't been enough time for Frank to reach the river.

The two riders were Ned Perkins and Tolliver Adams. Kate pulled her wagon to a halt and eased herself down off the hard wooden seat. Grateful for the chance to stretch, she was leaning back against the wagon when the two riders dismounted and approached her.

Ned Perkins touched the brim of his hat in greeting. The big, lanky foreman was the shyest man Kate had ever known, but he was one fine cattleman and she respected him.

"Real hot, ain't it?" said Tolliver.

"Yes, it is."

The two men exchanged glances; neither one, it appeared, seemed eager to speak first.

"What is it, Tolliver?" Kate prodded.

Tolliver cleared his throat nervously. "Kate, I think maybe we got a problem."

"I'm listening."

"This here herd is very thirsty. It ain't had good water since noon yesterday."

"I know that, Tolliver. So am I. But there's plenty of water up ahead."

"That's just it," broke in Ned Perkins, his concern making him forget his shyness. "The herd's already smelling that water. And when they reach the river, they won't charge across like they should. They'll start to drink. Or worse, start to mill."

"So?"

"If they do that, Kate," said Tolliver, "they'll get stuck in the quicksand in the shallows. And we'll have one devil of a time hauling them out."

"Another thing," said Ned. "The cattle might stampede toward the river. If they do that, we won't be able to control them worth a damn. Some will go on down them steep cutbanks and break their necks."

"Or get trampled by them coming up behind," added Tolliver.

Ned said, "It'll be a real mess, Miss Kate."

"So what's the solution?"

"Don't drive 'em across today," said Tolliver.

"When should we?"

"Tomorrow."

THE TEXAN

"But how will that make it any easier?"

"We can turn them aside right now and head for a stream I spotted west of here."

Ned broke in then. "You see, Miss Kate, what we'll do is let them fill up, then bed down for the night. In the morning they fill up again, and then we'll drive them real nice and peaceful across the Red River."

"They won't stand in the water to drink," Tolliver explained. "They won't mill. The crossing'll go fast, and we'll get the entire herd across by noon."

Kate thought it over. Remembering what she had heard the night before, she realized that the two men were making good sense.

"Sounds like a good idea to me," Kate told them.

"The trouble is," said Tolliver, "Frank won't hear of it. He wants us to push on. He's all-fired anxious to get the critters across today, before nightfall."

Kate frowned. That sounded like Frank. "Well, you go tell Frank I think we should do what you suggest," she said. "You tell him there's no reason for us to chance the crossing today."

Pleased, Ned and Tolliver thanked Kate, turned, and mounted up.

Watching them ride off, Kate pulled herself back up onto her wagon seat and took up the ribbons, a frown on her face. It bothered her that Frank had not thought of this himself.

Kate had felt uneasy watching Frank perform these past weeks. She had not found it a pleasant chore, and it had forced her to examine her relationship with him—and also, after all these years, her reason for hiring him in the first place.

In the beginning it was his strength and stubbornness she admired. He was tough enough to handle other men. In San Antonio, the first time she had observed him in action, with one punch he had flattened a bullying slob who had elbowed him aside while climbing a saloon porch. And there was no doubt that his sleepy, outlaw eyes had intrigued her as well. And so, she realized now, out of anger and loneliness she had indulged herself.

For close to six years she had not found Frank wanting when it came to standing up to trouble. But the death of Tim O'Hare and Bart Hardison had shaken her confidence in Frank pretty deeply. She had accepted his explanation of the tragedy only because his testimony was backed up by the other two hands—and because she had no alternative.

Since the trail drive had begun, however, Kilrain had driven the men with an arrogance so blatant and uncalled-for that it was turning most of the men against him. Relying almost entirely on his two long-standing buddies, Cullen Barker and Carl, he took little advice from others even when he should have listened to them. Seeing this almost immediately, Kate had hired extra hands at Crow's Creek and put them under Ned Perkins, who now reported only to Tolliver Adams. Though Kate knew this made for a divided leadership, she did not care.

For it also kept a closer check on Frank Kilrain.

The sudden clatter of hoofbeats broke into her thoughts. Frank was riding toward her. He was alone. Kate pulled her team to a halt. Reining in alongside Kate, Frank gazed at her angrily, his hard eyes blazing with contempt.

"Kate, I just told Perkins where he could shove the crazy idea that he's got to stay on this side of the river tonight. I understand he came sniveling to you. That right?"

"He wasn't sniveling, Frank."

"Yeah?" Frank snapped. "Well, if that mealy-mouthed son of a bitch comes near me with any more of his tomfool notions, I'll send him back to Texas afoot."

"Now, you know you wouldn't do a thing like that."

His eyes became sullen. "Don't be so sure, Kate."

Kate had difficulty keeping her temper. But she had long experience on this where Frank was concerned. "Frank, what Ned suggested made good sense to me. We don't want them cattle to get bogged down while we're crossing the river, do we?"

"They won't. Hell, Kate, they'll be across that river before they know it. And I don't need you or anyone else to tell me how to do it."

"Getting pretty big for your britches, ain't you?"

He smiled. It was a nasty smile. "You been inside my britches often enough. You ought to know how big I am."

With a cruel laugh he took up his reins and spurred past her on his way back to the herd.

Kate had pulled her wagon to a halt on a knoll overlooking the river. Alongside of her was Herman's chuck wagon. The cook was sitting on a bench peeling potatoes. Every now and then he would look up to see if the men were coming.

"Here they come," Kate told Herman.

The cook got to his feet and stood alongside her, craning his long neck. At first he saw only the dust from the herd, hanging like smoke on the horizon. Then gradually there came a deep, rumbling sound—like thunder. But it was not thunder. There was not a cloud in the sky. The low, sinister, trembling sound increased. Then she knew what it was—the herd was stampeding.

Ned and Tolliver had been right on the mark. The cattle, smelling the water and unable to contain their need, had bolted full-tilt toward the river. Before long, Kate glimpsed the lead steers and behind them the heaving backs of those following. As the herd thundered closer its width increased, along with the dense cloud hanging over it. Nearing the river, it resembled a bobbing forest of horns.

Frank had said he would get the herd across in a hurry, but Kate found it impossible to believe that this stampede was Frank's idea—until she saw that the men riding on the herd's flank were not trying to turn the stampede at all. They were firing into the air, urging the frantic beasts on still faster!

But the riverbanks were too steep. The lower banks and more solid fords were farther upstream. If the cattle kept on their present course, they would plunge over several of the embankments and injure themselves, perhaps fatally.

Yet the cattle pounded on.

The first steer went tumbling headlong. Another followed, slipping sideways and twisting completely around as he plunged into the river. Then there were too many to count as the tide of lunging steers surged over the lip of the embankments and tumbled into the water. Some steers, clambering frantically over the backs of those in front, found themselves in deep water. Lifting their heads, they began to swim across the river, only their long horns and noses protruding above the surface. Soon the current carried this lucky group downstream, and Kate lost sight of them.

By this time the embankment was alive with great, twisting bodies as those behind kept coming, piling up onto the rest. And almost immediately, cattle who reached the river slowed and ducked their heads to drink, ignoring the shouting cowboys on the bank or those steers still piling up behind them.

The herd was not crossing the river.

Cattle in the deeper water were milling frantically, while up and down the shoreline, steers were wallowing in the deep muck and quick sand as they tried to drink their fill. Some of the animals began to realize they were stuck fast and, in sudden terror, began to bleat and bellow frantically. This did not stop the animals behind them, however, who kept right on coming, piling into the now mud-darkened river until the south bank of the river, for at least a quarter mile in each direction, was a pitiful mass of stuck and bawling critters. Some of the cattle had already begun to sink out of sight, their miserable lowing filling Kate with pity.

By now the riders were swarming down to the river's edge, roping animals and trying to pull them out, shouting and making as much commotion as the longhorns.

Herman was appalled. A lean, weathered man with slicked-down hair and a long handlebar mustache, he kept shaking his head.

"*Mein Gott*," he said. "They all be drowned!"

"I'm going down there, Herman," Kate told him. "I can't just stand here and watch this."

Swiftly Kate unhitched one of her horses, saddled up, and rode down to see what help she could give.

By now the men saw the foolishness of trying to stampede the herd across and were busy cutting off the cattle that had not yet reached the river. Riding up to Ned Perkins, who was working with two of the riders she had hired at Crow's Creek, she shouted, "Why not drive what's left over to that stream you mentioned?"

"That's what we're doin', Miss Kate!"

She saw Tolliver and a few others trying to cut off a determined number of steers and galloped over to help them. In a minute or so, her extra horse had turned the trick, and Tolliver had a sizable bunch heading after the others.

Other hands, acting on their own, turned the remaining cattle westward, following Tolliver's example. In less than an hour the only cattle in sight were those lucky few who had made it across to the other side and those pitiful creatures bogged solidly up and down the riverbank—in some cases on both sides. Estimating roughly, Kate figured there were close to fifty or sixty head of cattle trapped along the riverbanks.

Dismounting, she moved cautiously down the

torn riverbank, a rope in her hand. She saw two cowpokes trying to pull a steer out of the quicksand and moved in their direction, coming to a halt beside them. They were too busy to question her appearance at their side, and soon the three of them were working together to rope the steer. Before long, others joined them, these newcomers carrying heavy corral ropes and horse hobbles.

The steer they were trying to pull free was not more than forty feet from the bank. With one horn broken off and a long, dark gash along one flank, he looked wild enough to kick them to hell and gone, if only he could get his legs free of the relentless quicksand.

As soon as they roped him they left Kate holding on to the ropes and waded out to the bogged animal. Kate could not help noticing how treacherous the quicksand was. As soon as one man paused to look the situation over, he began to sink almost immediately. Only if they kept moving along the bottom could they keep themselves from sinking.

There were four of them struggling fruitlessly to lift the steer's tail out of the quicksand. Giving up at last, they bent over and burrowed in the quicksand until they freed the tail. But as soon as they did so, it sank back almost immediately.

The men laughed, then cursed, then excused

themselves hastily when they remembered Kate on the bank, hanging on to the ropes. The next time they freed the animal's tail, they coiled it up and tied a hobble around it. Then, dropping a corral rope over the steer's horns, they tossed it up onto the bank for Kate to hold. This done, they turned the steer over as far as possible and burrowed into the quicksand, freed the fore and hind leg, then quickly doubled back the legs, tying them up with the hobbles. Then they turned the steer over onto his other side and hobbled the remaining legs in the same manner.

Kate had to laugh, despite herself, when she saw how swiftly the soaking men scrambled out of the water, grabbed the ropes she was holding, and dashed up the slope onto their horses. Snubbing the ropes around their saddle horns, the word was given, and working as a team, they dragged the steer clear of the quicksand. They kept going until the steer was on solid ground before they released the hobbles.

Kate scrambled up the embankment and watched in fascination as the steer, angry and sullen, rose once more onto his feet. He was a mess. One horn was broken off, his tail and legs gleamed with quicksand, and his undercarriage was a tangled mass of mud and hair. When he caught sight of Kate standing on the edge of the bank, he lowered his head and pawed at the ground, obviously pleased to find someone he could blame for his troubles.

One of the men, screaming like a Comanche, dashed past the unhappy steer, distracting him with a blanket. With surprising agility considering his recent ordeal, the big steer swung around and took after the man. But when others distracted him with waving hats and shouts, he pulled up, bewildered and defeated, and trudged over to a group of mud-coated steers building up some distance away.

Kate watched the steer go, took a deep breath, then went back down the embankment. There were plenty of other steers that needed the same treatment, and the day was still young.

As they worked into the evening Kate thought she heard the distant rumble of thunder. But there were no clouds in the sky, and she gave it no further thought. Close to midnight, the sky so bright with stars they could see clearly what they were doing, the men finished their task. On the far side twenty steers had been pulled free, and on this side, close to thirty-five. Kate's original estimate had been a good one.

They were not able to free every steer that got bogged, however. At least ten, the men estimated, had been pulled into the quicksand and drowned—and one of the steers had lost its hobble and plunged a forefoot into the mud just as the hands reached their horses. Not until they pulled the poor critter up onto the bank did they see it no longer had its right front foreleg.

The poor brute was put out of his misery with a single shot, and later, while the men worked into the night, they could smell Herman's fire—and the near maddening aroma of the unlucky steer's haunches turning slowly on the spit.

Kate rode wearily toward her wagon. Glancing up at the Big Dipper, she saw it sitting on its head alongside the North Star. Midnight. She shook her head in wonderment. It seemed that the last time she had looked up, the western sky had been ablaze with red. Never before in her life had she worked this hard. From this moment on she would always have an abiding respect and affection for every man on this drive.

With the possible exception of Frank Kilrain.

But she was too weary to think about Frank. She dismounted and clambered up into her wagon. A few moments later, in dry clothes and feeling a little more civilized, she was in the act of combing out her mud-streaked hair when she heard someone riding up to the wagon.

"Kate?" It was Tolliver Adams.

She poked her head out of the wagon.

"Herman's got a feast going down there. You're welcome. There's plenty of steak and coffee."

Kate realized how famished she was. "Be right there," she said.

"I'll wait."

The two rode down the slope to the camp together and dismounted. Weary, mud-splattered men were hunkering down around the fire, eating like silent wolves. The herd was to the west, bedded by the stream Ned and Tolliver had discovered.

Looking around at the men, Kate expected to see Frank. But he was nowhere in sight. She didn't ask anyone of his whereabouts and moved along the serving board Herman had set up on two barrels. She found slabs of steak and son-of-a-bitch stew for starters, with hearts and livers and brains simmering in it, the entire batch brought to sizzling life with Louisiana hot sauce. Kate ladled a sizable portion of the stew into a bowl, being sure to include some hefty chunks of beef, and found a spot under a tree. Tolliver joined her.

The stew finished, Kate went back for a thick steak, sourdough biscuits, pinto beans, and coffee. She was leaning back against a tree, polishing off her meal, when she felt the ground under her begin to tremble.

The first thing she thought of was another stampede. The men got to their feet, obviously thinking the same thing. As Tolliver got up he looked down at Kate.

"It's the river," he said.

At once Kate remembered that distant thunder she had heard earlier. She had seen no clouds overhead because the cloudburst had taken place in the mountains to the west. Now they were to see the results.

They hurried back to the river and peered down. In the dim starlight Kate could see a frothy tongue of water sweeping down the river's channel from the west, carrying before it a litter of heavy brush and broken trees. It looked to Kate as if everything that grew or put down roots had been plucked out of the ground and flung headlong before this incredible flood. The crest swept on past them. In seconds, it seemed, the river had risen from a few inches to perhaps six feet. And still the water rose. Before long it was swirling past the trees sticking out of the embankment.

Then came the grisly climax. Steers that had been sucked under that day were swept from their sandy graves and bobbed to the surface where they began swirling downstream, their horned heads spinning lifelessly in the flood. Some were swept close enough to the bank to be snared by the tree's branches. Once caught, they remained stuck in them, their stiff carcasses washed clean by the onrushing waters.

Kate and the others turned back to the wagon—and found Frank Kilrain standing with spread feet in front of it. He was grinning at them.

"See that?" he called out to the men. "If we'd

waited till tomorrow, we wouldn't have gotten across, anyhow! This flood would've seen to that."

Kate walked toward him.

"That's right, Frank." Her voice was heavy with sarcasm. "You sure planned that perfect. Good thing we spent the day pulling them steers out of the mud. Kept us from getting into mischief."

She brushed past him, as did the rest of the hands, not a single man saying a word to him. Kate glanced back at Frank as she slumped down under the tree next to Tolliver and watched the trail boss stride off angrily. He wasn't hungry, it seemed.

Well, she told herself, Frank had no one to blame but himself for today's debacle. He had been warned. Perhaps now he'd begin to listen when others offered good advice.

The next day, the men rested. The day after, they found the level of the river steadily subsiding, and Frank—a sober, more tolerant trail boss at this juncture—decided that it might be a good time to drive the herd across.

Everything went smoothly. The steers were almost placid, and the men were too weary to allow any more difficulties. Without looking back, the cattle plunged into the river and began pulling for the far shore. All Kate could see were the tips of their horns and the ends of their noses, their calves plunging fearlessly in alongside them, their little heads barely visible alongside their mothers.

Kate's wagon and the chuck wagon had already been floated across, while Kate herself had sat high on her black's saddle as he swam across the stream. Herman had taken off everything but his red union suit and, clinging to one of the biggest steers, let the big brute pull him across. Everyone laughed at the ungainly German as he clambered up on shore beside the steer, but in a moment all that was forgotten as the hectic business of the crossing continued.

The herd was over by noon, and the two mossbacks that had led them this far fell into place at the head of the trail herd. Someone had looped a bell around the biggest steer's neck, and as the herd started north for Kansas, the sound of the cowbell perked everyone up, including the cattle.

Climbing up onto her seat, Kate looked back at the Red River. In crossing it, she realized, they had passed a significant boundary. Behind them was Texas. Ahead of them was Indian Territory, lawless for the most part and settled by Cherokee, Creek, Seminole, Choctaw, and Chickasaw.

And the hated Comanche.

Kate slapped the reins down onto the backs of her horses to get them going. She had brought her rifle and Colt with her. They were in the wagon behind her, wrapped in a blanket. It might be a good idea, she decided, to take them out when they made camp that night and clean them thoroughly. They could have gotten wet during the crossing.

And from then on she would keep them beside her on the wagon seat—loaded.

Chapter Twelve

When Bart, Scott, and Nils rode into Tule, they were not alone. Raoul and three other Comancheros were escorting them. Raoul directed them through one of the gates in the warehouse wall and called them to a halt before a cellar door. Raoul and three Comancheros dismounted first. Then, with a quick movement of his head, Raoul indicated Bart and his companions should dismount.

As soon as Bart reached the ground, Raoul stepped closer and swung the stock of his carbine, catching Bart on the side of his head and sending him slamming back against the warehouse wall. Though his head spun crazily, Bart somehow remained on his feet. Raoul was annoyed.

Still smiling, he jabbed the barrel of his carbine deep into Bart's midsection. Doubling over in awesome pain, Bart managed to grab hold of the barrel and yank the weapon out of the Mexican's hand. Swinging the rifle like a bat, he caught Raoul on the side of his head, sending him reeling.

He then turned to the other three Mexicans, who were in the act of clubbing Scott and Nils to the ground. Bart lunged at them, but Raoul caught him from behind. The three Comancheros pounced eagerly on Bart, caught him around the waist, and threw him to the ground, clubbing him on the head with their revolvers.

Bart felt himself being dragged down cold stone steps into a cellar and remembered little after that except for the hollow clang of a cell door as it slammed shut.

Bart lifted his head. He did not know how long he had been unconscious. His clothes were clammy; a bug was crawling over his hand. Despite the swelling under his right eye, he could see Scott and Nils in the dim light filtering in through a window above him. Both men had makeshift bandages around their heads, and Scott had a gash behind one ear he hadn't bothered to cover. Nils, facing Bart, was gazing out the window.

Pushing himself upright, Bart scooted back against the damp wall.

Nils grinned at him. "That Raoul sure has a

warm spot in his heart for you, Bart. I wondered why he was so glad to see us."

"I should've remembered how unhappy I left the son of a bitch. De Santos warned me about him. Raoul has a long memory. Any word from de Santos while I was out?"

"Nope."

"He ain't here," Scott said. "If he was, I figure Raoul would've treated us a mite more gently."

"How long was I out?" Bart asked.

"Through the night. You didn't miss much."

"What now?" asked Nils.

"Hell," said Scott, laughing softly. "We told you we'd get you here and we did. What more do you want?"

"You're right," Nils said. "I am very grateful."

Bart looked over at Nils. Kristen's brother had filled out some these past weeks, but noting his drawn face and hollow eyes, Bart wondered if the young man would ever regain his old vitality. Bart had seen others like Nils, men hurt so grievously that even though they appeared fully recovered, they could never again be what they once had been.

"I'm hungry," said Bart. "They been feeding you?"

"Yeah. And wait'll you taste it," said Nils. "You'll never want to leave."

Bart groaned.

They endured the filth of their cell and the

slop they were served to eat. But after the first week they complained so much about their food, the guard kicked the tin food dish against the wall and brought them nothing more.

Late one night the cell door was pushed open and de Santos entered. Holding his lantern high, he looked them over. Behind him stood a tall, handsome Comanche, whose features looked more like those of a white man than of an Indian.

"So! It *ees* Señor Hardison," de Santos said, his obsidian eyes gleaming coldly as he stared down at the men. "At first I could not believe you would be so foolish as to come back here."

Bart got slowly to his feet; Scott and Nils stood up also.

De Santos bore little resemblance to the suave, well-manicured man of leisure Bart remembered from his first visit. His black sombrero, pants, and jacket were grimy from windblown sand and the smoke of many camp fires; he smelled of horses and dust.

"Come out of here, my foolish friends," de Santos said, his teeth flashing in his swarthy face. "This cell, it does not smell so good."

With Bart going first, the three men followed de Santos out of the cell and down a dank hallway, at the end of which they turned into a small office, the Indian following in after them. Caught in such a confined space with so many white men was obviously not to the big Comanche's liking.

He shifted his feet nervously, like a caged mountain cat. Looking more closely at him, Bart saw that he had very blue eyes—and a louse crossing his forehead.

"Who's your Indian friend?" Bart asked de Santos.

"A Comanche chieftain. The very famous Quanah Parker. I am sure you hear of him before this."

Looking quickly back at the tall Comanche, Bart felt his scalp pickle. So this was the fabled offspring of Cynthia Ann Parker, the girl taken by the Comanche at nine years of age from Elder John Parker's fort! The band of Comanche that took Cynthia Ann had left behind two women grievously wounded and five men dead. The attack had outraged all of Texas, since one of the men, John Parker, had been pinned to the ground with Comanche lances and his genitals ripped out.

Bart nodded to the Comanche. Quanah Parker looked him over with the calm indifference of a savage appraising a stolen horse and made no sign of greeting.

De Santos sat back on his cluttered desk. "*Señors,* I have been riding for weeks. This Comanche chieftain and his band have not been much comfort. What is it you want in Tule? I am a busy man."

Bart turned to Nils. "You tell him."

"Señor de Santos," Nils said, "I am Kristen's

brother. I understand she is living with you now. I would like to see her."

"Kristen's brother...?" De Santos was genuinely astonished. "But Kristen said you were dead—killed in the war!"

"Not quite. Though most of my left lung is gone, the rest of me is very much alive. And I am sure Kristen would want to know that."

"Yes, yes! Of course! I am sure she would."

"May we see her, then?"

"Unfortunately, that is not possible."

"Why not?"

"Kristen is not here."

"What do you mean?"

"I mean, she has left. I have just discovered it. She has left with Estrellita. They go to California. I ride off to do business with Quanah's people—and this is what I find when I get back. Believe me, *señors,* it was not my wish that she run off." He shrugged fatalistically. "But how is one to fight a woman? As the wise men say, 'The whim of a woman is light and perfumed with the breath of flowers, yet nothing can stand before it.'"

Nils's eyes revealed the bitter disappointment he felt. Bart knew what he was thinking. Kristen could be anywhere between here and California—and California itself was an enormous state. Both Nils and de Santos could spend the rest of their lives looking for her with little chance of success.

Nils glanced wearily at Bart. "Let's go to Kansas."

"Señor de Santos," Bart said, "could you perhaps get your man Raoul to escort us to the Kansas border? We got some beef headin' that way."

De Santos smiled. "I could give him the order, *señor*. But I do not think Raoul would let you get that far. He wants you very bad, I think—the way a famished cat wants a mouse."

"You mean, he wants me dead."

"That would please him greatly."

"What's wrong with him, then? He had the chance while you were gone."

"He is a loyal and devoted lieutenant. Earlier— because of Kristen—I had ordered him to see that no harm came to you. I forgot to rescind the order. As far as Raoul was concerned, it was still in effect."

Bart smiled. "And have you told him of the change?"

"I have advised Raoul that since Kristen is no longer with us, he must not allow *tejanos* or any other gringos to come and go as they please. But if you are willing, I have a suggestion."

"I don't see that we have much choice in the matter."

"You mentioned Kansas."

"Yes. We have a trail herd heading for Abilene."

"Then I could suggest to Quanah that he escort

you at least to the Kansas border. I could make it part of the deal I am arranging with him now."

"Sounds fair enough to me. Thanks, de Santos."

He smiled. "I do it for the brother of a woman I loved very much. I am sorry she has gone. It is a great disappointment for both of us, I assure you. But I must warn you, Hardison. If any of you come here again, I will remember that you are gringos, and this time I will let Raoul feed on you."

"Fair enough," said Bart.

De Santos pulled Quanah to one side and spoke quickly, urgently, to him in the Comanche tongue. There was a brief argument, it seemed; but it did not last long, after which the chief took one quick look at Bart and his companions, then turned and vanished from the office.

"It is done," de Santos told them. "Quanah will get an extra box of carbines, and for that he will take you as far as the Kansas border."

As if Bart and his two companions were lepers, the Comanche kept a good distance ahead of them. All that concerned Quanah, it appeared, were the heavily laden carts carrying the goods they had obtained in trade from de Santos.

They knew what the Comanche had offered de Santos in trade. Now that the War Between the States had ended, the other Comanche bands and Kiowa tribes closer to the Indian nations were having no difficulty acquiring whatever arms and goods they needed from the traders in the agencies, now run by Quakers. These Quakers were considerably more honest than those they replaced; but on the other hand they were, almost without exception, incredibly naive in their dealings with the Indians, who found them notoriously easy to bully.

But Quanah's Comanche, the Antelope Band or Kwahadi, remained on the Staked Plains, as aloof and remote as ever, distrusting all intercourse with the white men—except for their traditional trading partners, the Comancheros. De Santos was anxious to hold on to this trade with the only remaining Comanche band not being seduced by the goods of white traders—and this meant taking from the Kwahadi all the horses they could bring him. And most of those horses came from Texas.

In fact, the horse Quanah Parker himself was riding was remarkably similar to a horse belonging to a string Bart's father had been bringing along before the war.

On the sixth day out, a little after midday, Quanah and his entire troop of warriors left their wagons on a distant ridge and peeled back toward Bart and the others, coming toward them in a wide, inverted V formation. Sweeping on around the three men, the Comanche proceeded to put on a spectacular demonstration of their riding prowess.

Bart found himself wondering if perhaps their string had run out. Having taken them this far, were the Comanche now about to forget their deal with de Santos? After all, what proof did they have that Quanah's deal with de Santos said anything at all about letting the three of them continue on to Kansas?

"You thinking what I'm thinking?" Scott asked Bart.

"Yeah. But it's a little late for that now."

As suddenly as it started, the riding circus ended. As most of the Comanche, the air trembling with their battle cries, raced back to their wagons in the distance, Quanah Parker rode up to them. Six proud warriors sat their ponies behind him, their implacable gaze resting on the three men.

"You are Texans," Quanah said.

Bart nodded.

"You know my mother's people?"

Bart did not know any of the Parker clan personally. But he had sure as hell heard a lot about them. The whole damn Texas frontier had ruminated on nothing else since that infamous attack on Parker's Fort. The stark, brutal accounts of the murder and dismemberment, the taking of the women and the children—all this had been branded indelibly into the consciousness of every Texan.

"I know of your mother's people," Bart replied.

"Good. You tell Texans my mother, she no more Texan. She is Nadua, the woman of Nokoni, my father. Speak no more of ransom. Leave her with her people. Tell this to the Texans."

"I will do that," Bart told Quanah solemnly.

Quanah looked deeply into Bart's eyes, measuring the sincerity of his response, no doubt. Then, apparently satisfied, he lifted his lance and pointed back the way from which they had come.

"Look," he said.

The three turned to see a thin trail of dust lifting into the sky. Riders. A good number. Bart figured them to be at least three miles back.

"Quanah leave you now," he said. "He go toward his land. You go on to Kansas. But first I think maybe you watch out for riders who come after you. De Santos not your friend."

At that he wheeled his pony and led the Comanche with him in a charge back to the ridge and their waiting wagons. A few Comanche leapt from their ponies onto the wagons and, whipping the mules mercilessly, drove off, the entire band soon lost in the shimmering distance.

Looking back at the dust cloud, Bart said, "My hunch is it's Raoul."

"Yup," said Scott, rubbing the red stubble on his face as he squinted in the distance.

Nils spoke up then. "I think Quanah knew all along Raoul was on our tail."

"Sure he did," said Bart. "And this was where he was supposed to hold us until Raoul came to take us off his hands. Only it looks like he had second thoughts."

"Yeah," said Scott. "He wanted you to deliver a message for him."

"To the Texans."

The riders coming after them were visible now—but only as wavering blobs sitting above the horizon or lost entirely in the heat shimmering up from the prairie floor.

Nils pointed to a low line of rocks rearing up out of the ground a good distance ahead. "I think maybe we'd better make for them rocks."

"Good idea," said Bart.

Changing gaits to rest their horses but never stopping, the three men kept on through the blistering heat and reached the shelter of the rocks not long before sunset. Once in the rocks they dismounted, led their horses higher, then found vantage points that gave them clear, unobstructed views of the mesquite-pocked flat they had just crossed. Each took a drag from his canteen, then waited patiently.

It was Raoul, all right.

He came on steadily, following Bart's tracks,

THE TEXAN

then pulled to a shambling halt in front of the rocks, clouds of dust momentarily obscuring him and the other riders. Raoul's big sugarloaf sombrero made a fine target as he stood up in his stirrups and brandished his rifle in defiance.

"Hey, gringo!" he cried.

"I think he wants to challenge you to a duel," Scott said, letting fly with a gob of tobacco juice.

"Some other time."

Bart released the safety on his Henry, then rested his sight on the Mexican's big hat. Raoul was well beyond the carbine's range, so he lifted the barrel and squeezed off a nuisance shot. He was surprised to see the round kick up dirt just in front of Raoul's horse. Immediately Raoul sat back down and led his men off to the east at a hard gallop, disappearing quickly beyond the rocks.

"Soon's it's dark, they'll be comin' around behind us," said Scott.

"If we wait here," replied Bart.

"So maybe we shouldn't wait," said Nils.

"I say we go after them," Bart replied.

"Let's go," said Scott.

They picked their way back down out of the rocks, mounted up, and rode after the Comancheros.

Chapter Thirteen

Kate pulled her wagon to a halt and leaned back. Ahead of her the prairie unfolded in an unbroken panorama. For mile upon mile she could see only a trackless expanse of grass.

It was dangerous for her to continue riding ahead of the trail herd like this, but more and more Kate welcomed this opportunity to get away from the heat and dust of the trail herd and the weary, hard-driven men pushing it toward Kansas. Sometimes she was lucky enough to find a small stream where she could undress completely and scrub the trail dust from her body. She needed these few precious moments of privacy as desperately as she did the ablutions—and she insisted on it, despite the protests of Tolliver

Adams. The rancher had been sighting Indians, it seemed, since the day they left the Red River behind.

Kate got down off the wagon and straightened, her eyes taking in once more the vast expanse of grass, flowing like an unbroken sea clear to the horizon. Paradoxically these past weeks, as her eyes drank in this unbroken immensity stretching before her, she found herself gazing inward, down the pinched, arid stretch of her past six years.

Under these immense skies she felt as small and as insignificant as a dust mote caught in a sunbeam. And this sense of her vast unimportance did not dismay her; instead it seemed to free her. Whenever she got down from her wagon and walked around through the high grasses of the river bottoms, so alive now with the hot fragrance of berries and wildflowers and the small, hurrying animals of spring, she found herself filled with an intoxication that made her want to cry out—in pure joy as much as in sorrow for having shut herself away from all this for so long.

Leaving behind her the thick walls of her ranch house and moving out into this wide, spacious world had transformed her, had flooded the dark corners of her soul with a light pitiless in its clarity. The claustrophobic self-deception of Nordstom's Fort fell away from her, revealing what she had become—and what she had lost. The truth of this came with the painful clarity of a knife. It did not make her feel any less bitter about herself, but it gave her hope. If she had done this to herself, perhaps she could undo it as well.

Only first she had to accept what she had done.

When Seth had returned to her without Nils, she had wanted him dead as much as Frank Kilrain had. And whether she had killed Seth or the Comanche had, in her heart she was equally guilty. Now Seth was gone, as was Nils. And Kristen would never return to Nordstom's Fort.

All she had now was Frank Kilrain's unclean thrall. A bitter reward, indeed. Why was it, she mused, that a man got the notion he owned you just because he dropped his pants by your bed?

The distant, muffled beat of an approaching rider coming from the south broke into her thoughts. She turned. Ned Perkins crested a knoll and bore down upon her. As soon as he realized Kate had seen him, he waved his arm frantically. So fast did he come at her, he had to swing his charging horse around the wagon before coming to a halt.

Leaning down, his big, friendly face filled with concern, he cried, "You got to come quick, Miss

Kate! Our boys riding drag saw Indians coming up."

"A war party?"

"I don't think so, Miss Kate. Tolliver says they maybe just want beef."

"How far back is the herd?"

"Less'n a mile, ma'am."

Kate climbed up into the wagon and lifted the reins.

"Lead the way," she told Perkins, "and ease up on that horse, Ned. We'll need it all the way to Abilene."

"Yes, ma'am," Ned said, pulling his mount around.

Kate slapped her team's backs with her reins and gave them a shout. They charged after Perkins, and before long, Kate rattled up alongside the trail herd.

As she took in the situation she tried not to laugh out loud. The Indian scare consisted of three Indians mounted on gaunt ponies. They had halted halfway up the slope of a steep hogback on the far side of the herd. One threat was a squaw holding a youngster on her thigh. The other threat was a thin, white-haired old man. The third Indian was a young brave who was holding up his right hand, palm out, in the traditional Indian sign for peace.

Tolliver hurried over. "Don't laugh, Kate," he

told her. "Where there's one Indian, there's a lot more."

"I believe you, Tolliver," she told him. "Thanks for sending Ned after me."

At that moment Kate saw Frank, with Cullen Barker and Carl riding alongside him, breaking through the herd, scattering the cattle so briskly he almost caused a stampede as he headed toward the three Indians. The rest of the trail herd's drovers followed well behind Frank. All told, it was a formidable formation to handle one old man, a squaw, and a single brave.

Watching Frank's bent, vengeful figure, Kate felt a sudden foreboding.

"What in hell's Frank up to?" she asked an anxious Tolliver.

"Hell, Kate, I don't know. He didn't consult me."

One of the riders Kate had hired in Crow's Creek yelled over to her, "Frank says he's goin' to teach 'em a lesson."

"Ned Perkins!" Kate cried. "Stop Frank! Get him back here!"

Perkins promptly spurred his horse through the herd on a direct line to Frank. Kate jumped down from the wagon and called for a horse. The wrangler ran up with her gray. Tolliver helped her saddle it. As she buckled the cinch strap she saw Perkins overtake Frank and pull his horse around to face him.

Only reluctantly, it seemed, did Frank and his two partners come to a halt. Kate swung into the saddle, pulled her horse around, and raced through the now milling herd toward Frank.

As Kate neared him she saw Frank arguing heatedly with Ned. At the sound of the hoofbeats of her approaching horse Frank glanced in her direction. She could see his mouth working angrily and could almost hear him curse. He looked back at his two cohorts and gave Cullen an order.

Cullen promptly turned his horse and, lashing it furiously, headed toward the three Indians.

Pulling to a halt alongside Frank, Kate demanded angrily, "What in the hell is Cullen up to?"

"I'm the trail boss, Kate. I'll handle these Indians."

"What do you mean, you'll handle them? If they want a few head, let them have it, Frank. We don't want trouble!"

"Hell! We start giving our beef away now, we won't have any left when we reach Kansas."

"Frank! Call Cullen back!"

"Damned if I will!"

Kate stood up in her stirrups. Cupping her hands around her mouth, she called out to Cullen, demanding that he come back. But by this time the distance was too great for Cullen to hear her above the pounding of his horse's hooves, and he kept right on. Desperate, Kate called out to Cullen a second time; but she was too late. As her cry echoed across the grassland Cullen exploded into the midst of the three Indians.

His gun hand lashed out, catching the white-haired Indian on the side of his head. As the old man went flying backward off his pony, the young brave yanked his mount around and tried to bring up his lance. Cullen shot him twice at point-blank range. The Indian slipped off his pony. At this his squaw broke away and spurred frantically back up the slope, still holding her child on her thigh. Cullen overtook her easily, snatched her reins, and pulled her pony around.

Then he galloped back toward them, a triumphant grin on his face.

Kate felt sick. She had not realized what unbridled brutality resided in Cullen. Brushing angrily past Frank, she rode out to intercept Cullen. He was still grinning in triumph when she snatched the reins of the squaw's pony from him and tossed them back to the squaw.

With only a quick, grateful glance, the squaw pulled her pony around and rode swiftly back to where the old man and her husband lay sprawled in the grass. Kate turned on Cullen, furious.

"You're fired, Cullen," she told him, tight-lipped. "Get your bedroll and ride south."

"Hell, I will. It was Frank signed me on!"

Her crop worked so fast, it astonished her as

she snapped its braided rawhide across his face. The force of her blow knocked Cullen off his horse. He came to his feet spluttering, his hand covering the growing welt on his chin.

"Maybe Frank signed you on, Cullen," she told him. "But I'm the one firing you! Now get your gear and ride out!"

She was turning her horse to ride over to the three Indians when she glanced up in time to see an astonishing sight. On the crest of the ridge above them stood a long line of mounted warriors. Outlined against the sky, their lances gleaming in the late-afternoon sun, she guessed there had to be at least fifty in all. They were so silent, they hardly seemed real. The only visible movement was the wind lifting the tails of their ponies. They weren't Comanche; of that Kate was certain. Nor Kiowas, since Kate did not see a single buffalo-horn headdress. They were Southern Cheyenne probably, or Arapaho.

It was obvious what had happened. These three Indians had been sent down here to ask for beef. They had been testing the water. If the three got beef, the trail herd would have been allowed to pass. If they did not get any cattle, then the Indians had the excuse they needed to take what they wanted.

And when Frank sent Cullen after those three Indians, he had played right into their hands.

Close to panic, Frank rode up beside Kate.

"Jesus!" he exclaimed. "There must be fifty of 'em!"

Ignoring Frank, Kate addressed Perkins. "Let me have your gun, Ned."

Nudging his horse closer, Ned handed his Colt to her. She took it, checked its load, cocked it. Then she pointed it down at Cullen.

"Drop your gun belt, Cullen."

Cullen hesitated, alarmed. He glanced quickly at Frank, then back at Kate.

"What're you goin' to do?" he demanded.

"Just do what I'm telling you, Cullen. Now!"

His hands trembling, Cullen unbuckled his gun belt and let it slip into the grass at his feet.

"Ned," Kate said curtly, "take Cullen's gun and ride along behind me." Then she glanced at Frank. "You stay here, Frank."

"Kate, what in blazes're you up to?"

"Never mind that. Just stay here. And I'm warning you, I'll brook no interference."

By that time Tolliver and the rest of the crew had galloped up. The sudden appearance of the Indians had more than justified Tolliver's earlier concern. He looked ready to fight now if he had to, as did the rest of the riders backing him. But Kate was going to do everything she could to see that it did not come to that.

She looked down at Cullen. "Start walking, Cullen—up that slope."

"You mean, toward them Indians?"

"You heard me."

"But you can't! They saw what I done! They'll kill me!"

Kate sent a shot into the grass at Cullen's feet. He jumped back, looking up at her in horror.

"I can kill you here, Cullen, then drag you up the slope to them Indians—or you can walk up like a man and maybe let me talk them out of skinning you alive in front of us. Which is it to be?"

Cullen looked back at Frank. "Frank! You can't let her do this!"

But Frank just pulled his mount back, willing, at least for the moment, to let Kate play it her way.

Kate sent another bullet at Cullen. This one took a small chunk out of his calf. The man howled, turned, and began limping through the grass toward the slope. Kate and Perkins followed behind on horseback. They had almost reached the ridge's crest when a single Indian nudged his mount forward and rode down to meet them.

Somewhere up on the ridge, far to the left, a pony whinnied. It was the only sound in all that expanse of land and sky. As the Indian rode toward her Kate held up her right hand, her palm out, hoping for a better response than Cullen had given the old man and the young brave.

The chief pulled up in front of Cullen, who had collapsed onto the ground, sobbing in fear.

Behind her, Ned said softly, "This here's an Arapaho chief, Miss Kate."

The chief looked to be in his forties, Kate judged, though it was hard to tell. His face was scarred in several places, his brow flat, his nose bent. There was a fair sprinkling of wrinkles around his eyes. His chin was square and his mouth an inflexible line. Looking into the smoldering anger in his eyes, Kate felt only sympathy for his anger.

"Chief," she told him, "this man at your feet is a fool. He did not know the old man and the young brave were not dangerous."

"No, he not fool," replied the chief, his magnificent voice trembling with sarcasm. "He brave white man! He knock old man from horse. He shoot young brave. Such brave warriors we keep in camp to help women find roots and gather firewood."

"Take him, then," Kate offered. "Let him gather firewood for your people. We do not want such a fool and coward in our camp."

The chief looked with contempt at the cringing Cullen. "It would be better to kill him and be done with it."

Kate shuddered, aware that all the chief would have to do at that moment to carry out his threat was raise his right hand. In less time than it took to tell it, his warriors sweeping down from that ridge would turn Cullen into a pincushion.

and then they would sweep on down the slope and stampede the herd.

The chief's expression softened. "But Little Raven will think on what you say." Then the chief's eyes grew crafty. "The buffalo herds are thin. The winter was long and the cry of our women fill our lodges as the old and the weak journey to the Land Beyond the Sun."

"You want beef, do you?" Kate said.

The chief's expression hardly changed as he shifted on his pony. "Yes. How many beef will the Iron Woman let the people of Little Raven have so he not kill this foolish white man—and so he let you through his land in peace?"

Kate was startled by the name the chief had bestowed on her. She didn't know if it was all that complimentary. But she was relieved that Little Raven was willing to deal—despite the death of one of his braves.

"Take fifteen." She flashed five fingers at him three times in case he did not understand the word.

"Twenty," he countered.

"No. Sixteen."

"Nineteen."

"Seventeen."

"Eighteen. We bargain no more, or my braves kill this brave white man of yours."

"Eighteen it is, then."

Kate turned to Ned Perkins. "Go on back down

and cut out eighteen fat ones, hear? As fat and as sleek as you can find."

Ned wheeled his horse and galloped swiftly back down the slope.

From the grass at her feet Cullen cried piteously, "My God, Kate! You can't do this! You can't give a white man to an Indian—like he was some nigger!"

"You damn fool. I'm saving your life. They'd have had you one way or another. This way you got a chance to keep your scalp. They might even feed you and give you a place to sleep. In time you'll learn all about their lovely ways. All their brutish customs. You should be right at home."

"Kate! Please!"

The wail of the grieving squaw reached them from below, her sharp cries cutting into Kate's heart. The chief heard them as well. Turning to the Indians above him, he shouted something. Three braves charged off the crest toward them. When they reached the chief, he held one back and sent the other two on down to the wailing squaw. Then Little Raven gave the remaining brave a sharp command, pointing down to Cullen as he did so.

As soon as the Arapaho grabbed Cullen's arm the man let out a horrifying scream. He tried to pull away, struggling frantically, and was promptly clubbed senseless, then flung across the Arapaho's pony. In a moment Cullen had disappeared over the ridge, a few warriors peeling after him.

The rest of the Arapaho remained motionless on the ridge.

The chief looked at Kate. "That one you give me, he has bad medicine. He wail like woman. I am sure now. I do not think we will kill him. It would do us no credit."

Kate nodded, relieved.

"We will let him live. He will serve the mother and the woman of brave he kill. They will keep him busy so he will not think of death and cry like a woman."

"That's fine, Chief."

"And now hear me, Iron Woman. If this white man have horse, it would be fine payment for dead warrior."

Kate considered that. Cullen was brutal on horses, and it would not be a good policy to give this chief Cullen's sore-lipped horse. "I will give you a horse in payment," she told the chief.

Watching her shrewdly out of his obsidian eyes, the chief almost smiled. "I know you try to stop brave white man. I hear you call to him. Later I see you knock him from horse. He is the bad one—not Iron Woman or her men. That is why Little Raven and his people will not stampede your cattle and take what they want."

"That's right decent of you, Little Raven."

At that moment the eighteen cattle, driven up

the slope by Tolliver and Ned Perkins, reached them. They were as sleek as Kate had hoped they would be; and as she looked them over, she found herself hoping she didn't have to do this too often.

The chief waved six braves down from the ridge. They took the cattle from Perkins and Tolliver and drove them over the crest of the ridge.

Kate turned to Ned. "Ride back down and bring up my black."

"The black? You sure, Kate?"

"You heard me."

When Perkins returned with the horse, the chief grunted his pleasure, his eyes feasting on the animal's powerful flanks, the long snout, the wide, intelligent eyes. Kate felt a pang but knew there was nothing else to do.

Barely taking the time to nod his approval to Kate, the chief snatched the animal's reins and galloped back up to the ridge. As he rode on through the waiting line of warriors, they followed behind him and were gone—as swiftly and as silently as they had appeared.

"I wonder," Kate remarked to Tolliver as she rode back down the slope with him and Ned. "The chief says he's giving the black to the grieving family. What do you think?"

Tolliver snorted. "That pirate? If you believe him, you're crazy. That black is his now."

Kate sighed. "That's what I thought."

* * *

With the cattle bedded down for the night Kate paused beside her wagon. She could hear a night guard on the far side of the herd singing to the cattle to keep them quiet. The men were bedded down around the camp fire. She was about to climb into her wagon to make her bed for the night when she saw Frank slouching toward her. There was just enough moonlight to show the surly cast to his face as he pulled up in front of her.

"I want to speak to you, Kate."

"I'm listening."

"The men don't like it—what you did, I mean. Throwing a white man to them redskins, like a bone to wild dogs."

"You mean they would rather we lost the herd to them, is that it? When Cullen killed that brave, he was a dead man. I did the best I could for him. And it was more than he deserved."

"Dammit, Kate! You let that chief bully you!"

"You're singing a different tune now. You weren't talking like this when you saw those Indians on that ridge."

He shifted his feet uncomfortably. "Well, maybe so. But dammit, Kate, you crossed me back there—right in front of the men."

"I had no choice."

"Then we got to get something straight."

"Oh?"

"About us, I mean. You been leadin' me to think that we was going to get married someday and run the Circle N together. But if that's your intention, you sure as hell ain't actin' that way."

The man's incredible gall was almost amusing. "I see, Frank. You mean, I should act more like a dutiful wife—not stand up to you in front of others."

"Well, yeah," he admitted, almost grateful that she had put it so clearly for him. "And besides that, Kate, ain't you forgettin' I'm the trail boss?"

"No, Frank. I am not forgetting that. I wish I could."

His narrow, sleek face hardened. "Now, what in hell do you mean by that, Kate?"

She looked at him for a long moment. She had had enough of Frank Kilrain. And now was as good a time as any to tell him.

"What do I mean, Frank?" she replied wearily. "Are you that stupid? Considering what happened today—and after that miserable performance at Red River—do you think you have any authority left to lead this trail drive? You're out, Frank. Tomorrow Ned Perkins will be taking over as trail boss."

"Kate, you can't do this. I won't stand for it."

"You don't have any choice in the matter, Frank. You were worse than a fool today. You nearly cost us the trail herd—or worse. It was you who told

Cullen to go after them three Indians. I saw you."

"What if I did?"

"Thanks, Frank—for making it so easy for me."

"You can't do this, Kate, not with what I know."

"That sounds like a threat, Frank."

"I'm just remindin' you, Kate."

"Of what?"

"You ain't no better than me."

"You think so, do you?"

"You're goddamn right I do. It was you made me lock Seth out. I only did it 'cause I knew it was what you wanted. You're a great one for giving white men to Indians."

Kate tried to slap him. He grabbed her wrist, then swung at her hard, his clenched fist clipping her on her chin. She felt herself spinning, and then the damp grass slammed up against her face. Rolling over, furious, she looked up at Frank. He stood over her, making no attempt to apologize or to help her up. She waited for his kick or whatever he had in mind. It was what she deserved, she realized bitterly.

Running footsteps caused Frank to lower his fists and step quickly back away from her. Using the side of her wagon, Kate pulled herself up onto her feet as Tolliver and Perkins ran toward them. They must have seen Frank strike her, Kate realized.

Tolliver pulled up angrily beside Frank, his six-gun in his hand, his face fiery red with indignation. "I saw that, Frank! Ned did too!"

"Now, Tolliver, no harm done," Kate said.

"Dammit, Miss Kate!" said Ned Perkins. "Let me take a piece out of his hide!"

"No, Ned. I told you. No harm's been done." Then she looked at Frank. "Get your gear and ride out, Frank—and take Carl with you."

"You really mean that, Kate?"

"Yes, I mean it."

"I'm tellin' you, if me and Carl go, we ain't goin' alone. There's men in this outfit still backin' me. They won't follow no damn woman who'd give a white man to Indians."

"Then take those men with you, Frank," said Tolliver coldly. "If they'd follow a piece of offal like you, we don't want them on this drive."

Frank looked from Tolliver back to Kate, as if, even after all this, he still hoped she'd change her mind. When she said nothing, he spun around and strode off.

"How many men do you think he'll take with him?" Kate asked Tolliver, watching Frank go.

"Not many, I'm thinking."

"Two, maybe three hands," said Ned Perkins. "I wouldn't worry none about them, Miss Kate."

"I just don't trust him," Kate said. "There's no

THE TEXAN

telling what he'll do." Then she glanced at Ned. "Ned, you're trail boss from here on."

"Sure thing, Miss Kate," he said, brightening. "And don't you worry none. We'll get these here cattle to Abilene."

"I know we will, Ned."

As the two men walked back to the camp fire, Kate climbed into her wagon and undressed for bed. While she was making up the bed, she heard the sudden staccato of horses' hooves as Frank and Carl rode out. There were definitely more than two horses, she realized. She pulled the tarp over her and blew out the lantern.

Frank's terrible accusation had brought it all back. She saw herself planted with her back to the door and Kristen on the floor in front of her, pleading with her to let Seth in. And afterward, Seth's screams. . . .

She clenched her fists and squeezed her eyes shut, moaning softly. She had managed to keep that awful moment locked away deep inside her. Sometimes the memory would sneak out to confront her. But always in the past she had managed to push it back into a secret corner of her mind.

Only this time she could not do it. Frank had made perfectly plain what she had done. He had put her on the same level with him, and though the thought sickened her, there was no escaping the truth of his ugly words.

The terrible shadows of Nordstom's Fort closed around her.

Chapter Fourteen

Bart lay flat on his belly, peering down through a patch of scrub pine at Raoul and his fellow Comancheros. This high in the rocks, they were feeling pretty secure. They had not bothered to hide their morning fire, and they made no effort to curb their conversation and laughter as they threw off their tarps and started to get dressed. Some refused to get out of their sleeping bags, Bart noticed.

Scott moved up beside Bart. Scratching his red stubble, he peered down at Raoul's encampment. "Cheerful buzzards, ain't they?"

Nils cleared his throat. "We goin' to take them?"

"I'm thinking on it," replied Bart.

"When?" asked Scott.

"Right now."

"You got a plan?"

"Yup."

If a man learned anything from war, he learned how dangerous it was to hang back. Battles were never won by inching ahead cautiously, groping for a soft spot. Reconnoiter the terrain, check your opponents' capabilities, then move boldly— and keep on driving. How many times had Bart seen battles lost because some damn fool of a general wet his pants and called for a pullback?

Since the odds weren't good, Bart figured they would need plenty of firepower. In his mind he went over the weapons they possessed. They had the Henry, a rapid-fire carbine good for close-in fighting, his big Walker, and Scott's Navy Colt. Nils had a Colt and his Springfield; the rifle was not much good in close combat. Also, there was that sawed-off shotgun Scott had looped to his saddle horn. Bart knew how to turn that scatter gun into a cannon, and he had a hunch Scott did too.

"Scott," he said, "I figure we're going to be needing that shotgun—and maybe some of your chaw too."

Scott grinned, catching on instantly. "Maybe so."

Scott pulled back and returned a moment later with a handful of shells. In the dim, pre-dawn light the older man worked swiftly. He peeled

THE TEXAN

back the crimped ends, then mixed the buckshot with his chaw, stuffing the load back into the shell casing.

"I never would have thought of that," Nils said.

"The chaw holds the charge together so it won't scatter," Bart said. "Hits like a cannonball."

"What's the effective range?"

"Maybe a hundred and fifty feet. Right, Scott?"

Still working, Scott nodded. "That's about it."

While Scott worked, Bart outlined his plan. When Bart finished, Scott glanced over at him, a slight frown on his lined face. "Seems like you're carrying most of the load in this here action, Bart. You sure you can handle it without getting your ass cooked?"

"Can you think of a better plan?"

Scott reflected a moment, staring down the slope at the awakening camp. "Nope. Not with seven of them bastards against three of us."

"It's Raoul we want first off. And maybe a few more to send the rest packing."

Scott spat a dark wad of chewed-up tobacco onto his palm and mixed it with the last of his buckshot. "Beats me why de Santos didn't take us back in Tule when he had the chance."

"I'd like to know that myself," Bart told him, glancing thoughtfully down the slope at the Mexicans lounging around the blazing camp fire.

From this distance he could smell the fresh coffee perking.

A few minutes later, having given Nils and Scott time to take their positions, Bart mounted up. Working his horse carefully over to a dry wash, he suddenly spurred down the slope, heading straight for the Mexicans. The sudden drumming of his mount's hoofs had the desired effect.

The seven men around the camp fire jumped up, frantically grabbing their weapons. But Bart was already off the slope, pounding toward them. Wrapping his reins around his saddle horn, he lifted his Henry and flipped off the safety. He was looking for Raoul, but he couldn't make him out in the early-morning light. So he took out the nearest Mexican, sending him spinning back into the fire.

Galloping on past him, levering and firing as rapidly as he could, he plunged through the Comancheros' midst, spreading his fire. The Mexicans' return fire was hurried and wild. He had caught a few still asleep in their bedrolls. Cutting down two more, Bart cleared their camp and broke for the opposite slope. Keeping his head down, he cut onto the narrow trail leading up through the spruce. Behind him the Mexicans sent a solid fusillade after him, a wall of lead chasing him up the slope.

Then he was in the timber, pushing his mount hard. Behind him the aroused Comancheros raced

THE TEXAN

after him, cursing and shooting. His Henry empty by this time, Bart dropped it into his saddle boot, turned, and sent a couple of rounds from his Walker back down the slope at those pursuing him. He saw that four Mexicans had mounted up and were charging up the trail after him. The last one had a rifle in his hand and—except for his sombrero—was stark naked.

Then came the unmistakable smacking sound of a bullet striking flesh. Bart's mount collapsed under him, a bullet through his hind leg. Thrown clear, Bart hit hard, doing all he could to keep the big Walker in his hand. The gravel dug into his elbows and knees. He rolled off the trail and got to his feet, firing back down the trail at the oncoming Mexicans as he did so.

Then he ducked into the timber, firing as he went.

Scott watched the Mexicans galloping up the trail after Bart. He was pleased. Bart had done his part. Scott almost could have reached out and touched him as he galloped past. Cursing, screaming, the damn fool Mexicans taking after him were so outraged, they were liable to shoot their own horses out from under them.

Above him on the trail came the sound of Bart's horse hitting the ground, followed by its startled, terrified cry. Glancing up the slope, Scott saw the blood gouting from the animal's shattered leg. He winced as the horse, thrusting its neck up off the ground, continued to whinny in terror and pain. Scott hated that sound. He'd sooner hear a woman scream than a horse.

Lifting his shotgun, Scott waited in the timber, easing back both hammers, his finger curled inside the guard. He felt the tension of the first trigger. Then the air was filled with dust, and the ground shuddered under him as the four Mexican riders pounded past him up the slope.

When the last rider—as naked as a plucked turkey—whipped past, Scott stepped out of cover and brought up the twin barrels. The first ten-bore explosion caught the naked horseman in the small of his back. The packed round of his second shot caught a second rider in the head, his skull exploding like a ripe watermelon.

Bart stepped out of cover to draw down on the remaining two riders. Caught between Bart and Scott, the Mexicans flung themselves from their horses and dived frantically for cover. Nils stepped out of the timber a few feet from them, his Colt roaring twice in rapid succession. Both Comancheros went down.

Scott saw Bart running toward Nils to make sure the four downed Mexicans were no longer dangerous. Peering back down the slope to make sure no more Mexicans would be riding up after them, Scott rested the twin barrels of his shotgun on his shoulder and started up the trail to join them.

He heard someone in the timber beside him. Before he could react, there was a detonation. A Sharps, he thought, as the bullet slammed into his back. He was on his face, his chin plowing through gravel. There was no pain. It felt like someone had punched him in the small of his back. This was not the first time he had been shot, and he recognized the feeling. The pain would come later, after the shock wore off.

He tried to move his arms so he could pull himself into the brush he glimpsed out of the corner of his eye. It would be smart for him to get away from whoever the hell had sent that slug into him. But before he made another move, a second shot came from above and behind him. This one caught him in the back of the head, slamming him forward into darkness.

Running down through the thick timber, swearing silently, Bart broke past a heavy clump of scrub pine and came upon Raoul so suddenly that both men slammed into each other and went tumbling to the ground. The Sharps rifle in Raoul's hand went flying. Nils, racing after Bart, got caught up in the tangle. But he had sense enough to strip Raoul's six-gun from him, then duck away from the struggling men.

His Walker still clutched in his hand, Bart

clubbed Raoul repeatedly about the head and shoulders. Hunching his shoulders to absorb the blows, Raoul closed his fingers around Bart's neck. A second before his windpipe gave way, Bart slammed his knee up into Raoul's groin. Raoul doubled over and sagged back.

Swinging his Walker around with all the force he could muster, Bart caught Raoul on the side of his head. The man went down like a felled steer. When he made a sluggish effort to get back up again, Bart kicked him in the face. He would have sent a shot down through his skull if the man hadn't flipped over onto his back and stared glassy-eyed up at him, as helpless as a babe. Reaching down, Bart picked up Raoul's rifle.

"Make sure he doesn't go anywhere," Bart told Nils, "while I go see how bad Scott's been hurt."

Scott was lying facedown, his forehead resting in a bloody porridge of brains and bone fragments, a neat hole blasted in his skull. There was another hole in his back. This first round should have severed his backbone. Death must have come the instant that second slug smashed through his skull. Raoul had finished him off quickly, the way he would a horse with a broken leg.

Bart glanced up the trail. His own horse was still alive, kicking and whinnying feebly. He hurried up the slope. Long strips of saliva hung from its gaping mouth. He shot it through the

THE TEXAN

head, then looked at the sprawled bodies of the four other Mexicans. The stench of death hung heavy in the damp morning stillness.

Then Bart looked back down the trail at Scott. "Sorry, Scott," he said softly. "It happened too fast—before I could return the favor."

Bart's plan had worked well enough. Only Bart hadn't figured on Raoul getting Scott from behind like that. He hadn't figured on that at all.

When Bart came back to Nils, he saw the question in the young man's eyes and shook his head. Nils frowned but asked no questions. Bart looked down at the still unconscious Raoul.

He was shirtless, wearing only his long johns. There was a hole in the right side of his chest— more than likely a bullet from Bart's Henry. Though the wound was superficial, it was bleeding copiously, turning the dirt and pine needles plastered to his chest into a bloody smear.

The big Mexican shook himself and opened his eyes. Hunkering down beside him, Bart cocked his Colt and shoved its barrel into Raoul's mouth. When the startled Mexican tried to talk, Bart pressed the muzzle in deeper and shook his head.

Raoul froze, eyes wide.

"Listen and listen hard, Raoul," Bart told him. "If you won't tell me what I want to know, I'll kill you. Won't be no reason not to. Not after what you just done to Scott. You hear that?"

Dark gobs of sweat ran down the Mexican's forehead. He nodded quickly. Bart took the muzzle out of Raoul's mouth and stood up.

"Why did de Santos send you after us?" he demanded.

Raoul answered almost eagerly. "It is not personal, Señor Hardison. He just want you dead."

"Why, dammit?"

"Because you are the rival for his love."

"For Kristen?"

"*Si!* For the golden-haired one."

"Then why didn't he kill me in Tule when he had the chance?"

"Because if he kill you, he must also kill the brother of Kristen. But how could he do such a thing? For when he bring her back, she will hear of this and hate him for it."

"Bring her back?"

"Yes."

"Has he found her?"

Raoul smiled. "Señor de Santos is no fool. The golden-haired one say to tell everyone it is California where she go. But Estrellita, she go with her. And this mother of whores, all she talk about is Kansas—to make much money in the place called Abilene." Raoul smiled. "So we ask someone who know Estrellita, and he say we are right—it is to Kansas where they go."

Bart looked quickly at Nils, who appeared as astonished as Bart. "Did you say Abilene?"

THE TEXAN

"*Si!* It the place where all the cows from Texas go now. There they have many fine cantinas for the men to drink and the women to play. There is much money there, gringo."

"I know," Bart said grimly.

Nils spoke up then. "So de Santos wanted you to kill me out here where there'd be no trace left, is that it? Killing me was all right, as long as it didn't get back to my sister?"

"No. Señor de Santos tell me to let you live. It is only this Bart Hardison he want dead for sure."

"Get up, Raoul," Bart said.

Raoul struggled to his feet. He would survive, Bart figured. His flesh wound would barely slow him down.

"Bury your dead, Raoul," Bart said. "Then go back to de Santos and tell him what a fine success you had."

Raoul studied Bart through crafty eyes. *"Gracias, señor!"*

"And there's something else I want you to tell him."

"*Si, señor,* what is that?"

"Tell him I'll be waiting for him in Abilene. *Comprender?*"

His face impassive, Raoul nodded. "*Si,* I will tell Señor de Santos what you say."

"And I'll be waiting for you, too, Raoul."

Raoul threw back his shoulders, his assumed

273

servility of a moment before gone completely. Through unblinking, lidded eyes he regarded Bart coldly. He was safe, now that the gunfight was over. It was this foolish gringo's curious code of honor not to shoot him down in cold blood.

He smiled at Bart. "And I will wait for you."

"Then we will meet again."

"That is a promise, gringo."

Bart was satisfied. Raoul would deliver his challenge. If de Santos still wanted to get rid of his rival, Bart wold be waiting for him in Abilene, ready and eager to settle matters.

And Raoul, the man who had just killed Scott Tyrell, would be waiting there too.

Chapter Fifteen

Except for that last faint rumble of thunder, the night was quiet. Too quiet. Kate didn't like it. She was standing beside her wagon with Tolliver Adams. He had just announced that Ned and the boys had made sure there were no gullies, cutbanks, or deep arroyos nearby into which the fool beasts might plunge if they got the notion to stampede.

Still, Kate was worried. She felt the tension in the air. She had felt this same way a week ago, just before the sky opened up with hailstones the size of quail's eggs, raising welts on the men that later caused their skin to peel. Though they lost only two head, rounding up the herd afterward took the better part of the day. It was dark before they reached a decent bedding ground.

Tolliver shook his head apprehensively. "Can you feel it, Kate? I'm all prickly, as nervous as a hawk."

"Yes, Tolliver. I feel it. It's the same way I felt before that hailstorm."

Not long before, a night herder's horse stepped on a dry twig and every single steer lifted its head—in unison.

"I been thinking about Frank," Kate said.

"I figured you were."

"Now would be a nice time for him to try something."

"I know. But relax, Kate. He should be halfway to Texas by now."

"I hope so."

Kate liked Tolliver's company. Though the rancher was in his early fifties, he had a round, boyish face. The lines were there, of course, and the graying hair—but he was one of those men who had the curious ability to retain that youthful look well into maturity. It was his pale blue eyes, Kate realized, and the sandy, nearly invisible eyebrows that gave him the appearance of a man still surprised—and delighted—by the amazing world around him.

Despite his youthful appearance, Tolliver owned a trail-wise wisdom that was becoming a growing comfort to her. And the man was honest. Not

THE TEXAN

one to mince words, he had expressed his disapproval of her letting Little Raven take Cullen Barker. But once he had told her this, he said no more about it. He seemed to hold no grudges. He was able to accept the fact that Kate's action must have seemed the best possible course to her at the time.

Herman dropped a pan in the chuck wagon, then another. The sound seemed to radiate with tension, and the great, dark mass of cows stirred. One or two got up, startled, and only slowly dropped back down. Something else Kate noticed: Not a single steer was chewing its cud.

"The herd is sure not settling down any," Kate said. "You ever been through anything like this before, Tolliver?"

The cattleman chuckled. "Sure have, Kate. I've seen some herds where you'd have to ride back a hundred yards just to spit. Thing is, it don't do no good to mollycoddle cattle. Trailin' herds to Louisiana before the war, I used to bang around them somethin' awful when we first lit out—just so's they'd get used to the noise. Hardened them right up, it did."

"These critters should be hardened by now, Tolliver."

"Maybe so," Tolliver agreed, taking off his hat very carefully, "but if they ain't and they do take a notion to bolt, we ain't goin' to find all of them come next Christmas."

Kate nodded and leaned her head back against the wagon. Since that last tiny alarm, the one set off by Herman's clattering pans, the herd finally seemed to have settled down for the night. Not a sound came from them now.

"Looks like they're quieting," Kate remarked.

Tolliver took out his sack of tobacco and built himself a cigarette. He did it so casually and quickly, Kate was barely aware he had started before it was in his mouth and he was bent over a lit match, drawing it to life.

"Yep, Kate," he drawled softly. "They're quietin' down now, sure enough. But maybe they're too quiet. I like cows to sit still, sure, but I feel better when I hear some of them natural noises that goes with a herd this size. Let me hear 'em blowing off, or the sound of their joints creakin'. That means they're easin' themselves down into their beds, settling in for the night."

"I don't hear any of that."

"That's what I mean. Real spooky, I'd say. Better'n three thousand head of cattle only forty feet away—and you can't hear a blamed thing. Ain't natural."

Kate wondered why the night riders weren't singin' to the herd. They usually did. "Maybe the riders should sing to them."

"You think that calms down a herd?"

"Doesn't it?"

"Nope."

"Then why do the men do it?"

"To let the brutes know where they are. Gives the cows a chance to keep track of the riders. Let some cowpoke loom up sudden-like on a steer without no warning and that steer's off and runnin'."

"Maybe you'd better tell Ned. Perhaps the men should get ready for trouble."

"I do that and nothin' happens, the next time Ned raises an alarm, all Ned'll get will be a lot of hootin' and laughin'. Nope, Kate. We got to wait this one out and see what happens. But that's why I trailed my horse out here behind me. Where's yours?"

She nodded to a dark clump of oak about ten yards behind the wagon. "My gray's in the timber behind me."

"Tethered?"

"Yes."

"Good thing."

He dragged on his cigarette awhile, its tip glowing brightly in the stygian gloom.

Kate liked the smell of the tobacco. It was a companionable smell. She wished women could smoke cigarettes instead of having to stay inside with their pipes. Damned social conventions, she thought. Though, God knows, on this trip she had broken enough of them to fill a bushel basket. For a moment she seriously considered asking Tolliver to build her a cigarette, then thought better of it. He was a tough old-timer who didn't shock easily, but even so, she knew he would not approve.

There it was again, that dim mutter of thunder in the distance. She remembered having seen torn remnants of dark clouds on the horizon not long before sunset. The storm had moved off, she thought. It had been sultry all day, but a pleasant breeze had sprung up after sundown. It was gone now, though.

A single, silent wink of lightning illuminated them and the prairie around them. In its split-second flash she saw the cattle's gleaming backs. It *was* amazing she could not hear them even when they were this close. The darkness closed in, a heavy, threatening darkness—and she could almost feel the low storm clouds rolling in, shutting out the stars.

Ned Perkins was nervous too. Tired of sitting around the chuck wagon, he'd mounted up to help out in case hell came unstuck, and for the past hour the big puncher had been on his horse, humming half aloud to keep the cows from spooking. But it was so dark, even his horse was feeling its way. He felt as if he were moving through a black pot. The sky and the ground were all the same.

A few minutes earlier there had been a dim mutter of thunder, followed by a lightning flash.

THE TEXAN

Relieved that the herd had not spooked, he kept on around it through a darkness more profound than that before the lightning. When he heard cattle getting up around him, he realized he had blundered into the herd. It was a good thing he had kept on humming, he told himself. Otherwise the cattle might've panicked. Pulling to his left, he cautiously worked his horse clear of the herd.

It was useless to ride if he couldn't see, he realized. Pulling to a halt, he kept on humming, trying to think of a tune. There was no more lightning, but it was still growing darker. The slight breeze that had sprung up at sundown had died down completely. It was hotter than the hubs of hell now.

Then it came, from the far side of the herd—the snap of a blanket or a rope slapping the flank of a horse.

The ground shook. As one single, massive animal, the herd came to its feet and plunged blindly through the black night. Ned's horse took the bit and plunged after the herd, running like a scared wolf as it burned a hole in the darkness.

A brilliant flash of lightning played over them. Glancing to his left, Ned saw the herd pounding along beside him. Big drops of rain began slapping his hat. The storm had broken now for sure, and the lightning was bombarding the herd continually, showing it the way to hell. Another series of flashes and Ned saw a rider pulling alongside him, so close Ned could have hit him with his quirt.

"This sure is hell!" Ned cried through the pounding rain.

"What damn fool kicked the lid off?"

And then the rider was gone, swallowed up in the pounding night.

Ned's ears told him the cattle were running straight. There was no click of horns. What he heard instead was a kind of humming noise—like a buzz saw. Only it was a thousand times louder. He didn't think there was any chance they could turn the herd in this darkness, so he continued to ride wide of its thundering flank, keeping it well to his left.

Before long, Ned heard the cattle coming together. A brilliant series of lightning flashes showed the brutes milling frantically, their heads jammed together, their horns locked. Some were rearing up and riding others, the whole mass squirming like a nest of snakes.

Blinded by the rain, Ned's horse plunged over a bank, landing safely. It couldn't have been more than a four-foot drop, but in the darkness it felt like fifty feet to Ned. If it hadn't been for his chin strap, he would have lost his hat. Another flash and Ned saw he was in an arroyo, the cattle pouring over the edge after him, wriggling and squirming like army worms. Using his quirt ruthlessly, he managed to outrun the cattle and gallop up out of the arroyo just ahead of them.

Once again he found himself pounding alongside the herd.

They seemed to be slowing down now. Perhaps it was the rain. Pulling himself closer to the cattle, he pulled out his six-gun and began firing at the ground just in front of the nearest cattle. They swerved slightly, but not enough as the entire herd kept plunging straight on, unmindful of his shots. He holstered his gun and settled down to a hard gallop, intent on simply outrunning the herd.

He was beginning to pull ahead of the leaders when he thought he heard hoofbeats closing in on him from behind. He glanced back. A rope snaked out of the night and settled over his shoulders, pinning his arms. An instant later he was yanked backward, his feet pulling free of the stirrups. In midair he began to turn. A second before he hit the ground, he braced himself. But the impact was enough to send him tumbling into darkness.

When Ned regained consciousness, he was flat on his back. The sound of the herd had faded to a dim thunder. It was still raining, the heavy drops pounding relentlessly down onto his face and chest. He tried to open his eyes. But his lids were heavy—ponderously heavy. And he could not move his limbs.

With an enormous effort of will he managed to open his eyes enough to see the two horsemen looming over him. Bent under the rain's persistent hammer, they peered down at him, the rainwater pouring off their brims in a steady rivulet. It was their voices that had aroused him—that as much as the steady pounding of the rain.

One of them was Frank Kilrain, and the other was Carl. They were discussing what to do with him.

"... I say we finish him right here," said Carl. "We got no reason to care what happens to him."

"Dammit," replied Frank irritably, "if this here's to be an Indian raid, we can't finish him off with a revolver. We need an arrow."

"Tell you what. I'll slit his throat and scalp him."

"It'd be better if we had an Arapaho arrow."

"Well, we ain't got one, Frank. And we're gonna drown on our horses if we don't get after them beef. The others've probably cut out their share by now. And we better get ours."

"All right, then. Do it."

Ned watched Carl dismount and head for him, drawing his bowie knife as he approached. Ned took a deep breath and found he could move his shoulder a little. Life flowed into his limbs. His right hand was next to his holster. His six-gun was still sitting in it. Slowly, he closed his right hand over the grips.

Carl halted over him, his body shielding Ned from the rain. Hesitating for only an instant, Carl hunkered down beside Ned in the mud, and holding out his bowie knife, blade up, he leaned closer. He hesitated. He was deciding which to do first, slit Ned's throat or scalp him. He decided on scalping and was leaning over to grab Ned's hair when Ned thrust the muzzle of his Colt into the man's gut and blew out his backbone.

Flinging his arm around the dead man's neck to use him as a shield, Ned thrust his gun out from under Carl and sent a round up at Frank. Kilrain lost all his enthusiasm, pulled his horse back, wheeled, and galloped off. Ned flung off Carl's body to send one more shot after him. But the hammer came down on an empty cylinder.

Ned looked down at Carl's sprawled figure. Then, peering through the curtain of driving rain that enclosed him on all sides, he swore.

Where in hell was his horse?

Tolliver had been in the act of consulting his pocket watch when the loud snap came, sending the herd plunging through the night. He was already swinging into his saddle when Kate cried out, "I'll get my horse! Wait!"

"No you won't, Kate!" Tolliver shouted down to her, above the fearsome roar. "You'll get yourself killed! Stay here and keep an eye on the camp—if you can see it!"

And then he was off after the herd, the rest of the riders—including Herman, the cook—galloping after him.

Kate knew what they had to do. First they must overtake and turn the leaders. Once that was accomplished, they would make the entire herd mill until the exhausted cattle gave up their collective madness and allowed themselves to be bedded down for the night. After that would come the long search through the night and the next day for the cattle that had left the main body and were still running loose in every direction.

Kate was not happy to be left behind. She wanted to help, dammit! She could ride as well as any man. She stomped about her wagon a couple of times, then lit out for the oak clump where she'd tethered her gray.

Pushing her mount hard, Kate eventually caught up to some of the men.

Above the thunder of the herd, off to her left, she could hear the men shouting to each other as they kept alongside it. Then, far ahead of her, came the sudden bark of gunfire. The men were attempting to turn the herd. She headed for the flashes of gunfire and became aware that the herd was slowly turning away from her. A series of lightning flashes played over the landscape, and she saw the cattle milling, heads jammed together, some of them with their horns locked.

THE TEXAN

Then darkness came again, leaving only the flash of gunfire to tell her where the herd was.

She followed the men, keeping the herd's thunder on her left. Another flash of lightning showed a torrent of glistening backs, a pounding river of horned animals sweeping in a great circle across the prairie. She thought she saw two or three riders well ahead of the lead animals. Then she saw nothing and simply did her best to keep up.

It was going to be a long ride, she realized, before these brutes came to their senses—or dropped from sheer exhaustion.

Kate was right. Not until daybreak did the animals slow and begin gathering into small, weary bunches, then begin to graze. They had long since outrun the cloudburst and were spread out as far as Kate could see. When she rode up to Tolliver, she was saddle-sore and exhausted. Tolliver had looped his foot over his saddle horn and was building himself a smoke.

"I told you to stay with the camp," he remarked as she reined in beside him.

"You can't tell me what to do, Tolliver."

"I know it, Kate. I just didn't want you to get hurt."

"Everyone here?"

"Slim, Pye, and Donaldson are out after strays. Thing is, I don't know where Ned is. He might be back there somewhere."

"You mean...?"

"Now don't go thinkin' the worse, Kate. His horse could've gone down, that's all. But if he did go down, I don't like it. It was as black as a Comanche's heart last night."

"What are you going to do?"

"I'm torn, Kate. I'd like to send all the men back for Ned, but the remuda's all strung out. Our mounts are nearly done in, and we have to keep after the steers or they'll drift into the next county. I'll send Simpson back after fresh mounts, but that'll take time. Maybe he can hitch up your wagon and bring that along too."

"We going to stay here?"

"It's good grazin', and there's water beyond that flat. I figure these animals have lost enough tallow already. Better give them a chance to put it back on—and these men a chance to catch their breath."

"Good idea," Kate said, "and while you're doing that, I'll go back and see if I can find Ned."

"I'd sure appreciate it, Kate."

It was noon that same day when Kate saw Ned Perkins walking across the prairie toward her. Shading her eyes, she could hardly believe it was him. He halted, then waved his hat. Enormously pleased to find him alive and apparently well, she nudged her exhausted gray on toward him. When they finally met, Ned grinned up at her wearily.

"What're you doin' way out here, Miss Kate?"

"Looking for you."

"Well, now, looks like you found me."

"Where's your horse?"

"Over there." He pointed. Kate, squinting into the distance, caught sight of a roan horse standing on a slight rise, its head raised, peering alertly in their direction.

"I gave up trying to catch it, Miss Kate. The damn fool hoss thinks it's a game we're playing. He waits until I get close, and then he bobs his head and fiddle-foots away from me. I swear, last time I looked, he was laughing."

"Do you think this gray might help?"

"Let me try."

Kate dismounted. Ned climbed into her saddle and put the gray to a trot. Halfway to Ned's horse the foolish roan whinnied happily and galloped toward Ned. Ned reached out, grabbed the flying reins, and pulled his horse in. Aware of how weary Kate's horse was, he mounted his own and led the gray back to Kate.

"I got some news for you, Miss Kate," Ned said as they rode back together.

"Oh?"

"I didn't fall from this horse. It was a rope pulled me off."

Kate glanced over at Ned, frowning.

"Either Frank Kilrain or Carl roped me. They was the ones behind this stampede—them and those other jaspers they took with them when they left the herd."

"Ned, are you sure of this?"

"As sure as I am that Carl's back there where I left him, feeding them buzzards."

Startled, Kate looked back in the direction from which they had come. Tiny black specks, like cinders above a fire, were circling in the sky. She judged the distance to be four or five miles.

"Maybe you better explain it from the beginning, Ned."

Ned did, and when he had finished, Kate could only say, "I thank God you're all right, Ned."

"Guess I was lucky, sure enough."

And that was all Kate had to say. She was too numb to comment. When they reached the new campsite, Ned was greeted by a jubilant crowd of riders. Then he went off with Tolliver to tell him about Frank. Kate's wagon, she saw, had been brought up by Simpson. Dismounting, she offsaddled the gray and sent it to graze.

Then she climbed into her wagon and made her bed. She was asleep almost the moment her head hit the pillow.

It had been getting steadily hotter all day, the grasslands around them shimmering under the blazing sky. She had parked her wagon alongside the stream, beside which the cattle had been grazing all day. Sitting up on the seat, she was looking out over the diminished herd strung out along both sides of the stream as far as the eye could see.

All morning Kate had been wishing she could sneak off and find a place private enough for her to strip and bathe. She thought she might be able to manage it after dark farther downstream, but she was irritated at having to wait that long.

She saw Ned riding up to report to her. When he got to her, he pulled to a halt and leaned forward wearily onto his pommel.

"Well, Ned?"

"We sure are missing some, Miss Kate," Ned said, mopping his brow with his bandanna.

"How many head would you say?"

"Close to a thousand."

"That many?"

Perkins nodded.

"Have you told Tolliver yet?"

"Just did, ma'am."

At that moment Tolliver galloped over, pointing. "We got visitors," he told Kate.

Ned turned his horse to look. Kate shaded her eyes. Far up the stream, splashing across it and sending grazing cattle lumbering out of their path, mounted Indians were approaching—a long file of them. They were coming on quietly and peaceably, Kate thought gratefully.

"And look what's bringin' up the rear!" said Tolliver.

Kate could hardly believe her eyes. It was their cattle. A long, swelling tide of steer, moving into and merging with the rest of the herd. Arapaho braves were driving them across the stream, using their lances to prod the weary animals on.

"Hey! Ain't that Frank?" someone yelled.

It was. Frank Kilrain was riding alongside Little Raven. His hands were tied to his saddle horn, and his horse was being led by an Arapaho brave. He looked pretty miserable. He was hatless, and the side of his face was a bloody mess. He obviously was in pain. As he rode, he favored his right side.

By this time the rest of the crew had mounted up and ridden over to Kate's wagon, crowding around it protectively.

Little Raven reached over with his knife and slashed through the rawhide binding Frank's wrists. Then he slapped the rump of Frank's horse. The mount surged forward. Frank slid off its back. He hit hard but managed to regain his footing. As soon as he did so, Little Raven nudged him closer to the wagon with the gleaming tip of his feathered lance.

The riders pulled their horses back to let Little Raven and Frank through. The closer Frank got, the worse he looked. But he managed to keep on his feet almost to the wagon before collapsing facedown in the grass. Kate turned away at the sight of the gaping lance wound in his right side.

The chief reined in his mount. He was riding Kate's big black. She and Tolliver had been right. Such a fine horse had been too valuable a prize to give to a grieving widow.

"It is good to see Iron Woman!" Little Raven told Kate, his eyes gleaming in triumph.

"And I am pleased to greet my friend, Little Raven," Kate replied, not forgetting the elaborate courtesy required at such times. "What have you brought me?"

The chief was enjoying himself hugely. "A cattle thief! He make stampede. Then he and his men ride off with many cows. But Little Raven bring back cattle—and cattle thief too. Now maybe Iron Woman punish them."

"Where are the others who were with him?"

"They ride off. But they not ride far. Many carry Arapaho arrows."

"You have done us a great service, Little Raven."

"Yes. That is true. And we do not want much in return."

"Just some of the cattle you saved."

"Iron Woman understand the Arapaho. Maybe I not take cows. Maybe I take Iron Woman instead—if she want."

Kate could hardly believe her ears. The chief was proposing—or what passed for a proposal in Arapaho society. She felt her face flush and for a moment could not decide how to parry this unwelcome proposition. To her dismay, however, her silence served only to encourage the chief.

"I see you not say no," he noted cheerfully. "That is good. But you must wait, I think. I have many wives. My lodge is crowded. Maybe next winter, when the winds come and I need big woman like you to keep me warm. For now, only fifty cows do I need to satisfy my women and the people of my band."

"Fifty?"

He nodded vigorously.

"I say thirty."

"Forty-five."

"Forty."

"That is good," the chief said. "Forty."

Little Raven wheeled his horse and galloped back toward his braves. It did not take long for them to cut out the forty steers. Lashing at them with rawhide thongs, the Arapaho braves drove them back across the river and soon disappeared.

Tolliver and two other hands were on the ground beside Frank. Tolliver glanced up at Kate.

"Frank's been hurt bad, Kate. He'll have to ride in your wagon."

Kate was too upset to reply. But she knew they had no alternative. Grimly she nodded her assent.

What was that about bad pennies?

PART THREE
Abilene

Chapter Sixteen

First the buffalo. Now this. Kristen had no trouble believing in their luck. It was that bad.

For three full days the four of them had been forced to keep within a watery thicket alongside a narrow stream while an enormous herd of buffalo rumbled across the plains from east to west, turning the thicket into an island of green surrounded by a black sea of horns, humps, and clotted tails. In addition, moving calmly along with this vast buffalo herd were smaller herds of horses, elk, deer, antelope, wild cattle—even wolves. A real peaceable kingdom, Kristen had told herself.

And now there was this damned buffalo hunter.

He and his pack of skinners had come along as

soon as the herd had passed, setting up their camp at the fringe of the thicket. The wagons, piled high with still wet, rotting hides stank so bad that she and Estrellita had been able to smell them before they came into sight. In his train the hunter had eleven carts in all, two of them already filled to overflowing with buffalo hides.

As Kristen pulled out of the thicket she tried to avoid the hunter and his skinners; but her wagon had been spotted as soon as it had reached the flat. Shouts from the skinners came first; then the hunter sent a rifle shot into the air. Pancho and Esteban reined in immediately, and Kristen, muttering in frustration, hauled back on the mules.

Now, keeping out of sight inside the wagon with Estrellita, Kristen watched through a tiny hole in the canvas as a tall, bearded hunter approached, rifle in hand. He was wearing a flat-crowned plains hat and filthy, blood-soaked buckskins. His skinners followed behind him, smelling almost as bad as they looked.

Kristen called softly to Pancho, who was standing with Esteban beside the mules. "Go with them. Drink all you want. But tell them nothing about us or you won't get any of this gold—*they* will!"

"*Si!*" a very nervous Pancho whispered back.

The two Mexicans left the wagon and hurried

toward the hunter, who halted to wait for them. The conversation between Pancho and the hunter was brief, and at its conclusion the hunter pushed impatiently past him and continued on toward the wagon.

Stepping up onto its seat, he peered inside.

One look at Kristen—Estrellita crouched behind her—and the hunter swung back around to glare at Pancho and Esteban.

"What in hell's goin' on here!"

The skinners crowded around the wagon. One swarthy fellow who stank like rotten meat stepped up onto the seat beside the hunter and looked hungrily at Estrellita. The others behind him crowded around, looking into the cart in wide-eyed wonder at what the two Mexicans had just tried to hide from them.

Pancho, with Esteban right behind him, hurried back to the wagon. "What ees thees you want?" Pancho asked. "Thees woman are our wives!"

"You mean that blonde's married to *you*?" the hunter demanded, incredulous.

"Si, señor!"

"Hell, I don't believe it! You two're up to something! Where in hell are you taking these women?"

At that Estrellita jumped out of the wagon and planted herself between Pancho and Esteban. Arms akimbo, eyes flashing, she let go in Spanish with a stream of pure invective. Not a word of it was intelligible to the hunter, but he understood her message. He backed up hastily. Sensing her opportunity, Kristen clambered down beside Estrellita and let loose every choice Mexican invective she could recall.

It was enough. The hunter and his skinners backed away, willing to concede that it was possible for two cringing, unwholesome Mexicans to have such shapely wives—even if one of them was a blonde.

But as Esteban and Pancho were about to mount up, the hunter draped an arm over Pancho's shoulder and invited him and Esteban to join them in a drink. Pancho took off his huge sombrero and bowed in gratitude for this show of hospitality. A moment later he and Esteban disappeared behind the hunter's circle of wagons with the hunter and his men.

"I don't like it," said Estrellita. "Why they want Pancho and Esteban to drink weeth them?"

"To get them drunk."

"Why?"

"You know why."

"I think maybe we better get out of here."

"I think so too. We'll load what we can onto the horses and leave the mules and the wagon. Then we'd better keep to the river bottom until we're a good distance from here."

As soon as it was dark, they proceeded to pack as much of their provisions as they could onto the backs of the two horses. While they worked, the hunter and his skinners built up a huge camp fire. Before long their wild laughter rang out lustily through the night.

Hearing this, both women redoubled their efforts. When men drank in this fashion, there were no secrets between them. It would not be long before the two Mexicans revealed to their new friends that Kristen and Estrellita were not their wives and that they carried two saddlebags bulging with gold and jewels.

While Estrellita finished filling the canteens, Kristen tied the saddlebags down securely. A particularly loud burst of laughter prompted them to pull the horses hastily back into the brush along the riverbank. Then they hitched up their skirts and mounted. They looked back. The big camp fire was still leaping skyward, and from behind one of the wagons a skinner stepped into view. Then came a second, staggering slightly and holding up a jug. The rest, equally boisterous, followed close behind.

"Here they come!" whispered Estrellita.

"Looks like we're only a step ahead of them," Kristen remarked grimly.

"Come, Kristen! We go now!"

Kristen did not argue. She dug her heels into her horse's flanks. Estrellita did the same, and they rode back toward the river, their horses plunging through the heavy growth of grass and underbrush without slowing. Just before they reached the water, they heard the sudden cries of the men as they discovered that Kristen and Estrellita were gone. Bent grimly over their horses now, the two women pressed on through the dark underbrush. When they reached the stream, they moved out into the middle and splashed downstream through the shallow water.

Suddenly there came from behind them the high, yelping cries of a Kiowa war party. Kristen's scalp prickled. She recognized the Kiowa battle cries from the many attacks they and their Comanche allies had made upon her home.

"Hide!" Kristen called to Estrellita.

They turned their horses and splashed ashore. Dismounting quickly, they pulled the horses over the solid ground until they reached a thicket. Then, after some desperate struggling, they managed to pull the horses off their feet and keep them on the ground beside them. Huddled behind the mounts, they kept their hands close to the horse's snouts to prevent them from winnying if a Kiowa rode too close.

Three mounted Kiowa warriors in full war paint and regalia galloped up the river past them, *ki-yi*-ing like fiends newly sprung from hell. Soon the night resounded with the pounding of unshod hooves as the Kiowa spread out to look for still more victims on both sides of the stream. One mounted Kiowa charged across the river, vanishing into a clump of birch not fifty feet away, the sound of his horse crashing through the brush fading rapidly.

Meanwhile the sky in the direction of the wagons was lit by a growing fire as the skinners' wagons went up. More cries followed, but these were different from those emitted by the Kiowas. These cries came from the throats of the hunter and his skinners as the Kiowa braves went to work on them.

And perhaps Pancho and Esteban as well.

The screaming, howling, and hoarse pleadings continued, while mounted Indians rode back and forth through the breaks, searching for more victims. Kristen was sure they were looking for the white women who owned the feminine property left behind in the wagon. Had this attack come during the day, Kristen knew, the Kiowa would have had no difficulty at all in tracking them. Clutching their little derringers, they kept their heads down and prayed.

It was close to dawn when Kristen heard someone crashing through the brush downstream. She and Estrellita peered in that direction. The moonlight was strong enough for them to see it was Pancho. Hatless, his head a bloody mess, he came staggering out of the brush on the far side of the stream. Reaching the bank, he flung himself into the water and began paddling feebly.

Before Kristen could stop her, Estrellita jumped up. "Over here, Pancho! Hurry!"

Hearing her, Pancho began striding blindly through the shallow water toward her, Kristen, furious, pulled Estrellita down.

"Fool!" she hissed. "He'll bring the Kiowa right to us!"

"But eet is Pancho! They will kill heem!"

"And us!"

The sudden drum-beat of hoofs warned them. They ducked low. Down the center of the shallow stream rode a Kiowa, his pony kicking up a bright spray of moonlit water. The Indian had spotted Pancho and was heading straight for him. Hearing him coming, Pancho flung himself around and began to stumble back to the shore.

The Kiowa swung down his lance and, as Kristen watched in horror, caught Pancho in the small of his back, running him clean through. Still urging his pony on at full speed, the Kiowa used his lance to lift Pancho's skewered body and slam him down over his pony's neck. Uttering a high, piercing cry of triumph, the Kiowa swung out of the stream and galloped off toward the burning wagons.

"You see!" breathed Kristen, furious. "Another second and that Kiowa would have discovered us!"

Estrellita was petrified. Tears streamed down

THE TEXAN

her face. She did not have to be told how close they had just come to being taken.

"You are right. I am sorry. But how can we stay here anymore? We must get away from here!"

"No, we must wait! The Kiowa are all around us. They know we're here somewhere. As soon as we make a move, they'll catch us. Keep quiet and stay down!"

Obediently Estrellita nodded and crouched back down behind her horse.

Kristen had no difficulty understanding how Estrellita felt. Even though she had never had anything good to say about Pancho, he had been their companion of sorts, and she was not completely without feeling. Kristen, too, had been sickened by the sight of that Kiowa's barbarous act. But if they were to avoid capture by the Kiowa, they had to think only of themselves.

As Kristen knew only too well, death was infinitely preferable to capture by these savages.

The looting and burning of the carts went on unabated through the rest of that terrible night. But it was the sound of the tortured men that affected Kristen the most, for as the night wore on, the Kiowa braves warmed to their task. The sobbing cries and whoops of pain they drew from their victims rose to an awful crescendo.

Kristen tried to block out the horror of it by

pressing her hands over her ears. But then, fearful that this would make her unable to detect any savage creeping up on them, she pulled her hands away. She had no alternative, it seemed. She was forced to hear every panting scream, and though she fought against it, she found herself reliving that terrible night when her father had died.

There were those in the East, Kristen realized bitterly, who saw in these mounted plains-warriors a stirring band of glorious, freedom-loving hunters. In the poetry and novels they wrote, these Easterners portrayed the plains tribes as noble children of nature following a way of life they themselves wished they could emulate. To such romantic fools the plains Indians were a testament to the joy and natural goodness that could be found only close to nature.

But Kristen knew differently, as did every citizen of Texas who ever had the misfortune to come upon these Indians while they were displaying their plumed, full-throated savagery. To Kristen they were nothing more than insane children at such times. How else could anyone describe those whose greatest joy, it seemed, was to torture innocent men, women, and children to death?

It was close to dawn when the Kiowa band let loose a series of high-pitched yells. A moment later came the swiftly receding thunder of their ponies as they rode off to the south, the same direction the buffalo herd had taken. For a long while, well after the thunder of their hooves had faded into the early-morning stillness, neither woman dared believe in their good luck.

Slowly, cautiously, they stood up. Dawn was a faint red streak on the eastern horizon. Letting their horses up, they mounted them and rode across the river, then cut upstream until they came abreast of the hunter's camp, then rode cautiously toward it until they could see the smoldering wagons ahead of them through the trees.

Cautiously they peered out through the willows and beech at the devastation. Two small Indian ponies were grazing some distance away, along with one of the mules and a swaybacked gray. Evidently the Kiowa did not think they were worth taking with them.

The wagon belonging to the hunter had not been completely destroyed. Only a portion of its canvas top had been burned away. In the pale early-morning light, Kristen saw someone bound to its front wheel, his bloody, scalped head hanging forward. And on the ground surrounding the hunter's wagon the mutilated bodies of the skinners had been staked out.

But not all of them were dead. Kristen could hear a few of them moaning softly, feebly. Their pitiful cries seemed to come from the very blood-soaked earth itself.

"We go now?" Estrellita said hopefully.

"No."

"Why not?"

"Listen. Can't you hear them?"

Estrellita turned her head slightly, then glanced, frowning, at Kristen. *"Madre de Dios!"* she whispered in dismay. "Some of the men! They must still be alive!"

"We must help them."

"How can we help them?"

"Put them out of their misery."

"But, Kristen...!"

"We would do the same thing for a horse, wouldn't we?"

"But...how do we do such a thing?"

"We have derringers."

Estrellita sighed. "All right, you crazy gringo. But you go first, *por favor*!"

Kristen nudged her horse out of the thicket and rode into the burned-out encampment. As she glanced around, she found herself reluctant to dismount. Spread below her on the bloody grass, like a scene from Dante's *Inferno,* were souls in torment.

Only two men remained alive. One gasped his last breath as they rode closer. The only other man still alive was the one Kristen had seen hanging from the wagon wheel. Dismounting, she approached him slowly. His groans echoed from the very bottom of his soul. Kristen placed her hand under the man's chin and lifted his face.

It was the buffalo hunter.

Since this was the man who had directed the slaughter of their buffalo, the Kiowa had saved their greatest skill for him. Careful not to sever anything vital, they had sliced and peeled and cut with the prowess of surgeons trained in hell. The hunter's eyelids had been torn off; skin hung from his naked torso in long, raw strips. The Kiowa had made certain that though he must eventually die from his wounds, his death would come slowly—primarily of exposure, a truly terrible death.

He looked unblinkingly at Kristen, his mouth hanging open. He had no tongue left, only a stump so that when he moved his mouth to speak, nothing came out but a terrible, whining groan. Then he caught sight of the derringer in Kristen's hand, and she saw at once that he gratefully understood what she was about to do.

Behind Kristen, Estrellita dismounted and walked closer, her derringer in her hand. She gasped in dismay when she saw what remained of the hunter.

"He wants me to kill him," Kristen whispered to Estrellita. "I can tell he does."

"Then do it...."

Kristen let the man's head sag forward. Then she straightened and released the safety on her derringer. Cocking it, she aimed at a spot just above his ear, turned her head, and squeezed the trigger. She felt the faint spray of his blood on her wrist and quickly pulled her hand away. The other side of the hunter's head had exploded outward. Bloody particles of his brain were smeared on the side of the wagon.

Kristen thought she was going to be sick. But she didn't have time for that. Estrellita screamed. A shadow fell across Kirsten. Glancing up, she saw a Kiowa brave looming over her from inside the wagon. Stumbling back, she raised her derringer and fired.

The round caught the Indian in his chest. He glanced down at her in amazement, then toppled back into the wagon. Another Kiowa came at Kristen from the other side of the wagon, an upraised hatchet in his right hand. Kristen's derringer was empty. She turned and ran—just as Estrellita fired her own derringer.

Kristen heard the Indian hit the ground and, turning, saw Estrellita aim carefully down at the fallen savage, brace herself, and fire a second time.

Two weeks later, leading their gaunt horses across a broad, undulating sweep of grassland, they caught sight of a troop of cavalry on the horizon. The troopers were heading west, sunlight winking off their sabers. Shouting futilely at the distant formation, they mounted up and spurred their exhausted horses after them; but the poor brutes were soon close to foundering, and the two women were forced to jump off in order to save them. Slumping miserably down on the grass, they watched the thin line of troops vanish.

It was Kristen who spoke first. "Anyway, they weren't Kiowa or Comanche."

"Which way do we go now?" Estrellita sighed.

"East. In the direction those troopers were coming from. There must be a fort nearby. We can maybe get fresh horses there and buy what we need to continue on to Kansas."

"What you say make sense, but I think maybe God want us to walk all the way."

"First thing is to get out of this heat."

"Maybe it will rain," Estrellita said, glancing ironically up at the cloudless blue sky.

Kristen smiled wearily. "Come on. We can't stay here."

Two hours later, pulling their horses along under the blistering noonday heat, they saw a long cloud moving across the prairie. The closer it got, the darker it looked. Kristen knew at once what she was seeing—smoke from a locomotive. Still, no matter how hard they strained their eyes, they could not see the engine.

The smoke vanished behind a series of hillocks. They waited for it to reappear; but with the exception of a faint dusting of gray on the western horizon, the smoke from the locomotive never reappeared.

"Now what?" Estrellita asked.

"That's easy. That train was running on tracks. We'll just find the tracks and follow them east."

It was close to dusk when they finally reached the tracks. Patches of the prairie alongside them were burned black, Kristen noticed, as if the passing trains were spreading a sickness into the surrounding grass. For a moment Kristen was puzzled, until she realized what it was—sparks from the steam engine's smokestack were igniting the grass. She was surprised that the entire expanse of sun-browned grass had not already burned. Perhaps it was too early, she concluded. Later in the summer, when the grass was like tinder, it would be a different story.

"I would prefer a water hole," Estrellita muttered as she gazed up and down the shining rails that extended in unbroken lines toward both horizons.

"If we keep going along these tracks, we'll find better than that."

"What do you mean?"

"These trains run on steam—and that means water. Pretty soon we'll come to a water tank."

"How long will that take?"

THE TEXAN

Kristen shrugged. "We just have to stay on these tracks."

Without any more discussion they set out eastward, staying alongside the tracks.

They kept going until dusk when they found they could not trudge a step more. On a hillock close to the tracks they unsaddled their horses in the gathering darkness and made a miserable dry camp, eating what remained of their sourdough biscuits. They had long since run out of grain for their horses, and for the past few weeks Kristen had made heroic use of her fishhook. There were plenty of grasshoppers around, and every clear stream they came upon furnished them with fresh fish, which Kristen dressed with her bone-handled knife and cooked over glowing coals.

But in the past week they had not come across a single stream; and during this day's trek alongside the gleaming rails, they had gulped down the last drops of water remaining in their canteens.

As Kristen fell asleep, she had visions of a cool stream shaded by oaks and willows....

She awoke with the ground trembling violently under her. Her heart in her mouth, Kristen sat bolt upright. A locomotive, belching fire and smoke, tore past them, devouring the night as it followed the beam of its single, powerful lamp. The underside of the smoke plume was crimson with fire reflected from the boiler's open door. For a split second Kristen could see the fireman tossing wood into the roaring flames. Then the great black engine was past them, showering sparks, igniting patches of grass all around her.

They were both on their feet by this time, jumping and yelling crazily as a long line of flatbed cars and finally a caboose whipped past them. A few seconds later the train vanished into the night, leaving them more alone than ever. They collapsed futilely back down onto their blankets, staring dismally after the train.

"Maybe it is better if we sleep on tracks," Estrellita muttered. "Then maybe they see us."

"Don't talk silly."

"I am so thirsty, Kristen. I dream of water—and wine."

"Just water would do me for now, thank you."

Kristen slumped back against her saddle, then glanced away from the tracks down the far side of the knoll, expecting to see their two horses grazing where they had left them. They were not there. As far as she could see over the rippling, moonlit surface of the grassland, there was no sign of either horse.

She nudged Estrellita.

"What is it?"

"The horses are gone."

"Mother of God!" Estrellita cried, jumping up to scan the grasslands around them.

THE TEXAN

"The train must have frightened them."

"We did not think to hobble them," Estrellita admitted dispiritedly.

"We were too tired."

"Yes."

"Who would have thought in their condition they could gallop so far in such a short time."

"If we find them, they will not be alive, I think," Estrellita said. "To bolt like that was bad for them. It was their last run, I think. I could count their ribs."

Kristen nodded and lay back, feeling for the two saddlebags under her saddle. At least they had not lost the gold and jewels.

She slept.

She was awakened by the bright sun, sweat trickling down her temple and into the hollow of her neck. Shaking herself, she sat up, using her forearm to shade her eyes from the already fierce sun. Estrellita was still asleep. Kristen reached over and prodded her.

Without the horses they would have to bury the saddles and the rest of their gear nearby. Kristen dug a hole under the tough bunch grass with her knife, and there they hid the saddles. Farther up, at Estrellita's suggestion, Kristen dug another hole for the two saddlebags. Estrellita then took Kristen's knife and carved two deep crosses in the cross ties, bracketing the spot where they had buried the saddles and the two saddlebags.

By that time the sun was well above the horizon. They set out once more, following the tracks east. By noon they were staggering, but they kept on. Then Kristen saw it in the distance. A huge water tank shimmering alongside the tracks.

"You see!" Kristen cried through cracked lips. "There it is! The water tank for the trains!"

Estrellita did not question it; she just hurried on, gasping. But the distance was cruelly deceptive. They walked forever, it seemed. The water tank did not get any closer.

And then suddenly the tank was in front of them, looming up out of the ground, less than two hundred yards ahead. Kristen could see the wooden seams in its side and make out clearly the long, folding canvas hose that carried the water to the thirsty engines. But by this time she found herself fighting a painful stitch in her side and did not see how she could go on.

Estrellita stopped and sat down. Kristen pulled to a halt and stared down at her.

"Why not wait here until it gets cooler," Estrellita said to her.

"That's crazy, Estrellita."

Estrellita nodded slowly. She knew it was crazy, but she no longer had the strength even to respond.

Kristen heard distant shouts. Focusing her eyes,

THE TEXAN

she saw men gesturing wildly as they ran down the tracks toward them. Kristen tried to wave back. But she could not lift her arms; she could only collapse beside Estrellita.

She dimly remembered the feel of strong hands lifting her, and when Kristen awoke, Estrellita was lying in a bunk across a narrow aisle from her. Then she felt the cool edge of a tin cup against her mouth. A man wearing a green eyeshade was gently pressing water to her lips. As she gulped the water down gratefully she became aware of a steady, clacking sound coming from under her bunk. She was on a train!

"Where..." she managed between gulps of the water, "...are we going?"

"You just rest now," the man said. "You're goin' to be all right."

"But where are you taking us?"

"Never you fret, Goldie," the fellow said, refilling the cup and lifting it to her lips again. "We're heading for Abilene Town."

Chapter Seventeen

Kate was having a nightmare. She had just stepped off an outside stairway and could feel the wooden steps behind her in the darkness. Before her yawned the mouth of a back alley—as black and menacing as a rifle bore. Then she saw someone with a lantern coming through the alley toward her. The figure looked familiar—achingly familiar. Hurrying forward, she saw that it was Nils. With a cry she ran toward him.

Nils stopped, his lean, handsome face mournful.

"Nils!" she cried, reaching out to him. "You're alive!"

He stepped back in horror, as if touching her would defile him. "Ma," he demanded, "where's Pa? I can't find him! I've looked everywhere!"

"Your pa's dead! The Comanche killed him."

"I don't believe you, Ma. What happened to Pa? Where is he?"

He looked past her hopefully. She reached out to him again. But Nils ignored her outstretched hand and brushed past her.

"I'm going to find Pa," he told her.

"No, wait!" she cried, running after him. But before she could reach him, he opened a door, stepped through, and vanished. She tried to open the door, but it was locked. She collapsed to the alley floor, sobbing.

When she awoke, every sense was alert, her back crawling with perspiration. The hot sun poured down on the wagon's canvas top. It was late. Why had she not been awakened before this? Shaking off what shards of the nightmare still clung to her, she sat up and looked around.

Tolliver had been standing outside. When he heard her sit up, he poked his head into the wagon. "You was sleepin' too hard for me to wake you," he said.

"Give me a few minutes, Tolliver."

He nodded. "I'll be over by the camp fire. There's still some coffee left."

"Sent Ned ahead," Tolliver said, as Kate finished her coffee. "We're close to that cattle town, but I don't think we should go stormin' in with this much cattle—not till we got some idea of where we're supposed to go."

"I agree."

Kate looked around her at the herd. The cattle were on their feet now, grazing calmly. A couple of weeks before, not long after they crossed the Cimarron, she would not have given ten cents for their chances of getting this far.

Because of the unusually dry weather and the fact that they were slanting onto the Chisolm trail from the southwest, they were forced to drive the herd over a stretch of nearly forty miles without water. They did it without stopping, driving the herd on for two days and a night. It had not been easy. At one point the cows had been so crazed with thirst, they had begun to mill helplessly, attempting to go back to the last water they remembered.

Yet somehow the men managed to keep them going, and when the poor, half-blind critters finally reached the stream, they waded into it, moaning and lowing, and waited—some for half an hour—before allowing themselves to satisfy their thirst. Even then they drank only small amounts, after which they calmly waded ashore on the other side and began to graze.

Through it all, the men had been magnificent. Never out of the saddle for longer than it took to change to fresh mounts, they lived almost entirely on black coffee. Once or twice Kate saw a few of them rubbing tobacco juice into their eyes to keep themselves awake. Looking back on that incredible drive, Kate shuddered to think how they would have managed had Frank been the trail boss.

Which reminded her. She looked at Tolliver. "How's Frank?"

"About the same. But it ain't him I'm worried about. It's Herman. He don't mind cookin', but he sure hates to be a jailer. And he takes an awful lot of abuse from Frank."

"I can imagine."

"It just ain't easy to keep Frank tied up. Some of the men don't like it, either. They're sayin' maybe you should let Frank go. He's well enough to ride now."

"He's a cattle rustler and a would-be murderer. He's going to pay for that—either here or in Texas."

Tolliver said nothing more. But Kate could feel his disapproval, just as she could feel it from almost every man in her crew—with the exception of Ned. Behind her back they called her what Little Raven had called her—Iron Woman—but it was not meant as a compliment. It was intended to convey that Kate had no feelings, that she was a woman who could deal a white man to an Indian as easily as a riverboat gambler could an ace.

Just then Kate heard a faint shout. Looking

around, she saw a rider approaching at full gallop. It was Ned. As he galloped closer, he waved his hat frantically from side to side.

"Abilene!" she heard him crying. *"Abilene!"*

Kate turned to Tolliver and smiled. "It looks like we made it!"

"Yes, it does at that, Kate," he replied, grinning at her.

Not long afterward, two men from Abilene rode up, halting before Kate's wagon. They introduced themselves and were told to dismount. Both wore derbies and starched shirts with string ties knotted at their throats. A thin patina of dust lay on their hats and shoulders. They were smiling happily, obviously pleased to see so much beef.

The biggest of the two men was Henry Reed. His companion was Sam Mabry. It was Reed who spoke first. Looking at Tolliver, he said, "Would you be the drover, Mr. Tolliver?"

Tolliver glanced at Kate.

"Guess *I* am," Kate told Reed.

"Then you'll be handling the sale of these cattle, Mrs. Nordstrom?"

"Don't see why not."

Looking around at the trail herd, Reed's companion said, "My, it sure is nice to see all this Texas cattle."

"It was kind of you to come out here to greet us."

"We've been appointed by Mr. McCoy," said Mabry. "This here is the third herd in a week. And there's other trail herds moving up behind you, two from Fort Worth."

"You goin' to have enough room for all this beef?" Tolliver asked.

Reed laughed heartily. "Don't you worry none about that. We got pens aplenty."

"Shall we drive the herd right in?" Tolliver asked.

"That's one of the reasons we rode out," said Reed. "For now it would be best if you bedded your cattle down on the other side of the tracks, north of Abilene. There's plenty of grass there. By this time tomorrow we'll be able to handle your herd. We'll need your crew, though, to help drive the steer up the chutes and into the railcars."

Kate nodded. "What's the going rate?"

Reed looked at Mabry, who shrugged. "Guess it don't matter none if we let that out," he said. "We got buyers waitin' in the Drover's Cottage payin' close to forty dollars a head."

Kate could hardly believe it. She tried not to show her surprise. Glancing at Tolliver, she saw the cattleman calmly take off his hat, then mop his brow with a gentle, dabbing motion.

"We'll need help finding that bedding ground you mentioned," Kate told Reed.

"Our pleasure, ma'am," Reed said, mounting back up. "All you have to do is follow us. Soon's you're ready."

As the two men rode off to look over the cattle, Tolliver, grinning slyly, looked at Kate. "I still don't believe them figures."

"Makes it all worthwhile, don't it?"

"It sure does."

Ned Perkins moved closer. He had been standing within earshot and had heard everything. He was grinning too. Everyone in Texas who worked cattle knew what forty dollars a head meant.

Kate looked at Ned. "Cut Frank loose," she told him. "Tell him he's a free man—and tell him to move out fast. I don't want to have to look at him."

"You sure you want to do that, Kate?"

"I know how you feel, Ned. And I don't blame you. But right now all I want is to get that skunk out of my sight. We'll be in Abilene soon, and we won't want to be hauling that son of a bitch around with us everywhere we go."

"All right, Miss Kate."

As Ned disappeared, Tolliver looked pleased. "A smart move, that," he told her. "It'll make the boys feel better. Hell, we got here—and you'll be rid of Frank at last. Makes sense to me."

It made sense to Kate too. But at the same time she wondered how she could ever really get rid of Frank Kilrain.

* * *

That same night Bart and Nils—dust-covered and weary—rode into Abilene.

They came in past the acres of pens filled with bawling cattle. Long lines of railcars sent them back in the direction of the prairie in order to reach Abilene's broad main street. The town was growing fast, Bart could see, many of the buildings sided with fresh, unpainted lumber. Signs of bustling prosperity were everywhere.

It was past eleven, but the saloons were still open. The fast, bouncy tinkle of pianos filled the night, along with occasional shrieks of female laughter. On their way past the pens Bart sighted the red-light district, a place of rambling shacks and tents, its streets filled with swaggering knots of cowboys pulled along by their female friends. Every now and then the dance-hall music and shouts of laughter were punctuated by gunshots as some inebriated cowboy let loose at the moon.

Above some of the darkened stores on Texas Street, lighted rooms shone brightly, the windows open, laughter drifting down. Hotels and rooming houses of every size and description lined the narrow side streets. But as Bart and Nils rode on by, it was clear that many of the drovers and businessmen of the town were taking their pleasure in the center of Abilene, along the wide Texas Street.

"We need clothes," Nils called over to Bart.

Bart nodded. "And soon. If we stood our pants up, they'd run away."

"Wish they would."

Bart looked around, hoping to find a clothing store open, even at this late hour. As they approached Henry H. Hazlett's Farmer's and Drover's Supply Store, Bart was pleased to see it was still open for business.

Dismounting in front of it, they dropped their reins over the hitch rack and entered. They were greeted amiably enough by the owner, a small man with a tape measure around his neck. He looked very tired but not too tired to take their money.

As the two men brought over to the counter the fresh duds they had purchased, Hazlett cleared his throat. "Are you with that new herd waiting outside of town?"

"Which herd would that be?" Bart asked.

"The one from the Brazos country."

In the act of handing Hazlett two shirts and a pair of Levi's jeans, Bart paused and regarded the man more closely. "Brazos country, you say?"

"Why, yes. I believe so."

Bart was not surprised. But he was pleased. He and Nils had stopped at a little place called Newton, south of Abilene, and while there they had learned of a trail herd from the Brazos country that had passed by a week earlier on its

THE TEXAN

way to Abilene. The two men had pushed hard to overtake it—and it looked as if they had.

"Who's the trail boss?" Bart asked, just to make sure.

"Fellow name of Perkins. He rode in here this morning. All excited, he was."

Bart frowned. "Not Frank Kilrain?"

"No, sir. I don't believe so."

Bart was astonished. He wondered if it had been Indians or a falling-out with Kate that had finished Frank. He was also disappointed. He had come a long way to settle with Frank Kilrain.

"Who's the drover?"

"A woman, I believe." The man spoke as if he disapproved of a woman making the trip north with a trail herd—and all those men.

His voice reflecting his eagerness, Nils asked quickly, "And would that woman's name be Kate Nordstrom?"

"I believe so. Kate something or other."

"Is she in town?"

"She rode in with a cattleman this evening. A Mr. Tolliver Adams. They are registered at the Drover's Cottage."

Nils looked at Bart, his face glowing with expectation. How many long years had it been since he had last seen his mother? Close to seven, Bart figured. Nils turned back to the clothing counters, plucking from them a shirt and a pair of Levi's jeans in such a hurry that he paid little attention to price or style.

Bart asked the store owner, "Where can a man get a bath at this time of night?"

"The Abilene Tonsorial Parlor."

"The what?"

Henry Hazlett smiled. "The barbershop across the street, about a block down from the Alamo."

The Alamo, Bart figured, was a saloon or a gambling hall. He nodded his thanks to the store owner and finished making his selections.

"Doesn't this town ever go to sleep?"

Henry Hazlett smiled. "Not when there are flush cowboys from Texas in town."

When the rap came on her hotel door, Kate was sleeping so deeply that she almost refused to wake up—until the knocking assumed a nightmarish exaggeration, like a giant striding angrily toward her. She awoke with a start, the knock coming again, insistently.

"Who is it?" she called.

She knew it could not be Tolliver. The man did not have that much imagination; besides, he was easily as bone-tired and weary as she was.

When there was no response to her call, she flung back the sheets irritably and lit the lamp on her nightstand. Her robe was on the coverlet; the slippers she had thought to bring were on the floor beside her bed.

THE TEXAN

The knock came again, more gently this time, but just as insistently. Tying the sash to her robe, she stepped into her slippers and started for the door. Maybe it was Ned Perkins come to tell her the herd had stampeded clear back to Texas.

Pausing before the door, she asked again, "Who is it?"

"Ma?"

She flung open the door. Nils reached out to her. Uttering a startled, incredulous cry, she clung to Nils as he walked her over to her bed. Holding his face between her hands, she knew it was no dream. Her son had come back to her from the grave!

And at that moment Kate saw Seth staring out at her from Nils's face.

Chapter Eighteen

Stepping outside of the dress shop she had purchased a week ago, Kristen squinted in the bright sunlight, then went back inside for a broom. She called her dress shop Goldie's, the name given her by the railroad men who had brought her and Estrellita into Abilene. For almost a week afterward Kristen's account of their journey from the New Mexico Territory had created a sensation. By now, however, their notoriety was a thing of the past. The steady stream of trail herds flowing up from Texas was now the only news worth discussing.

Her eyes were smarting from the close work she had been doing for the past two hours. She was attempting to make a dress, two sizes too small, fit the wife of the biggest cattle broker in town. More than once she had almost given up on the impossible alterations, but nevertheless she kept at it. She needed this commission to make a success of the shop.

She kept the wooden walk in front of her store cleanly swept, not only because it needed it but also because it got her away from her sewing machine. Her ankles were sore from the foot treadle, and she had already broken two needles and sent a third clear through her thumb.

She paused now and then in her sweeping to peer at the men swarming past her shop. She knew that one of these trail herds now pouring into Abilene could be coming from the Brazos country. If so, she might meet someone she knew. Someone named Bart.

As if thinking of Bart could conjure him out of thin air, there he was, across the street, Kristen's mother and a rancher she recognized as Tolliver Adams striding along beside him. For a crazy moment her heart leapt at the sight of Bart and her mother; she almost dropped her broom and rushed across the street.

A cold, instant, bitter appraisal of the situation stopped her. She had already said good-bye to Bart. Once was enough. And she wanted nothing more to do with her mother. Not after what she and her hired ranch foreman had done to her father.

She hurried back inside the store. Two women followed her in, twittering like happy birds at the sight of the new fabrics.

When Bart strolled through the glass doors into the Alamo, he was impressed. The walls were lined with mirrors, giving the place a sense of spaciousness the other saloons and gambling halls sorely lacked. Behind the bar the glass tumblers were arranged in spectacular pyramids, each shelf crammed with glittering bottles of whiskey, brandy, and rum.

Huge oil paintings of scantily draped nudes hung on the walls. Some of the ladies were bathing; others were riding horses. This amorous splendor seemed to have the required effect on its male patrons. As Bart pushed through the crush of newly-affluent cowboys, he saw that most of them were filled with scamper juice and were more than eager to drink, fight, or gamble. Each had a dance-hall girl clinging to his arm, cheering him on as he bent over a crap or faro table—or ordered another round. Though a small army of bouncers prowled through the place to keep the roisters from getting out of hand and the noise level down, the lone musician banging away at the piano on a platform in the rear barely could be heard above the steady wash of laughter and shouting.

Bart stepped up to the bar and asked for a

THE TEXAN

bottle of whiskey. He glanced idly at a nearby gaming table and saw heavy gold coins rolling loosely over the green baize. He supposed that he could try his luck at one of the games—faro, perhaps. Or maybe a game of poker. He also supposed it would not be a very good idea.

The previous day, the deal for the herd had been closed, and Kate Nordstrom had given him his share of the sale. He was a poor man no longer. But he heard of some cattlemen from Texas who had already lost all they owned on the single flip of a card in this and other gambling halls lining Texas Street. Bart wanted no part of such foolishness. His mother and Dan O'Hare deserved better.

He paid for his bottle of whiskey and took it with him to a table in the back along the wall. No sooner was he comfortable than one of the Alamo's girls came over. She seemed concerned that he was sitting alone and asked if there was anything he wanted to play—including her, he gathered. He thanked her and said no, and as she got up from his table, obviously disappointed, Bart glanced past her and saw Estrellita hurrying toward him.

"Well! The *tejano*!" she cried. "He is here!"

"Join me, Estrellita," Bart said quickly, pushing out a chair for her. She was dressed as scantily and as gaudily as the other girls, but

333

her dark complexion and brilliant eyes made her something special.

She sat down quickly, her eyes gleaming as she took him in. It was obvious she had found a home in Abilene Town.

"Where's Kristen?" Bart asked.

She pushed an empty glass toward the bottle and pouted. "You see, it is always the same. Every time I am with you, it is this golden-haired one you sigh for. My feelings, they are very hurt."

"Come on," Bart said, filling her glass. "I know she left Tule with you. Where is she?"

"I do not think I want to tell you."

"Dammit, Estrellita. I've been looking all over Abilene for her. When I didn't find her, I figured either you hadn't got here yet or something might've happened to you two."

"It did, *tejano*. Very much." She shuddered and threw the whiskey down, then wiped her rouged mouth with the back of her hand.

"Is Kristen here?"

"Yes. She is here."

"Where?"

"She has a dress shop."

"A what?"

Estrellita nodded. "It is not far from here."

"Maybe you better explain."

Pushing her empty glass toward the bottle, Estrellita waited for Bart to fill it, then began her tale, her eyes bright with excitement. She obviously had told the story many times since arriving in Abilene. She left out nothing, including the incident with the Kiowa war party and how Kristen had ended the life of the unhappy buffalo hunter—and Estrellita's climactic execution of the second Kiowa.

Her story finished, she leaned forward. "There is more to tell," Estrellita said. "But this we tell nobody."

"I'm listening."

"Before we come to Abilene, when we near the railroad track, we bury Kristen's gold. Later we ride out and bring it back to Abilene. This is how Kristen have enough to start her store. And still we have money left."

"I see." Bart leaned back in his chair. "Well, that's some story, Estrellita."

"It ees all true, *tejano!*"

"I don't doubt it for a moment."

"Now I tell you something else."

Bart filled his glass and waited.

"Kristen does not want to see you. She knows you are here. She say she see you on the street with her mother. But she tell me it is all over between you and her. She says she have told you this already."

"Yes, she did. But I know she still loves me, Estrellita."

Estrellita shrugged. "That make no difference

to this woman. She has no heart, no warmth. I can see it."

"You said the same thing once before."

"And now I know it is true. Something else I know, something bad."

Bart said nothing as he waited.

"Last night," she told him, her voice low, hushed, "I see Salvadore de Santos and Raoul ride into Abilene. I do not know where they are now, but they are in this town, *tejano*. I think maybe they come after Kristen."

"Or me."

She leaned back in her chair and regarded him solemnly. "Then I think maybe you better be careful. Already I have warn Kristen, and I will myself be very careful until they are gone. Maybe you should ride out too."

"Not until I have finished what I came here to finish." Bart leaned closer to Estrellita. "Now tell me, Estrellita. Where's this dress shop of Kristen's?"

Estrellita shrugged and told him.

Bart nudged the bottle toward her in thanks, got to his feet, and left the saloon.

Entering the dress shop, Bart saw Kristen at once. Hidden away in a nook at the back, her head was bent over a sewing machine. Bart paused a moment to take her in. As usual, the sight of her caused him to catch his breath. She was thinner than he remembered, and more beautiful than ever. She did not look up as he walked the length of the store, paused beside a clothes dummy, and cleared his throat.

Glancing up at the sudden noise, she sat back, letting the thread ball up under the working needle.

"Estrellita told me you were here," he said.

"I was afraid she would."

"Estrellita's doing fine in the Alamo. I think she'll make a fortune."

"She will if she can get herself to drink less."

Kristen was looking at him with both wonder and dismay on her face. "I knew you were here. I saw you yesterday. Across the street."

"And you made no effort to see me?"

She shrugged wearily. "I told you before. There's no chance for me with you—or any man."

"You'd better be ready to tell that to de Santos. He's in Abilene."

"I know. He was in here last night."

"Did you tell him I was in town?"

"No, I didn't."

"Are you going back with him?"

"What I do—or don't do—is my business, Bart."

She got up and walked past him. Picking up a card that read CLOSED, she hung it on the door and locked it.

"Then you're going to stay here in Abilene—in this dress shop?"

"It's working out for me, but I don't think it's what I want."

"Too confining."

"Yes, too confining."

"Kristen, what about your mother? I haven't told her that you're here. But you must have seen her with me yesterday. Do you know the torment she's gone through since you were taken by the Comanche?"

"I can imagine," she snapped.

"And you don't care?"

"Listen, Bart. I've not mentioned this to you before. But as far as I'm concerned, my mother is as guilty as Frank Kilrain for the death of my father."

"Now, how in hell do you figure that?"

"Pa was up on the porch, but they wouldn't let him in. They slammed the door on him. They said if they let Pa in, the Comanche would get in too. But I don't believe it. My mother chose Frank Kilrain over her husband. She saw her chance and took it."

"Kristen, you can't believe that."

"You weren't there. I was."

"There must be a better explanation. Sure, it might have looked that way to you at the time, but if those Comanche got a foot in that door, you wouldn't be here now to make this accusation."

"It doesn't matter. I don't want to see my

THE TEXAN

mother and that's that. Please, Bart, don't tell her I'm here."

"All right," he said. "You can unlock the door now."

She looked wearily through the front window and shrugged. "Maybe I'll close for the afternoon and go upstairs. I'm tired, Bart. Very tired."

"Just do me this one favor. Open the door. Please."

"Why?"

"I sent word for someone to meet me here, the fellow who rode into Abilene with me."

"Scott Tyrell?" she asked, walking toward the door.

"He's dead, Kristen."

"I'm sorry. You and he seemed to be such good friends."

"We were."

She took down the sign and unlocked the door, pulling it open.

Bart walked up to her, took her by the shoulders, and led her gently over to a chair.

"I got some news for you, Kristen."

But he never got a chance to tell it to her. Glancing past him, Kristen saw Nils striding into the shop. With a startled cry she jumped up. Breaking into a wide grin, Nils hurried toward her. Brushing past Bart, Kristen flung her arms around her brother, sudden tears of joy coursing down her cheeks.

Bart moved quickly past them and out the door.

Later that same day, as Bart carefully cleaned his big Walker Colt, Nils knocked on his door and entered.

Bart looked up from the Colt. "What's the matter, Nils? You don't look so good."

"That's because I don't feel so good."

"What is it?"

"Kristen."

Slumping wearily into a chair, Nils looked for a long, desolate moment at Bart, then said, "She says Ma killed my father."

"She told me the same thing, Nils."

"She must be crazy! Ma would never do a thing like that."

"She tell you about Frank Kilrain?"

"Yes, but I already know all about him. He's been sent packing now, and that's the end of it as far as I'm concerned."

"And you don't think your mother and Kilrain conspired to kill your father?"

"Of course not. Ma told me what happened. She already blames herself, and I don't imagine it's easy for her to live with it. But hell, Bart, I can imagine what it was like in that house with them Comanche charging up onto the porch, one step behind Pa. It must have been horrible—but why make it worse with this kind of talk?"

"You got my vote there, Nils."

Nils shook his head. "And Ma doesn't even know Kristen's here!"

"You going to tell her?"

"Kristen told me not to. And I promised her I wouldn't."

"I got a suggestion, Nils."

"I'm listening."

"Take Kate out to dinner tonight—to the Drover's Cottage."

"Go on."

"If you do, you might find me there ahead of you. You could join me. I might even have a dinner guest."

"Kristen?"

"Let's give it a try, Nils."

Hope sprang into Nils's eyes. "I'm willing, Bart. And thanks."

Nils left the room then, and Bart went back to cleaning the Walker.

It was only four in the afternoon, but already the town was alive with the clattering of hoofs and the hoots and hollers of drunken cowpokes bursting in and out of the saloons and gambling houses.

Bart tried the Red Dog first, asking the barkeep where he might find Salvador de Santos. Then he purchased a drink and found a table in a corner, his gleaming Walker Colt strapped to his waist. The word got around, as Bart knew it would, and quite a few cowpokes left the place with a quick glance in his direction.

An hour passed without incident. Bart left the place, crossed the street, and entered the Bull's Head. Again he bought himself a drink and asked the bartender if he had seen de Santos. This time Bart described the Mexican Comanchero in detail. He took another table, this one along the wall opposite the bar, and waited for longer than an hour this time, but again without success.

It was nearly six o'clock when he left the fourth saloon on his tour and headed for Kristen's store. Finding it closed, he mounted the outside wooden steps leading to her apartment over the store and knocked.

"Hello, Bart," Kristen said, pulling the door open. "Won't you come in?"

"My, how formal."

She smiled. "I have a guest."

Bart followed her into the small living room and saw de Santos sitting casually in the corner of Kristen's sofa, a glass of wine in his hand. He got up politely, smiling.

"We meet again, Señor Hardison."

"I've been looking for you."

"I know."

"I have a score to settle with you. You sent Raoul and his boys after me."

"Let us say, there was no way I could stop

Raoul. Like I warned you, he has a very long memory."

"I still hold you responsible."

De Santos smiled and shrugged. "I am unarmed. Raoul gave me your message. So here I am, *señor*. Kill me if you wish."

"Will you two shut up?" Kristen said, out of patience with both of them. "You sound like two little boys daring the other to cross a line in the dirt!"

Bart smiled at Kristen. Her words were right on the mark, he realized. He looked at de Santos. "Guess she's got a point there, de Santos. But where's Raoul?"

"I am surprised you did not see him. When he hear you go all over town looking for me, he went to find you."

"He couldn't have looked very far."

"He will find you, *señor*. I would not worry about that."

Bart looked at Kristen. "Kristen, I want you to have dinner with me."

"I'm sorry, Bart. As you can see, I have a guest. And we were talking of dinner ourselves just now."

"For old time's sake, Kristen," he told her. "I promise. It won't hurt you."

Kristen looked at Salvador.

"Go with him," de Santos told her. "It does not

matter." Then he glanced coolly at Bart, a thin smile on his face. "I will wait here for you."

Kristen looked back at Bart. "I'll need time to change."

"I'll be back in half an hour."

"All right."

Nodding curtly to de Santos, Bart left.

Chapter Nineteen

The headwaiter escorted Bart and Kristen to the rear of the Drover's Cottage dining room. A spectacular chandelier hung from the ceiling, and everywhere they looked they saw gleaming brass, elegance, and glitter, all on a grand scale. Texas beef was bringing prosperity to Kansas.

They ordered wine before the meal, and while they sipped it, Kristen remarked, "I'm glad you aren't wearing that cannon you had on earlier."

"Well, I do feel kind of naked."

"Why?"

"You heard de Santos. Raoul's out looking for me."

"Here. Take this."

She opened her purse and slipped him a small pearl-handled derringer.

"Where'd you get this?"

"It was a gift from Salvador."

"You're going back with him, aren't you?"

She shrugged. "Rather than make the man I love miserable, I will make Salvador de Santos miserable."

Though Kristen was admitting that she loved Bart, Bart decided not to press the point. He realized now that Kristen Nordstrom was, in her own way, as stubborn as her mother. It would do no good for him to pursue her. Something cold and unyielding had entered Kristen's soul during their long separation. Kristen was lost to him now, and there was nothing either of them could do to change that fact.

"You know," Bart reminded her gently, "that wasn't very nice—what you told Nils about your mother."

Kristen flushed.

"He was very upset."

"Yes, I know. And since then I have felt ashamed."

"You mean you're willing to admit that you might be wrong about what happened?"

"For the first time, yes."

"Nils will be glad to hear that." He glanced up. "And you can tell him after dinner."

Kristen followed his glance and saw Kate

approaching their table with Nils by her side. Her eyes wide, Kate pulled up when she saw Kristen.

"Kristen!" she cried.

Kristen hesitated for just a moment. Then, unable to hold back any longer, she jumped up and rushed into her mother's arms. For a moment the two rocked in each other's embrace. When they finally broke apart, both women had tears of joy in their eyes.

Seated at Bart and Kristen's table, Kate smiled happily at Kristen. "When Nils told me you were joining us for dinner, I could hardly believe it." She shook her head in wonder. "Nils back from the dead, Bart alive and well after a fearful wound—and you, Kristen, here now.... It is all like a wonderful dream."

"You look fine, Ma," Kristen said. "All tanned and rugged."

"That trail drive from Texas was some experience," she admitted. "But it did me good to get out of Nordstrom's Fort."

"Nordstrom's Fort?" Nils asked, frowning.

"That's what they call our ranch house, Nils," explained Kate. "It's what we needed to fend off them damned Comanche. I made the walls thicker and sodded the roof, then shingled it over. We've boarded up the runways too." She shuddered. "A fort is a good name for it. And until this trail drive, it seemed, that ranch house was my entire universe."

A moment later, when Kate asked Kristen to describe her escape from the Comanche, Kristen refused, gently but firmly. Nils, however, was eager to speak of his years in Washington after the war, and then it was Kate's turn to describe the trail drive north. And she did not forget to mention Little Raven's offer to the one he called Iron Woman.

When the conversation turned to more general topics, Bart expected Kate to ask Kristen to return with her to the Circle N; but the older woman seemed to sense that this was no time for that. Bart could only agree. It was best for the two women simply to enjoy each other's company for now. It was enough that they were reunited— that Kate Nordstrom had her two children back to help her wipe away some of the anguish of the past six years.

Kate's gasp alerted Bart.

Glancing up, he saw Frank Kilrain approaching their table. His face distorted with hate, he came to a halt less than a table away and brought up his six-gun, aiming it at Kate. At this distance he could not miss.

Bart's move was instinctive. He flung the table up, pushing Kate out of the line of fire. As Kate went down the gun in Kilrain's hand thundered. A chunk of the table flew into the air as the bullet took a bite out of it. Sudden screams filled the restaurant. Bart leapt at Kilrain, but his foot got tangled in an overturned chair. He went down heavily yet still managed to grab Frank's leg. When he tried to pull Frank down, however, Frank beat him off with his heavy gun barrel, the sharp, numbing blows raining down onto his head and shoulders. Bart felt his hands dropping away from Frank's leg. As he slumped back onto the floor he saw Frank fleeing from the dining room in such haste he knocked over a table.

Bart scrambled groggily to his feet. Kate remained on the floor, chalk-white with terror. The headwaiter and the hotel manager hurried over to them. The dining room's patrons, silent now, were on their feet, staring in stunned dismay at the fight they had just witnessed.

"Kristen," Bart said, shaking off his grogginess, "take Kate to your place while I see to Frank Kilrain."

Kristen nodded hastily as she and Nils helped Kate to her feet. Bart turned to the hotel manager.

"Is there another exit from here?"

The manager pointed to a door at the rear. Bart handed him enough for the dinner and the damage, and with Nils and Kristen doing their best to comfort a near hysterical Kate, they hastened her toward the rear door. Bart hurried through the dining room and out onto the hotel porch.

He searched the street for some sign of Kilrain. The boardwalks were crowded with cowboys, but he caught no glimpse of Frank. Moving back through the restaurant, he hurried out the rear exit after Kate.

A short flight of wooden steps led down to the alley. Bart saw Kate facing the mouth of the back alley. Nils and Kristen were trying to get her to hurry into it, but for some reason Kate was frozen with fear and refused to go any farther.

As Bart descended the stairs Nils took his mother's arm.

"Ma!" he told her. "It don't matter now! He's gone!"

"I can't!" she cried, staring in wide-eyed horror at the alley in front of her. "Don't make me go in there!"

Kristen took her mother's arm. Then, with Nils helping her gently, Kate gave in, moving along with Kristen and Nils, as if in a dream. Just ahead of them Frank Kilrain materialized. He had doubled back. He still held his revolver. Flinging it up, he aimed quickly and fired—twice. But Kristen was faster than his trigger finger as she flung herself in front of Kate and took both bullets in her chest.

Frank turned and ran.

Bart raced after him, chasing him out of the alley and into the street. A large crowd had gathered, drawn by the gunfire. Still holding his

THE TEXAN

weapon, Frank fled down the middle of the street, Bart following close behind him. The light from the saloons and gaming houses flooded the street. There was not a spectator in the crowd who could not see what was happening.

Abruptly Frank Kilrain stopped running. Turning to face Bart, he threw his revolver away and thrust both hands high over his head.

"I ain't armed!" he cried. "You can't shoot me!"

Bart stopped less than ten feet from Kilrain. Bringing up Kristen's derringer, he fired pointblank, emptying both barrels into the man. Two neat holes appeared in Kilrain's shirtfront. As Frank staggered back and dropped to the ground, an angry mutter swept through the crowd. To the onlookers it seemed that Bart had just shot down an unarmed man in cold blood.

"He just killed that man!" someone cried.

"Get him!" cried another. "Get the son of a bitch!"

"He's a murderer!"

Bart threw the empty derringer to the ground, turned, and pushed back through the crowd. A few men tried to restrain him, but he angrily brushed them aside and ran into the alley. He saw Kate cradling her daughter's head in her lap. Beside her stood Nils, numb with shock.

Bart didn't need to be told that Kristen was dead.

* * *

Bart heard a soft, urgent knock on his hotel door. Drawing his revolver, he hurried to the door, then stepped to one side.

"Who is it?"

"Nils."

Bart pulled the door open. Nils ducked inside. As Bart closed the door Nils said, "Tolliver has your horse downstairs in the alley at the back of the hotel. You better make tracks."

"Is it that bad?"

"One of the men who left the trail drive with Kilrain has been shooting off his mouth. He says you goaded Frank into coming after you, that Frank was aiming at you in the hotel, and that you opened fire on him in the alley—that Kristen was hit with stray bullets."

"That'll never stand up in court."

"That ain't your problem. The town council's got itself all steamed up. It seems they like Texas beef, but they sure as hell don't like Texas cowboys. There's talk of bringing law and order to Abilene—of making an example of you."

"With a rope."

"Yeah."

"Well, I can see their point. I did shoot that unarmed son of a bitch down in cold blood."

"I would've done the same thing."

Bart slung his saddlebags over his shoulder and grabbed his rifle. "You remember that place where we camped outside Newton?"

"Yes."

"Meet me there with provisions in a week or so."

"All right."

As Bart pulled the door open he paused to listen. He could hear the sound of a crowd. Nils heard it too. He went to the window and looked down at the street in front of the hotel. It was filling up with torch-bearing citizens.

"You better make it quick, Bart," Nils said.

He turned away from the window. The door was still open, but Bart was gone.

It wasn't a posse following Bart. Just one man. Judging from the sombrero, Bart knew who it was.

Raoul.

Bart dismounted and propped himself behind a cutbank, the Kansas River at his back. Raoul was in full view now, riding calmly toward him over the gently undulating grassland, occasionally disappearing as he dropped into a swale. It was mid-afternoon and as hot as the hinges of hell.

Bart levered a fresh round into his Henry. Raoul was still out of range, but he saw no reason not to annoy the Mexican if he could. He pumped a shot into the air. A small puff of dust exploded at least twenty yards in front of Raoul's horse. Raoul kept coming and was soon within range. Bart levered another cartridge into the firing chamber and tucked the stock into his shoulder. Raoul pulled up suddenly.

"Hey, gringo!"

Bart lowered the Henry.

"We make promise. Ees that not so?"

"That's right, Raoul."

"You say you wait for me, gringo. You say we meet again."

"I'm waiting now, Raoul!"

"All right! I come to meet you now."

Raoul dismounted, his six-gun in his hand. Crouching low, he suddenly darted to one side and disappeared in the tall grass. Bart waited for the tip of Raoul's sombrero to show itself. It did not take long for Bart to realize Raoul was not that dumb.

He looked in both directions along the cutbank. Raoul could come at him from either side, he realized. He put down his rifle and drew his Walker, then edged himself up over the lip of the cutbank and snaked his way through the grass, heading for Raoul's horse. When Raoul returned to it, there would be a surprise waiting for him.

Nearing the Mexican's horse, Bart heard the sudden pound of footsteps behind him. He spun. Raoul was less than ten feet away, racing toward him. Bart brought up his Colt, but Raoul fired first. The shot went wild as Bart returned Raoul's fire. The Mexican staggered, but did not stop coming, and fired twice more, his third round catching Bart in the shoulder, violently spinning him around.

Then Raoul's bloody torso slammed down onto Bart, his strong hands grappling for Bart's neck, his fingers tightening around his windpipe with the strength of steel cables. Bart brought his gun up close, thumb-cocked it, and fired, pumping a slug into Raoul's gut. Convulsively the Mexican's fingers tightened.

Again Bart cocked and fired up into the hot, sweaty body covering him. But Raoul's fingers still closed around Bart's neck. For a desperate moment he felt a clammy darkness enveloping him. He couldn't breathe. Dropping his Colt, he clawed at Raoul's fingers. Before blackness claimed him, he managed to rip the dead Mexican's fingers from around his throat. Shuddering, Bart pulled himself out from under the dead Raoul. Slowly the numbness in his shoulder gave way to a searing pain worse than a toothache.

The son of a bitch had sure as hell kept his promise.

Bart made camp a couple of days later a few miles outside Newton, beside the creek he had mentioned to Nils. The next morning, at daybreak, Nils and Kate arrived in Kate's wagon. It was filled with provisions, a sizable portion of which they promptly transferred to Bart's saddlebags and onto the packhorse they had brought with them for Bart.

While Kate finished putting a clean bandage on his shoulder wound, Bart studied the wanted dodger Nils had brought with him. The pen-and-ink sketch was accurate enough, except for the eyes. But at least the information about him told the plain, unvarnished truth.

Kansas was no longer a state where Bart could rest easy, not for someone who calmly executed an unarmed man in cold blood while the rest of Abilene looked on. And if Bart returned to Texas, that was the first place the law would look for him.

Since he could not return, Bart asked Nils to take the money realized on the sale of the Anchor cattle to his mother and Dan O'Hare, and also to help Ellen and his mother run Anchor during his absence. When Nils readily agreed to this, Bart was pleased. There was little doubt in his mind that before long Nils and Ellen would be running Anchor as man and wife.

The packhorse loaded, Bart looped its line around his saddle horn and thanked Nils and Kate for coming. Favoring his shoulder, he mounted up slowly.

"Where you headed?" Nils asked.

"Don't ask, so you won't know."

Kate shaded her eyes as she looked up at him. Her hair was streaked with gray. It had come on suddenly, Bart realized, after she buried Kristen. Bart was not surprised. Since Kristen's death there had been an aching emptiness inside him, one he knew he would never be able to fill.

"Take care of your shoulder," Kate said.

"Thanks, Kate. Tell Ma I'll write—and to look for me when she least expects it. And Nils, you take good care of Ellen."

"I'll do that, Bart."

The two stepped back. With his shoulder bound so tightly, Bart could not wave. He nodded to them, clapped his spurs to his mount, and headed out. He heard Nils calling good-bye one last time, but Bart did not look back.

That was something he could never do again.

Get the whole story of
THE RAKEHELL DYNASTY

___Book One: THE BOOK OF JONATHAN RAKEHELL__
  by Michael William Scott   (D32-018, $3.95, U.S.A.)
                                           (D32-019, $4.95, Canada)

___Book Two: CHINA BRIDE__   (D30-948, $3.95, U.S.A.)
  by Michael William Scott   (D30-949, $4.95, Canada)

___Book Three: ORIENT AFFAIR__   (D30-771, $3.95, U.S.A.)
  by Michael William Scott   (D32-134, $4.95, Canada)

___Book Four: MISSION TO CATHAY__ (D90-239, $3.95, U.S.A.)
  by Michael William Scott   (D32-055, $4.95, Canada)

The bold, sweeping, passionate story of a great New England shipping family caught up in the winds of change—and of the one man who would dare to sail his dream ship to the frightening, beautiful land of China. He was Jonathan Rakehell, and his destiny would change the course of history.

THE RAKEHELL DYNASTY—
THE GRAND SAGA OF THE GREAT CLIPPER SHIPS
AND OF THE MEN WHO BUILT THEM
TO CONQUER THE SEAS AND CHALLENGE THE WORLD!

Jonathan Rakehell—who staked his reputation and his place in the family on the clipper's amazing speed.

Lai-Tse Lu—the beautiful, independent daughter of a Chinese merchant. She could not know that Jonathan's proud clipper ship carried a cargo of love and pain, joy and tragedy for her.

Louise Graves—Jonathan's wife-to-be, who waits at home in New London keeping a secret of her own.

Bradford Walker—Jonathan's scheming brother-in-law who scoffs at the clipper and plots to replace Jonathan as heir to the Rakehell shipping line.

WARNER BOOKS
P.O. Box 690
New York, N.Y. 10019

Please send me the books I have checked. I enclose a check or money order (not cash), plus 50¢ per order and 50¢ per copy to cover postage and handling.*
(Allow 4 weeks for delivery.)

_____ Please send me your free mail order catalog. (If ordering only the catalog, include a large self-addressed, stamped envelope.)

Name _____
Address _____
City _____
State _____ Zip _____
*N.Y. State and California residents add applicable sales tax.   37

THE BEST OF BESTSELLERS
By Ronald S. Joseph

___THE KINGDOM___   (A30-541, $3.50)
Out of the rugged brasada, a powerful family carved THE KINGDOM. Joel Trevor was willing to fight Mexicans, carpetbaggers, raiders, even Nature itself to secure his ranch. Then he won the beautiful Spanish Sofia who joined her heart and her lands to his. When control passed to Joel's daughter Anne, she took trouble and tragedy with the same conquering spirit as her father. These were the founders—and their story blazes from the pages of THE KINGDOM, the first book of a giant trilogy.

___THE POWER___   (A36-161, $3.50)
The children of Anne Trevor and Alex Cameron set out at the turn of the century to conquer the world in their own ways. Follow Dos, the reckless son, as he escalates youthful scrapes into crime. Travel with Maggie from boarding school to brothel to Congress. Meet Trev and the baby daughter to whom all the kingdom, power and glory will belong.

___THE GLORY___   (A32-128, $3.95, U.S.A.)
                                                            (A32-129, $4.95, Canada)
Meet the inheritors: Allis Cameron, great-granddaughter of the pioneers who carved a kingdom in southern Texas. Go with her to Hollywood where her beauty conquers the screen and captures the heart of her leading man. Cammie: Allis's daughter, who comes of age and finds herself torn between a ruthless politician and a radical young Mexican. They were the Cameron women, heirs to a Texas fortune, rich, defiant, ripe for love.

WARNER BOOKS
P.O. Box 690
New York, N.Y. 10019

Please send me the books I have checked. I enclose a check or money order (not cash), plus 50¢ per order and 50¢ per copy to cover postage and handling.*
(Allow 4 weeks for delivery.)

_____ Please send me your free mail order catalog. (If ordering only the catalog, include a large self-addressed, stamped envelope.)

Name _____

Address _____

City _____

State _____ Zip _____

*N.Y. State and California residents add applicable sales tax.   36

By the year 2000, 2 out of 3 Americans could be illiterate.

It's true.

Today, 75 million adults... about one American in three, can't read adequately. And by the year 2000, U.S. News & World Report envisions an America with a literacy rate of only 30%.

Before that America comes to be, you can stop it... by joining the fight against illiteracy today.

Call the Coalition for Literacy at toll-free **1-800-228-8813** and volunteer.

Volunteer Against Illiteracy. The only degree you need is a degree of caring.

Ad Council Coalition for Literacy

Warner Books is proud to be an active supporter of the Coalition for Literacy.